CANDLE LOVE

MINTY MARIE

CONTENTS

CONTENT CONSIDERATIONS

This book, at its heart, is a cozy why-choose romance with a lot of spice. That being said, there are a few things I would like to share with you, dear reader, so that you can make an informed decision on continuing.

Julie has been diagnosed by a doctor with obstructive sleep apnea and uses a continuous positive airway pressure (CPAP) machine when she sleeps. Julie's airway becomes blocked by relaxing soft tissues in her throat during sleep that close off her airway. Her brain then sends signals that wake her when oxygen levels in her body drop too low.

Any information and mentions of Julie's sleep apnea condition are for entertainment purposes only and definitely not a substitute for professional medical advice, diagnosis, or treatment. Readers should always consult with a qualified healthcare provider before making any health-related decisions.

While this author also has sleep apnea, I attempted to make Julie's situation vague for those who do not have this condition, so I do not get into all the small details involved in living with sleep apnea and CPAP machines. (Does anyone have any distilled water I can borrow? IYKYK).

There are many swear words and lots of sexual content, including MFM (one woman dating/engaging with two men who do not participate with each other).

Julie was adopted as a baby into a different family after the death of her parents.

Julie was encouraged to move out from her childhood home even though she wasn't hundred percent ready to do so.

Julie volunteers at a food bank where she assists with donations for those experiencing food insecurities.

The merchandise store Julie works at is involved in a car accident in which a vehicle smashes into the storefront (while there are some injuries, there are no deaths).

A coworker of Julie's is said to frequent clubs and bars, and it's suggested he may over indulge in them.

The characters in this book are all human-based but share qualities with other mythical entities and may exhibit different kinds of personality traits. This book features a human as the main character, but her two love interests are not fully human. (See the next chapter on "The Creatures of New California" for more information).

THE CREATURES (PEOPLE) OF NEW CALIFORNIA

Fox Folk—one of Julie's love interests, Trent, is a Fox Folk. Similar in size and coloring to humans, these human/fox hybrids are known for their large, furry ears and multiple fluffy tails. Nine is the optimal number of tails to have and any Fox Folk born with less is considered a "Runt" to be shunned by their entire family. They also tend to keep their social circles within their own kind and are relatively reclusive, but the bi-monthly heats every female goes through are common knowledge to all.

Demonnie—Julie's coworker, Eddie, is a Demonnie, a human/demon-type hybrid. They vary greatly in size, shape, and coloring but are tall with human-like features. Most, but not all, sprout horns of different sizes, shapes, and colors from their heads, and all have skin tones ranging from light gray to darker stone colors. Though they all have amber or copper eyes, some feature extra appendages such as tails, wings, and multiple body parts.

Dragoon—Julie's adopted family, best friend, and Julie's other love interest, Chalice, are Dragoons: creature types with human qualities along with long tails and scales that cover the upper half of their bodies and sides of their faces and necks. Some even have pointed teeth and blow small streams of fire from their mouths. They are the largest of the different creatures and like the Demonnie, some have wings. Their skin and scales range from fair to onyx, but they almost all have a shimmering quality to them.

Minotaur—large creatures with hoofed feet and fur covering the majority of their bodies. The Minotaur are a smaller creature set than the Dragoons; however, they remain imposing with their large heads and bullish horns. While many of them are big creatures, some have been known to be similar in size to the smallest of the creatures of New California: the humans and Mousequeeks.

Mousequeek—Small human/rodent hybrids known for their big, round ears, long hairless tails and voracious appetites. They have similar coloring to that of humans and Fox Folk but also have small button noses and long whiskers. Most of them are even smaller than the average human, but their big personalities tend to make them feel like giants.

Human—your standard human. You may actually be one yourself!

Dedicated to vanilla scented candles.

CHAPTER ONE

"Don't do it, Julie. Don't you dare do it!" My best friend, Frankie, takes a big gulp of her iced coffee and waves the cup aggressively toward the house. Most of the contents spill over her wrist, but she tilts her arm and licks it off. "I'm warning you, it's a bad idea."

Everyone needs a supportive and overly caffeinated best friend like Frankie.

But she's giving me that look again. The kind of disappointed gaze that says she's holding back on what she really wants to say and hiding it amongst the sharp, calculating look all Dragoons, human and dragon hybrid creatures, tend to have. I can even see the glint of disappointment in the smooth, copper brown scales covering her neck and sides of her cheeks.

I know this kind of look well because she's been using it ever since we were five years old. It started when she realized I couldn't run fast with her using my short, human legs and that she had to wait for me to catch up. She said I was the slowest creature in New California, and I cried the entire day afterward, but she then picked (stole) some flowers from our mutual neighbor's yard and gave them to me as a peace offering. We've been best friends ever since.

"I want to take one last look at the place, okay?"

"Julie, you're just going to make yourself sad. It's time to move on," she says while struggling to cram in one last packing box into my small car. Her brown, leathery wings twitch in agitation when it pushes another box out and to the driveway.

"Easy for you to say, Miss Dragoon. I don't think the way you do," I reply.

"Why not? You know, for living your entire life with Dragoons, you still act painfully human sometimes." One shove and the last box containing my entire life is loaded up in my car, ready to—like Frankie just said—move on.

"Frankie, stop being an ass." I swat her shoulder. "Moving out on your own is a big step for humans, just like it is with Dragoons. It's, like, a rite of passage, but that doesn't mean I have to like it."

"I know it is, but I remember the last time something made you sad and you cried for three weeks."

"And what was that?"

"When they cancelled that one vampire show. I can't remember the name . . . *Blood Diaries*? Something like that."

"Goddess, that was over ten years ago!"

"Not worth crying that much over, but I guess it was an okay show," she muses. "*Midnight's Kiss* was better."

"Ugh, I couldn't stand that one. Everyone was so . . . sparkly and pale. How can you be that pasty and still sparkle? It was weird."

Frankie thumps her tail on the ground in thought.

"I guess they were creepy looking. I'm glad the world moved on from vampire-based romance."

I actually think it could benefit from having more but to each their own.

I love Frankie like a sister, but I also wish my parents had stuck around long enough to help me move. They packed up last week and made their way to New Las Vegas. Even my brother, Jordan, moved up north last month to live with some friends. Frankie was the only creature left to help me haul away everything I own before closing up the place one last time.

She's right that going back to look at the house will make me sad, but it's something I feel like I need to do. After all, this house I'm moving away from has been my safe haven for over twenty-five years. Ever since my Dragoon parents decided to adopt a different creature type than their own and picked me up from the hospital. This is the only home I can remember and my little human heart is going to miss it.

Frankie folds her wing in and leans against my car. She gives me another long look and wave of her iced coffee.

"Just don't take too long, I want to get lunch."

"Aren't you full of coffee and whipped cream?"

"Yes, but I still need actual food in my belly."

"Ugh, fine."

Drifting away from my car, I walk down the cobble stone driveway and let my fingers trail over the velvety buds lining the purple rose bushes that separate the house from its neighbors. I guess I won't be around to see them bloom in the spring and that simple thought makes my eyes sting with tears.

I wipe them away quickly before Frankie can see and walk up to the front door. The brass knocker is still attached to the freshly painted wood, but someone has buffed it to a pretty shine and there is a newly purchased pot of pink daises growing off to the side. It looks the same but yet . . . it doesn't.

Fuck. I haven't even opened the front door before making myself sad. From where I'm standing, I can't see the empty rooms and bare kitchen, so I can almost pretend that everything looks the same inside the house. That I'm just leaving for camp or a sleepover at Frankie's place down the street. That in no time at all, I'll be back here and making chocolate chip cookies in the kitchen with Frankie and watching movies, not the old TV, until I fall asleep on the yellow couch.

No, I don't really want that last look inside to see the emptiness I know looms behind the front door. There is such a swirl of emotions inside me and it's super annoying. I'm excited to start a new life on my own, but . . . I don't want to. I'm not sure if I'm ready.

I'm also nervous about my condition. When I'm asleep, my throat closes up and stops my breathing. Because of this, I have to use a specialized device called a CPAP (which stands for "continuous positive airway pressure") to keep my airways open by blowing air into my nose and mouth. No one outside of my family and Frankie's immediate family has ever seen me use it at night before, and I'd like to keep it that way for privacy's sake.

Sleeping somewhere new might mean someone will see me using it, unless I do a good job at hiding it from them. It's not exactly the sexiest thing in the world.

The only other thing I'll probably keep to myself are my art journals. Drawing is just a hobby and I'm really not good enough to share my creations with anyone new, especially those I'll be living with. Not yet at least.

"Julie?" Frankie calls out, and I can tell she's trying to be kind and understanding but starting to get impatient. "We should get going."

"Yeah, okay." I turn my back on the house and walk back to the car with thoughts of my CPAP machine making way for the impending 'fresh start" I'm headed to.

I wonder how difficult it is for her, and my family, to understand my situation. Dragoon children leave home as soon as they start attending University or when they are at least old enough to attend. It's just the way things are with their creature types. My parents went against the norm and stayed a few extra years since they knew it would be hard for their adopted human daughter, but it was eventually time for them to move on. So they did, which led me to find a new place to live. It took a while, but a friend from a University class last semester hooked me up with some of her coworkers who needed a new roomie. It would mean sharing a bathroom with a Dragoon, but that's nothing new to me.

"Ready to head out?" Frankie asks.

"I'm not really ready, but it's not like I have a choice."

"I guess not. It is the Dragoon way." She rolls her lip piercing around with her tongue. I feel like I see a glimmer of sadness peak through her expression, but that might just be the light reflecting off the lip ring's metal stud.

It's the Dragoon way. Sure. That thought has been swimming though my mind for the last few years when I realized I would need to leave soon. While I understand the process, I can't help but feel a bit bitter about it. As well as a little betrayed, but this family of Dragoons raised me when I had no one else and I'm using everything in my being to trust and respect their traditions.

I'm still going to miss this house though.

"So what food sounds good to you?" I ask Frankie.

"Burgers, definitely," she says and despite everything, I smile. She's always been obsessed with burgers, even as a kid.

"There's a Burger Bliss on the way. We could stop there," I say, pulling my phone from my pocket and showing her the address.

She cracks a big grin.

"Okay, I've been to that one before. It's in the center that had that water main break. Remember how crazy that was?"

"We could see it from Candle Love and we're all the way across the parking lot. Everyone was talking about it all day."

I've worked at Candle Love for several years now. It's a shop that sells mainly—you guessed it—candles. But we also stock soaps, lotions, and various body care products. It's a fun job, even if it doesn't pay that well, but at least you get to take home a lot of the unsold merchandise. I've smelled good for years because of that stuff.

"Well, come on, let's rip the proverbial Band-Aid off." Frankie casts one last look at the house and another down the road at the home where she grew up. Her parents still live there though, even if she moved out a while ago.

I do the same before climbing quickly into my car. I feel the tears starting to come, but I hold them back. I need to be strong for today. There'll be time to cry later.

Right now, I need to act like a Dragoon and not the silly little human that I am.

"Ugh, they're always so busy here." I swivel on the plastic chair to make room for Frankie's swishing tail. Burger Bliss is packed today but we found a very small, two seater table in the back corner of the dining room.

As a huge contrast to my mood, it happens to be a gorgeous and sunshiny day. The holidays are just around the corner and everyone—and I mean everyone—seems to be out and enjoying themselves. And by enjoying themselves, I mean they're here eating burgers.

But if you are going to go out for a veggie burger, fries, and radish chips, then I guess this is the place to do it. Frankie and I have been coming here ever since she first got her driver's permit and could take us after school. And before that, my family used to come here every few weeks on the weekends.

It's packed as always today and our table is super cramped with a Minotaur family sitting way too close to us. One of their kids has been crying about wanting to eat another burger, and the other two are fighting over who gets to place stickers on the restaurant's walls. Their parents look like they're doing their best, but the constant noise from them, and everyone else around the restaurant, is making my palms sweat and my vision jagged.

I've never felt completely well inside a large crowd. The most people I can usually stand is the group during my volunteer work at the New Harvest Food Bank, and we're usually in such a big warehouse where I hardly ever see them all in one place.

It's just too loud in here right now. And it smells like grease and fries which makes me wish for the cool, scented air of Candle Love. I don't think I could ever pick up a job here. Just looking at the workers behind the counter makes me cringe thinking of how hard they must work. Working over a hot grill or fryer in such close proximity with other creatures while sweating my ass off? Nope, not for me.

"You can't beat the food, though." Frankie takes a long sip of her diet soda and nods seriously. "But apparently everyone feels the same way. Maybe we should go eat in the car?"

Burger Bliss does seem busier than usual, but that's to be expected. It's a popular restaurant. It makes me wonder how Candle Love is doing on the other side of the parking lot. We tend to get a lot of Bliss's customers after they're finished eating. They usually leave their food wrappers and empty cups in the parking spaces by our store. We're always fighting with each other about who will need to go outside and pick it up.

"This is fine," I say. "We won't be very long. I let Misty know I'd be there by five and she seemed pretty adamant that I get there on time. I think she has something she's going to."

Frankie checks her phone for the time and makes a face.

"Shouldn't be an issue, at least I don't think it will. Well, it did take a while for our food to be ready, but we're probably fine." Her words do not fill me with confidence and neither does her frown, or the way she keeps refolding her wings. "So, anyway, how is work going over at the candle store?"

I swirl a last fry inside a little paper cup to pick up the last of the ketchup before answering.

"Oh, okay, I guess. You know, it's the same old, same old. We're getting some new Litha themed candles next week. Stuff like lemon, orange, mint and ginger and lots and lots of honeysuckle. The store always gets busy around holiday releases."

Busy might be an understatement. There's been some releases, especially limited edition candles, that we've had creatures line outside the store before opening. It's never a huge line, but it's certainly weird to see people lining up just for an interestingly scented candle. I think the worst I saw was for Lemon Bacon Pancakes, followed closely by Oceanfront Bookstore. Books and water smells do not mix in my opinion.

I guess it's just the fear of missing out. Something I just can't relate to. I'm fine where I am . . . well, I was fine. Now I don't know what I am. Everything feels so displaced now.

I hate it.

I know Frankie is trying to create some normalcy for me, but I still hate it.

"Sounds like fun to work there, getting to sniff all the new scents."

She sounds interested but I doubt Frankie would ever be caught dead working in a place like Candle Love. She co-hosts a mildly successfully podcast about romance novels and volunteers to run haunted history tours in the older parts of town. In her spare time, she creates and sells these amazing works of sculpted and painted art. Working retail doesn't fit her brand.

We have very different personalities, but share enough in common to make us best friends. And it helped that she only lived three houses down from my adopted parents, so we saw a lot of each other growing up. Frankie always liked the edgier music and fashion, speaking her mind and being loud with her thoughts. A big difference to my more quiet and reserved nature.

I was happy to live my experiences through her, but that never stopped her from trying to push me out from my comfort zones. Of which I should be grateful . . . but it can be annoying when she won't let me sulk.

"It's usually pretty fun," I mutter, taking a bite out of a radish chip. I don't mention how boring it can be sometimes, but at least I get paid to stand around and talk about how things smell. My coworkers aren't so bad either, and it's much quieter than this place.

"You look so glum. Are you still thinking about the move?" Frankie frowns and points a fry at my face. "Don't worry, everything is going to be fine. It'll be weird living with people you don't really know, but you'll get to know them soon enough. I went through the same thing years ago, and I'm still standing. I'm sure your new roomies will be great, and if any of them give you trouble, just let me know."

"Thanks, but I don't really know much about them other than the fact that Misty and Chalice are siblings, a Fox Folk Runt with five tails lives there, and I'm replacing some guy named Pauly."

"That's a start. Are any of them cute at least?" Frankie asks and I roll my eyes.

"I . . . I don't know yet, but why would that matter? It's probably not a good idea to start fucking my roommates as soon as I move in."

"It might make things interesting." She snickers. "There are books like that, you know. Roommate tropes and all that, but I'm not sure how they apply to real life. You'll have to do some investigative work for me. You know, for the podcast and all."

"Well, if it's for the podcast then I'll tell you all about my experiences or lack thereof." I laugh and finish the last of my soda. "But I seriously doubt any of that will go down. I have too much going on right now to focus on getting involved with anyone, in the same house or otherwise. I picked up some extra volunteer shifts at New Harvest and Candle Love, plus I have more University classes to think about eventually. Besides, like I said, it'd be weird to move in and start fucking everyone right away."

"Eh, that's debatable, it might be fun! I get it, though. But really, Julie, I'm worried about you. You can call me if you need to talk, okay? I may not understand fully about the hesitation to leave home, but I'm happy to listen to you talk about it anytime you want."

"Don't worry, I'm sure you'll hear from me if things go badly."

"So if I don't hear from you, then can I assume things are going well? Like, I can assume you are fucking one of your roommates?" Frankie chugs the rest of her drink. "Because you still need to call me even if that does happen. I'll need the details!"

"Oh, Goddess, Frankie." I laugh and poke at the remaining ice in my drink with my straw. "But sure, you'll be the first to know."

"Good. I worry about you sometimes. I mean, even for a human, you're fairly low on the confidence level charts. Maybe a good romp in some forbidden sheets will be good for you, but I am super proud of you for doing this, I know you weren't exactly keen on moving out to begin with. It's a big step."

"Thanks for being there for me, Frankie. You're an awesome friend."

She thumps her tail happily on the ground and earns herself a disgruntled look from the Minotaur family. True to her nature, she doesn't care and flashes me a big smile.

"Aw, thank you! I do my best. Now hurry up and finish your food, we've got to get you started on your brand new life!"

CHAPTER TWO

When we leave the restaurant and suddenly realize it's almost five o'clock, Frankie and I book it to 1414 Cumberbatch Way—my new home.

"Shit, I think we lost track of time," she laughs nervously, tapping her long fingernails aggressively on the dashboard while we wait at a red light.

"You think?" I laugh. "I guess as long as we get there before five, I should be okay. Though I really don't want this to be one of my new roommate's first impressions of me. Oh Goddess, what if she holds a grudge?"

"I mean, most Dragoons do that kind of thing, but I don't know if being a few minutes late would warrant that kind of punishment. Besides, we still have a little time left. I'm sure we'll be there before five . . . like right before five. Maybe."

"Frankie!"

"Sorry, sending positive thoughts into the universe that we don't hit another red light!" She laughs and I step on the gas.

We're in a part of town I've not been to in a while. It's not like it's a bad area or anything, I just never had reason to come down this way. My whole life seems to revolve around my home, um, old home, several miles in the opposite direction. So the streets and shops we pass by are all unfamiliar, though I can tell their specialties instantly by their signage.

Passing by on my left is a large shop catering to footwear designed for Minotaur feet, their large cloven hooves need special padding and unique designs. After that is another, smaller shop that sells horn polish. While Minotaur always have horns, the shop has placed a sign indicating they also serve Dragoon and Demonnie, human and demon-like hybrids, who are sometimes born with them as well.

"Fuck!" Frankie growls as we stop at yet another red light.

I look over at her and see her flexing her tightly-folded wings pressed against the back of the car seat. Not all Dragoons are born with wings, just like only some of the Demonnie, but they all have long tails and scales covered at least half of their bodies. They also tend to be slightly larger than your regular human.

"It's like the universe wants me to go back home," I chuckle nervously but Frankie casts me that disappointed look again.

"Oh no you don't, no chickening out now. You're going to get us there before five!" Frankie snaps, and I keep my mouth shut when I see a small stream of smoke slither up and around her lip piercing.

While Dragoons don't really breathe fire, they have been known to release small streams of flame on occasion, and it's not necessarily something I want to witness today inside my car.

"Oh, what's that place?" Frankie says suddenly, and presses herself against the window to look at another shop we're passing.

It's a Mousequeek (small human mouse hybrids) bakery and, wow, it does look good. There's even a short line coming out the door into the parking lot with all different sorts of creatures, so you know it has to be good if Minotaur, Demonnie, Dragoon, Mousequeek, and even Fox Folk are lining up for it. A big sign out front says they sell the best donuts in all of New California.

Mousequeek are known for being small creatures with long tails and huge appetites, so I guess it makes sense that one, or someone related to one, would run such a successful bakery. I'm more surprised that there seems to be a few Fox Folk standing in line.

The human and fox hybrid, Fox Folk, I've known in my life always seemed, well, too posh for something like a downtown bakery selling donuts. At least the ones with the full nine tails, maybe not the Runts, those born with less than the proper nine. I think according to Fox Folk tradition, they're somewhat neglected or ignored by their families, so it wouldn't matter if they were seen at a donut shop versus some fancy, overpriced place.

"I'm so mad we don't have time to stop there," Frankie moans, pressing her nose closer against the window. "Promise me you'll try them soon or we'll go together when I come by to check up on you."

"Excuse me, check up on me?"

"Yeah, I mean, someone needs to come by and make sure you're still in one piece and haven't been split down the middle by one of your big ole' Dragoon roomies or their friends."

"Goddess, Frankie! Look, we're almost there, do you think you can pull yourself together so I can make a good impression?"

She cackles in laughter before responding.

"Sure, I can try. I'll even help you move some stuff inside. Did you pack your CPAP machine?"

"Of course," I reply softly. "It's in the pink duffle bag behind the seat along with some of my journals."

Frankie knows I like to try and keep my artistic talents a secret. She's the complete opposite and is always creating some sculpture or painting that she sells to the local art galleries.

"Gotcha, I'll take special care of them."

I don't respond, not wanting to make a big deal about it. I just hope the door to my new room has a lock so no one accidentally sees me using it at night. At least I can trust Frankie to keep my secrets.

In a matter of minutes, we're pulling off the main street and cruising down the small side street of Cumberbatch looking for number 1414.

"Hmm, older part of town means older houses," Frankie murmurs next to me. "But it doesn't look half bad. Kinda pretty in a vintage way."

The homes lining the streets all look nicely painted and have their lawns neatly trimmed. One has way too many plastic flamingos adorning their front yard, but the house itself is pristine. In fact, everything looks so well taken care of and uniform that it reminds me of my parents' old home.

The pain of nostalgia hits me in the gut, and I take my eyes off the homes and stare blankly forward as I drive down Cumberbatch Way.

"Okay, so at least it's in a nice area, and you have great food options just down the street. It's so nice, I would even live here."

"No you wouldn't," I say, glancing at her. "You'd never give up your tiny apartment."

Frankie lives in a little studio apartment in the oldest part of town. It's barely big enough for her, which is why I couldn't just stay with her after moving out.

"Alas, you've got me. I wouldn't, but what I mean to say is that this place is nice and I think you'll like it here."

"It's not so much the house, it's the creatures inside it. I won't know anyone and I'm expected to live with them? And share a bathroom? It's all so weird."

"Weirdness is part of life, my dear." She shrugs. "Everything will be okay, just be confident in thinking that it will and I guarantee you that everything will work out. Anyway, shouldn't we be there by now?"

Frankie leans out the window to look at the painted house numbers on the curb of the street but doesn't notice what I see directly in front of us.

Sitting at the very end of a quiet cul-de-sac is a house that someone has painted a ghastly shade of yellow. It appears to be single story except for a large expansion on top of a two car garage, and the whole thing is surrounded by a patch of dead grass.

But the most striking aspect of the property is a community center-sized flag poll sticking up from the ground near the front door.

"Is that . . ." Frankie squints at the flag flapping happily in the breeze. "The flag from *Marsh Lurkers Four*?"

"The video game? Yes, I think it is."

"And are those your new roommates?" She points to the lawn, and I see what I failed to see at first because I was so absorbed in the massive flag. I park along the curb and look over for a better view.

Placed in the center of the dead grass are two plastic kiddie pools filled with bubbles and several rubber duckies. In one pool, there is a male Fox Folk with dark, almost black hair and white tipped black ears, and in the other one, there is a golden scaled Dragoon. Both of them look fast asleep in the warm, late afternoon sun, so when Frankie and I jump out of my car, it startles them awake.

The Fox Folk shifts a lazy gaze over to us, first to me, and then immediately at Frankie with wide, blue eyes. He trails one of his black-painted fingernails through the bubbles and winks.

"Hey Chalice, wake up, we have company," he calls over to the dozing Dragoon. "Chalice!"

"Huh?" Chalice grunts, rubbing his eyes and looking up at Frankie and I. "Oh shit! What time is it? Fuck!"

He jumps up, stumbling from the kiddie pool in a blur of golden scales and skin. Bubbles and rubber ducks fly everywhere as the Fox Folk laughs loudly from the safety of his own pool and cracks open a beer.

For a moment, Chalice stands there staring at us and I can't help but admire the beautiful way his golden scales creep up the sides of his throat and cheeks and ends in a twisting, iridescent pattern around his eyes. My eyes trail lower, following the combination of smooth, tan skin and gold until they rest on . . . his enormous cock.

Oh, Goddess. This guy is totally naked.

"Ha! You got out first so I win!" The Fox Folk takes a big swig of his beer.

Chalice looks over at him with a scowl but quickly lowers his hands to cover his expansive cock and gives a startled yelp when he notices us standing there.

"Oh shit, shit, shit! Misty is gonna kill me!" He charges toward the house's front door in a sprint, bare ass on full display and the Fox Folk still laughing uproariously in his wake.

Frankie joins in on the laughter to a point of shedding a few tears, but I'm too stunned to do anything more than stand there.

"Oh, Julie." Frankie wipes a tear from her eye. "You're going to have a fantastic time here."

"Julie, huh?" The Fox Folk takes another swig of his beer and turns an interested look my way. "You're the new roommate."

"Uh, yeah. I am." I shuffle my feet and glance at the front door, now closed after Chalice's mad dash inside the house. "Misty said I should be here at five."

"You're a little late, aren't you?"

Another swig of beer and an intense stare down.

"Sorry about that," I stammer, avoiding looking directly at him as he rises from the pool and grabs a small towel. He drapes it around his slender waist, and it makes Frankie and I stare openly at the bubbles melting off his tattooed skin.

"No reason to be sorry, least not to me," he says with a smile before turning to look at Frankie. "Who's your friend?"

"Frankie!" She practically throws herself forward and nearly knocks me over with one of her wings. "And you are?"

"Trent," he says with another smooth smile. "Nice to meet you, Frankie. Hope we see more of you around here."

Frankie rustles her wings with pleasure and grins.

"I'm sure you will."

"Looking forward to it." He pauses again and looks me up and down. "See you inside, Julie."

He saunters off, still dripping water and bubbles, and walks inside, leaving the door wide open behind him with a trail of wet footprints in his wake.

"Should we, uh, follow him?" I ask Frankie and my voice breaks her from the trance he left her in.

"Yup! Let's do that." She unfolds a wing and drapes it protectively around my shoulders. "You ready for this? Looks like your two roomies are going to be trouble."

"Trouble? You mean the one drinking beer in a kiddie pool on the front lawn or the naked one that ran away screaming?"

"No, no, no. I mean the flirty Fox and the guy with the golden ass. I mean, take your pick, but leave one of them for me, okay?"

"How about you just take them both?"

"I mean, I could . . . but I don't want to be greedy. Unless you want to do that, then you have my blessing. Come on, let's get inside and find Misty."

Frankie and I are hardly two steps past the front door when a tall, silver-scaled Dragoon comes barreling down a set of stairs that must lead to the suite above the garage.

"Good, you're here!" Her silver scales line the bottom of a set of very pretty cheekbones and have a familiar twist around her eyes. This must be Chalice's sister, Misty.

"Hi, Misty. Um, I'm here!"

I've never felt more awkward in all my life. This first introduction to my new home has been anything but normal, but Misty puts a silver hand on my shoulder and smiles.

"First time moving out?"

"Um, yeah . . . this is my friend, Frankie. She's helping me move."

She and Frankie share a knowing look, and I suddenly feel so small and so, so very human. Misty takes her hand off my shoulder and gives me a very sage-like nod of her head.

"It's a big step in any Dragoon's life, and I'm sure in any human's as well. But don't worry we're a pretty chill house, I think you'll be just fine here. Did you bring in your stuff yet?"

"No, it's still out in my car."

"Chalice!" Misty suddenly screams, and I swear I feel the house shake a little. "Get your golden ass over here and help our room-mate with her things!"

Frankie nudges my ribs and leans down to my ear.

"I like this one."

I roll my eyes at her.

Chalice bounds over to us from a nearby hallway and is now, thankfully, fully clothed. It gives me a good chance to take a full look at him.

Like Misty, he is tall, a lot taller than a normal Dragoon and towers over Frankie. His hair is the same golden color as the thin layer of scales covering about half his body, including his long tail. I notice that he and his sister do not have wings like Frankie does, which isn't uncommon, but I don't think he needs them. He looks every bit the perfect specimen of a male Dragoon, or any male creature for that matter.

"Did you get Julie's room ready for her?" Misty asks him, and he scratches the side his face with a short, stubby fingernail.

Now that is certainly uncommon. Most Dragoons keep their nails long, kind of like talons. It's strange to see one of them who looks as if he clips his nails regularly and keeps them very short.

"Well, you see . . . Trent and I were, uh . . ."

"Busy playing a game." The Fox Folk Runt in question walks in from the hallway now wearing an old band T-shirt and shorts. He folds his arms and looks at Chalice. "By the way, you now owe me five dollars."

Misty narrows her eyes at them and a thin stream of smoke slips through her lips. I take a big step back.

"And what, dearest brother, was this game you were playing?"

Chalice avoids looking at her, or anyone for that matter, and stares at the ceiling. When a moment goes by with no one saying anything, Trent is the first to speak up.

"Seeing how long each of us could survive being outside naked in the front yard."

Misty blinks at them as Trent flips his five white-tipped, black tails lazily around his legs.

"Naked . . . out on the front lawn. On. The. Day. Julie. Moves. In. Are you two fucking nuts?"

Chalice takes a step back from her, and his arm brushes against my shoulder. He smells like this one special edition candle we sold at Candle Love a few years ago. I think it was called Midnight Ginger Sun that had a dark and smoky scent with hints of amber and ginger.

He turns to look down at me, and I'm momentarily lost in his hazel green eyes.

"Yeah, I kinda lost track of time. Trust me, Julie, it's not every day we're hanging around naked outside."

"That's too bad." Frankie snickers by my side.

Trent just starts laughing.

"Unbelievable," Misty mutters, running her hand over her face. "Can you at least make yourselves useful and go get her stuff from the car?"

"You got it, sis!" Chalice says brightly and clasps a large hand on my shoulder. "Welcome home, Jules!"

"Uh, thanks," I squeak out, but he's already out the door and jogging to my car.

"If you want to hang around naked every day, I'm down if you are," Trent says with a wink at both of us as he follows Chalice outside.

Misty groans and Frankie snickers again.

"I'm so sorry we're late, Misty," I say. "I remember you said you had somewhere you had to be tonight."

"Hmm? Oh yeah, it's okay. My ride to the airport is running late anyway. I'm headed up to Northern New Cali to visit a friend up there, so I'll actually be out of town for your first few weeks here."

"Hear that Julie? You're gonna be all alone with two of your new roomies!" Frankie's smile is anything but innocent as she jabs me in the ribs.

"Yes, I got that part, thank you, Frankie."

"Just make sure they don't throw any parties, and everything will be fine," says Misty. "Those two can get into some real trouble if they're left home alone with each other, so it's a good thing you'll be here to help level them out."

The thought of a house party in the place I'm currently living in doesn't sound very appealing. How can you go home to escape a crowded place when that crowded place is your home?

Misty checks the time on her phone.

"I have a few minutes, can I show you around the house before I take off?"

"That would be great, thank you."

"While you do that, I'm going to go help them," offers Frankie, though I think she just wants to go watch two hot guys lift heavy things.

"Thanks, Frankie." She gives me a wink and hurries outside.

"Alright, Julie. Ready for the grand tour?"

No, I'm honestly not ready. All I want right now is to get back in my car and drive back to my parent's empty house. Maybe I can break through a back window and just . . . stay there.

But that isn't something I can do. This is my life now, and just how it is. I have Frankie's support, and Misty seems nice enough. The two so-called trouble makers make me a little nervous, especially when I think back on Chalice's green eyes and Trent's lazy smile, but I'll get through this because I have to.

I take a deep breath.

"I . . . yes. I'm ready."

CHAPTER THREE

Misty glances outside and frowns. The front lawn is covered in a blanket of foamy white bubbles, and a few beer cans poke up around the scattered rubber ducks.

"I can't believe they put bubble bath in those pools. It's going to wreak the lawn." She lets out a big sigh. "Though it's not like it isn't already full of dead grass. When we were down a roommate, we tried to cut corners with the water bill. Watering the lawns was the first thing to do. Who knew grass can shrivel up and die do quickly?"

"You could consider it more eco-friendly, I suppose."

Misty blinks at me and then lets out a big, snorting laugh.

"Yeah, that's a good point!"

We walk a few steps away from the front door when she points to a long hallway in front of us with a nearby staircase. The walls are bare, but there are a few well-placed holes where it looks like pictures once hung and one lonely band poster taped up down the way.

"The staircase to your right leads up to my bedroom suite above the garage, and the hallway here leads to the other two bedrooms, but I'll show you that last."

I walk with her past the entry way, and we end up in a large, expansive room with a giant TV attached to the wall. A huge brown couch takes up most of the space and hooks around the wall in a "U" shape. A coffee table that has definitely seen better days rests in front of it and is covered with empty beer cans and discarded potato chips.

Everything is built just a little bit bigger since Misty, Chalice, and even Trent are all very tall. But it's nothing I can't handle as long as I can get my hands on a step stool or sturdy chair.

"The living room," Misty waves her hand and tail around the space. "Feel free to watch whatever, whenever you want. We got the TV from a friend, so it's kind of everyone's property. First come, first served."

I take note of an expensive collection of movies on a nearby shelf sitting next to another extensive collection of porno films. Yikes, I do not want to walk in on anyone watching one of those. Not that I have a problem with stuff like that, it would just be super awkward. Especially with roommates as attractive as the two I met out front.

To the side is a fireplace that looks like it hasn't been used in some time, which isn't uncommon. New California rarely gets cold enough to need the extra warmth, but the sight of the empty mantle brings a smile to my face. It looks like the perfect place to set up some of my candles.

Next, Misty shows me the kitchen. Unlike the living room, this place looks immaculate. The smooth marble countertops glitter as she turns on the light and we walk inside. There's a big, double door refrigerator that she opens and points at with one long nail.

"Label your food, for the love of the Goddess, label your all food. I will throw it out if it's not labeled. I will also throw it out if it's bad or expired." She turns to me with a wicked grin. "I take my job as fridge monitor seriously."

"Good, I like a clean fridge." I give a nervous chuckle at her comment, but my attention is quickly caught on the contents of the fridge itself. It's full of fancy cheeses, imported butters and jams, and small brown, paper packages of meats. There is even a pitcher of infused water with perfectly sliced cucumbers and lemons.

"Wow, there is a lot of stuff in here."

"Yeah, Trent is an aspiring chef. I think he's going back to school for it next year and Chalice . . . thinks he can cook. Seriously, though, don't let him make anything for you unless you're there to supervise."

She shuts the door, and I catch a glimpse of an old photo held up by a small black magnet. It's a photo of Misty and Chalice as kids, and they're scowling at the camera and covered in pasta sauce and noodles. To the side of the photo is a dusty brochure for The Mad Demonnie, which is a pit-stop on the way to New Las Vegas, a take-out menu for a pizza shop I remember seeing on the drive here, and a save-the-date wedding invite for a Demonnie and Fox Folk.

It's like a glimpse into someone else's life and the fact that I'm coming into an established household with its own history, friends, and favorite take-out restaurants makes me feel even more like an outsider.

"And over here is crown jewel of 1414 Cumberbatch Way." Misty pulls open a sliding glass door, and we step outside to the backyard.

Okay, besides the grass being brown and crunchy under my feet, the backyard is stunning. A big barbecue sits protected under a tarp next to the house, and there is a pool, long and rectangular, situated under a wall of tiles with several spouting fountains pouring into the deep end. There is even a connected hot tub off to the side with comfortable looking seats built into its circular sides.

It's a little cold for the pool, but the hot tub looks warm and inviting. Sitting in there after a long day dealing with people sounds wonderful.

"Fair warning about the hot tub." Misty scratches the side of her face with one of her silver colored nails. "If you see Trent or

Chalice in it alone, be warned, they're probably naked. I'm sure they wouldn't mind sharing the water, but . . . yeah."

"Do they get naked a lot?"

The image of Chalice's golden ass running into the house flashes through my mind and a small chuckle escapes my overwhelmed senses.

"Not as often as you would think, but more often than what I consider normal," she replies. "They're harmless, really, but Trent is a big flirt and Chalice can be pretty absent-minded sometimes."

We walk back inside, and I can faintly hear Frankie outside talking with Trent, and then a deep rumbling laugh, I'm assuming, from Chalice.

Misty points to the stairs again and says that her door will be locked while she's away, but Trent has the key in case we need to get in there for any reason. She says he's also the one who collects the rent money.

"The room beside that hideous poster belongs to Trent. It's the downstairs master, so he has his own bathroom attached, but there's only one other bathroom in this hall that you'll need to share with Chalice and any company that comes over. I hope you don't mind the, uh, setup."

She opens a door which leads to a large, fairly unremarkable bathroom with blue tile walls. It has been custom fitted to Dragoons, though, and the shower stall is long and slender to accommodate their tails and the shower head is set rather high, but it's nothing I haven't seen before. The showers at home were just like this.

"I grew up with a Dragoon family and shared a bathroom with my brother, so I'm used to it. I should manage just fine."

"Oh, that's right. You mentioned that to me already, sorry. Well, hopefully my brother will keep this place clean for you, but if he doesn't, just let me know."

We then make our way past another door that Misty points out as Chalice's room and then move on to mine directly next to his. She opens the door, which gives a little squeak, and we step inside.

Chalice, Frankie, and Trent have already made good progress moving my things inside, even my small bed has already been set up against the wall and a box marked "sheets" has been neatly placed on the mattress next to the pink duffle bag with my CPAP machine. I have to take a deep breath from the emotional feeling of seeing my normal bed that I've had for years now in a totally new and foreign place.

Misty takes out her phone and checks it.

"Looks like my ride is here," she says. "I need to go get my things. Do you have any questions before I leave?"

"No, um, I don't think so."

"Great!" Misty begins to walk out but turns around and gives me a warm smile. "If you grew up with Dragoons, then I'm sure you have a little bit of our spunk in you. Moving out is just one of life's big steps that everyone, no matter what creature you are, go through at some point. You'll be okay."

"I . . . thank you." Those are the only words I can get out as she smiles once more and leaves me in my new room.

Alone.

I'm only alone for long enough to unpack one box containing some of my artwork when the door to my new room swings open to allow Frankie and Chalice carrying a large box between them. I have to side step out of the way to avoid getting whacked by either of their tails as they place the box next to the closet.

"You're lucky we're such good friends, Julie. Helping someone move sucks, and I don't intend to help anyone ever again," says Frankie. She rustles her wings and rolls her shoulders. "I'm going to be sore for days!"

"I could have helped you bring everything inside!"

"Yeah, but no offense, I got it done much quicker than you would have." Frankie laughs and flashes me a smile. "Or maybe, I just wanted to stick around and get to know those guys you're living with now."

"Frankie"

"You'll be glad to know that I approve of both." She turns and gives a big exaggerated wink to Chalice.

"Um, thank you?" Chalice laughs awkwardly and looks away. "It would have gone a lot faster if Trent hadn't bailed. I'm actually surprised he lasted as long as he did."

Frankie's face flashes with equal parts amusement and disappointment.

"Yeah, Trent took one box inside and never came back." She lets out a sigh. "Well, it just means I'll have to come by another time to properly assess him and make sure he'll make a suitable roomie for my bestie. At least, all those tattoos really did it for me."

"What do you think of me?" Chalice asks.

"Eh, you lift boxes well," she responds. "But you've passed the first test."

"Which is . . ."

"You're a hottie with a nice golden ass!"

"Frankie!" I feel my face flush scarlet as she doubles over in laughter and Chalice spins in a circle trying to look at himself.

"Glad you like it!" he responds, crossing his arms over his chest and giving her a strange look. He turns to me with a softer smile, but I'm too embarrassed to make eye contact. I can hear him shuffle around, perhaps waiting for me to say something to him.

"Yes, we did like it and would love to see it again, but this time, as it exits this room and leaves me alone with Julie to help her unpack."

Chalice chuckles and turns to leave, giving us a wave over his shoulder. I can't help but notice his short nails again.

"Alright, well, nice to have you here Julie! I'll catch up with you later!"

No sooner does the door close behind him than Frankie spins around and stares at me with wide eyes.

"I am so jealous of you right now! This is amazing, you're living with two of the hottest creatures I've ever seen. Ugh, is it too late to switch apartments?"

"See, you joke about that, but I know you're not serious. You love living in little loft."

"Yeah, but," she gestures toward the door, "I can feel the hottest of those two literally oozing through the walls."

She falls atop my bed holding her sides as she laughs madly.

I laugh as well and rip open the big box they just brought into my room. It's full of clothes, most of which are still on their hangers. I start hanging them up in the closet, and Frankie finally comes over to help, but not after she lets out one more wild cackle that I'm sure the entire house can hear.

"In all honesty, this feels like the perfect place for you. After all, you're used to dealing with crazy Dragoons like myself and your own family for that matter. You're going to fit right in here."

I hang up a pretty pink camisole I've had for years and think about Frankie's words. This place does seem like a good fit for me. It's a little bit of what was familiar back at home, but with a touch of newness. And yet, it still feels so . . . weird.

"I know it'll be okay, but it's still sad to just move on so suddenly and have everything be so final. Like, I couldn't even visit my parents back in the place I grew up, I can never truly return home again. Still, it is exciting, but Frankie . . . what do I do if Trent and Chalice just, I don't know, run around naked all day?"

"Uh, call me immediately? Duh."

"Goddess, Frankie!"

We laugh together while putting away the majority of my things, and then Frankie helps to make my bed with clean sheets and pillows. Seeing everything put together eases some of the anxiousness in my stomach, it looks more like a home now instead of an empty room full of cardboard boxes.

Frankie very carefully rests my pink duffle bag on the bed.

"What kind of sheets are these? How old are you again?" Frankie points a long fingernail at my freshly made bed and grimaces. "These are not sexy."

"Hey, these are expensive, high thread count sheets."

"Made for who? Five year olds?" Frankie shakes her head at my pink and blue sheets covered in rainbows and unicorns. "You need some adult sheets."

"I don't think she does, they're kinda cute," a deep voice comes from the doorway and we both turn to see Chalice standing there.

He really is nice to look at, super tall with lightly gold skin and a matching sheen of scales covering the outer areas of his arms, cheeks, and neck. They dip down past his collar bone toward his chest, and the grey V-neck shirt he's wearing gives me a little peek at his well-defined, golden muscles.

"I mean, to each their own, but I already know I'm getting her some new bedsheets for her birthday next year," says Frankie, standing up and linking my arm with her own. "Come walk me out."

I give Chalice a small smile as I follow Frankie from my room and down the hallway.

"Please keep me informed of everything. Every look, every touch, every . . ." She waggles her eyebrows at me after I open the front door for her. "Every fuck. I need to know you're doing okay out on your own."

"I'll be fine because I have to be."

"That is a terrible way to think about it. You'll be fine because you are a strong, independent woman who may not be an actual

Dragoon but has the heart of one beating fiercely inside her. Besides, it's just moving out. It's not that big of a deal."

"Well, it is for me. I mean, those two in there are hot, what if . . .
what if they find my CPAP machine? That'd be so embarrassing."

We walk outside and pause on the dead grass. The bubbles have
since evaporated in the sun and it appears someone has come by
and picked up all the empty beer cans.

"Hey, we've had this discussion before." Frankie rustles and
stretches her wings. "It's not a bad thing to use something that has
been medically prescribed to you. It doesn't make you weak."

"Yeah, but . . ."

"Nope. End of discussion. If you're that concerned about it,
lock your door when you're asleep and put the thing in a drawer
during the daytime. I respect how you feel, but trust me, you don't
have to hide something like that."

"Maybe," I mutter, shuffling my feet while Frankie does a couple
more wing stretches.

I've always been secretly jealous of her ability to fly, as I'm sure
half the populace of Dragoons and Demonnie are as well. Not all
are born with wings, such as the case with Misty and Chalice, but
Frankie and her family all have huge leathery wings that allow them
to fly short distances.

"No 'maybes about it, everything will be fine. Now, as soon as
I'm airborne, go back inside and finish unpacking, then get your

ass in the kitchen and . . . I don't know, bake a cake. That could lure those hunks out and get to know them better."

"Do I have to?"

"Yes, because I need you to choose one so I can hit on the other without feeling bad. Or don't and take them both!" She laughs before leaning down to engulf me in a tight hug. "I wouldn't leave you alone if I thought you couldn't handle yourself. Remember that I'm a phone call away and you can ring me anytime you want to talk."

"I will; thanks, Frankie. You're an amazing friend."

I take a step back as she spreads her wings and gives me the same exaggerated wink that she gave Chalice. She really is my best friend, and one of the worst things about moving out is that I'll be even farther away from her now, but knowing her, she'll make it a point to show up here unannounced to 'check up on me' whenever she feels like I need it.

"I know, but so are you. Now go back inside and let your new roomies know how amazing you are!"

I watch she takes off into a purple and pink tinged sky. This day has gone by so quickly that I didn't even notice the sun had started to set already.

It's been a long ass day.

CHAPTER FOUR

O nce Frankie literally disappears into the sunset, I go back inside the house and head to my room. The place seems quiet, and it feels like Misty has been long gone. The stillness feels unnatural but luckily doesn't last long because I begin to hear someone, probably Trent, tuning a guitar in his bedroom.

I start to really notice the bare and empty walls as I pass down the hallway. Maybe I could sneak some of my drawings up. No one has to know I was the artist because I could easily lie and say I picked them up at a thrift store. Yeah, I could get a couple of cheap frames, scruff them up, and put a random signature on them. No one will ever know.

My artsy thoughts haven't taken over as I walk into my room, so I don't notice Chalice standing next to my bed until I'm closing the door behind me.

"Oh, I'm sorry!" I stutter and open the door again with a forceful shove, nearly tripping over my own feet in the process. "I didn't realize you were still in here."

The side of his mouth lifts in a grin, and he scans my room with a thoughtful eye. He has really pretty eyes. They're golden like his skin but have flecks of some undetermined color similar to green. Like uncut, hazel-colored diamonds.

And that tail! If Frankie were here right now, she'd make some joke about connections between cock and tail size, but she really wouldn't need to. I can tell already that Chalice is big because the sweatpants he's wearing certainly don't leave much to the imagination. I also saw him run by me completely naked earlier today.

"I'm in your room, and you're apologizing to me?"

"Uh, yeah." I grimace when I notice the smirk on his face because he noticed me checking him out. "I don't know, force of habit? It's what I get for working retail for several years."

His eyes brighten, and he turns his head to the side as he considers me with his golden expression. I'm a little bolder this time, maybe because I'm surrounded by my things and in the safety of my new room, but I actually make eye contact with him and wow, I can't look away.

"I work at Burger Bliss. Not exactly retail, but I bet we can trade some good horror stories. No secrets among those in the service industry!"

Frankie would be so disappointed in me because I have no idea what to say to him. He's staring at me now with those eyes and those muscles, and his golden tail is twitching slowly behind him and tapping at the side of my bed. Goddess, he's so big, he would probably crush my bed if we really got into it.

Come on, Julie! You got this. Just say something to him!

"Mmm hmm, yup."

Ugh. I'm so awkward.

"Sorry we have to share a bathroom, but did you know that you got the best room in the house?"

"I did?"

"Yup, coolest in the summer and warmest in the winter. There's also a tree we've managed to keep alive just outside your window and you can see hummingbirds sometimes at the feeder we hung up. You'll be comfortable here for years to come."

Thinking of being in this little room for years makes my head hurt, but that's a problem for future Julie. Present Julie needs to make sense of what she's feeling right now and what words to say.

"I like birds."

Brava, Julie. Bra-fucking-va.

"They are nice to look at."

We stand there in the silence, and it's the worst. I'm not sure what else to say to him and wish I was more free with my words, like Frankie. She'd have no problem telling him that when he crosses his arms, like he's doing now, it makes the muscles of his chest and shoulders bulge, or that his hazel eyes look deep and mysterious in the darkening room.

Wait, darkening? Why is it so dark in here? Shit, I need to unpack a lamp or I'm going to be really annoyed later.

"Did you paint this?" Chalice asks and I glance over to see him picking up one of my paintings. It's a very nice one of the parking lot at work. I did it in watercolor, and it took me forever to get the sunset just right because there were just too many colors.

"I did, but it's not very good."

"You've got to be kidding, it's amazing! This is the same parking lot by Burger Bliss. I recognize the landmarks."

"I work at Candle Love. I think we're just across from you guys. I did that one night in my car."

I immediately regret telling him that, but it's too late now.

"You did this? In your car? In watercolor? That's impressive, Julie! Do you have more I can see?" He places the painting gingerly on the bed.

"Some, but they're still packed away in the boxes. Speaking of which, I really should get going on that. It's gotta be close to seven."

"Right, right. You should get on that out of the way so we can have some roommate bonding time."

"Wait . . . what?"

"Bonding!" Chalice says with a wicked grin. "Don't worry, nothing nefarious, just some initial initiation stuff."

"Right."

Chalice turns to leave, but his tail swings out and bumps against the bed, causing my pink duffle bag to shuffle forward and nearly fall to the floor. I make a lunge for it, but he catches it before I do and hands it to me.

I clutch it to my chest, breathing heavily. If it had fallen, my CPAP machine could have been damaged, and it would be a pain in the ass to get a replacement. Besides, I kind of need it to sleep at night, and it would be a hard couple of days trying to get a new one as soon as possible.

"Sorry about that," he says, blushing and rubbing the back of his neck. "What's in there? Was it something breakable?"

I clutch the bag tighter, and he gives me a strange look when I don't answer. This is a secret I still want to keep a hold of.

"Alright, well, I'll catch you in a little bit."

He gives me another charming smile, and as soon as he leaves the room, I bolt to the door and close it behind him. I release a breath I didn't even know I was holding and gently set the duffle bag back down on the bed.

Once I hear his door open and then close, I begin to slowly unpack my CPAP machine and arrange the power cables so I can safely store it inside the drawer of my nightstand. I'll just have to take it back out every night, but it's a small price to pay. As long as no one comes in while I'm sleeping, no one will ever know.

I know it's a common condition, I really do know that in my heart, but I'm so embarrassed at wearing the giant mask when I sleep. It's the opposite of sexy, at least in my opinion. None of the glamours stars you see sleeping in the movies have their faces connected to plastic tubing. Maybe it's possible they do in their personal lives, but I feel like it's never talked about anywhere. I didn't even know it was a real condition until I was diagnosed by my doctor.

It's not the only thing I'm embarrassed about. I can't believe I let slip that I was the one who did that parking lot painting. Sure, it was a great conversation starter, but now he knows I like to draw and paint. There was just something in the way he asked about it, or maybe it was the look in his eyes that made me come clean. Should I—I don't know—trust him?

Fuck, it's all so overwhelming. I just met the guy, and he's my new roommate. A fucking sexy as all get-out roommate, but also the guy sleeping in the room next door to mine. We're even going to brush our teeth using the same bathroom sink, so perhaps he's even more like a brother. I've had a Dragoon brother before, so it shouldn't be weird.

No, that's weird to think of it like that. Ugh, it's been a long day and I'm ready for bed. Crawling under my bedsheets and shutting the world away sounds like bliss right now.

There's just one problem.

I can feel my stomach pinching in hunger, and I don't think I've ever gone to bed after missing dinner before. I'm going to have to reluctantly drag myself out to the shared kitchen for food and . . . bonding time.

Fuck.

Might as well get it over with.

I spend some time putting away more things before deciding to leave my room and as soon as I close the door behind me, I'm hit with the smell of baked dough, herby tomato sauce, and greasy pepperoni. It wafts down the hallway from either the kitchen or living room, and I'm drawn toward it like a moth to the flame of a special, limited edition candle from Candle Love.

Another trip through the barren hallway brings me to its source in the living room where I find Chalice and Trent sitting on the couch. In front of them is the coffee table piled with pizza boxes, paper plates, and what looks like Yule-themed napkins decorated with peppermint sticks and pine cones. A little out of season for those, but I appreciate the effort it seems they made to set the table.

"Julie!" Chalice jumps from the couch when I enter the room, but Trent stays seated and only tilts his head back to gaze at me with his icy blue eyes. "Trent ordered pizza in honor of your first night here. It's from our favorite place, Second Class Pizza!"

"Second Class? That's an odd choice for a name."

"Their motto is 'where the customer comes first.' But you're right, it is a fucked name," replies Trent. "Doesn't really matter, though, because the food is fucking delicious.

"Come sit with us and have some!"

Chalice sits back down and pats the open middle spot between them. I have to fight back the blush that threatens to creep up my cheeks at the thought of being sandwiched between the both of them and take a step back.

"That's okay, I can take a slice to the table in the kitchen. I, uh, don't want to spill anything on the couch."

"Too late for that." Trent laughs and points a black tail at Chalice. "He's already wrecked this couch beyond repair with his terrible eating habits. Trust me in saying that nothing you can do will compare to either the chocolate stains on the armrests or the persistent wine splashes he's sitting on."

"Hey, the wine stains are from Misty and her friends. I don't drink that stuff." Chalice huffs and piles a few slices of pizza onto one of the plates. "But I can claim ownership of the nacho cheese stain behind Trent."

"Join us and we can watch a movie or something." Trent flashes a smile and Chalice gives me such a sad-eyed, pleading look that makes me give in and sink onto the middle cushion between them.

There isn't much room and both my thighs are pressed against their own, and it suddenly makes me very self-conscious on how loud I'm breathing, or what my breath might smell like. Chalice hands me the plate of pizza slices, and I jam one into my mouth because I figure pizza breath is better than possibly bad breath.

They're right to claim it as their favorite because it is really good, even if it does have mushrooms on it. I stomach a few but finally have to pick them off. The spongy brown things simply do not belong on pizza.

Chalice raises an eyebrow at me and holds his plate over my lap.

"I'll eat them for you," he says with a wink, and I gratefully dump them off and wipe my hands with one of the peppermint napkins.

Chalice makes a face when he seems to notice the napkins they've chosen to use.

"Sorry, I couldn't find non-holiday-themed napkins." He laughs and holds one up for closer inspection. It's already used and has pepperoni grease smudges between the pine cones and peppermints. "But we have a ton of these leftover from a Yule party we had several months ago, and Misty is always going on about how we need to use them up. I said we should just chuck them."

"If you don't want to use them, there are, um, places you can donate them," I say.

"Like where?"

"I, uh, volunteer at the New Harvest Food Bank. They're always looking for donations and they're not picky about napkins. I bet you wouldn't have guessed it, but this isn't the first time I've used with napkins with peppermint sticks and pine cones this time of year."

"I have a buddy who does some work there," Trent says between mouthfuls of pizza. "Fun place." He winces as if realizing what he just said.

"I wouldn't exactly call it a 'fun' place, but the people there are nice and I have a good time helping out."

"That's really cool of you, Julie." Chalice's words sink into me like butter, melting into my soul as if it's a warm piece of toast, and I momentarily panic because I don't know how to respond.

"Uh huh."

Another fantastic, top-of-the-class response, Julie. A plus.

We continue to munch on pizza and the topic of conversation thankfully moves away from anything related to my hobbies and interests, and I find out more about two of my three new room-mates.

Trent, it seems, is an aspiring chef and day-time computer consultant, and according to Chalice, that simple fact makes him irresistible to almost everyone, and I'm warned that if I ever see him poking around in the kitchen after midnight, it's probably because he's experimenting with cooking something new.

He's considered a Fox Folk Runt, due to only having five tails instead of nine, plays guitar, has an unknown number of tattoos (he
refuses to tell anyone the actual number because apparently some
of them are very embarrassing), and is the undisputed champion
of any and all board games. He might be the second coolest person
I've ever met. After Frankie, of course.

Chalice and Misty are twins, and they both work at Burger Bliss,
though Misty dropped down to part-time so she could focus on
school. He's also a heavy sleeper and gifted with the ability to fall
asleep wherever and whenever he feels like it. Something I'm a little
envious of. It sounds like he's single, and from the way Trent tells
it, he has a hard time keeping a girlfriend.

"I just haven't found that special someone," he replies to Trent's
wry comments about his choice in women. "It'll happen one day."

Trent lets out a snorting laugh before turning toward me.

"What about you, Julie, you dating anyone? Any little humans
we'll need to watch out for, or perhaps big, manly Minotaur?"

"Oh, Goddess no, I . . . I'm not seeing anyone right now."

I pick at my last slice of pizza and take a sip of my drink. I don't
really want to talk about my dating life, or lack of one, to my new
roommates. I don't have the dating experience Frankie has, but
I do have some. It's just not very interesting, or recent for that
matter. My last relationship was terrible because he was, simply

put, an awful creature, and I sort of took a break after that. Though the "break" has been going on a few years by now.

"Hmm," Trent hums, setting his empty plate on the coffee table and grabbing the TV remote. He gives me a wink. "Well, just make sure to hang a sock on your door knob in case you decide to do any fucking."

I choke on my soda, and Chalice pats my back. His hand is large and warm between my shoulder blades, and the tingling feeling it leaves behind makes me cough even more.

Trent chuckles and waves the remote toward the TV.

"Alright roomies, it's my turn to pick the movie tonight and I've got the perfect pick in honor of Julie's first night with us."

Chalice grins and stretches both his arms across the back of the couch. One of them comes extremely close to grazing my shoulder. I chew on my lip to keep from saying anything dumb.

"Nice! Is it that zombie flick you were talking about the other day or the one with dinosaurs?"

"Neither, it's . . ."

I watch as Trent points the remote at the TV and starts pressing buttons. Instead of a normal streaming service popping up, I hear the tell-tale sounds of an old style DVD player coming to life as it loads up a movie. And then . . .

"Oh yeah . . . oh yeah . . . oh ya-ya-ya-yeah!" The high pitched squealing of a busty blonde Minotaur fills the room as the image of her being absolutely hammered from behind by what appears to be a Mousequeek with a cock as large as he is. Two humans appear moments later, one jamming their cock into the Minotaur's mouth and another pulling her hair.

It's porn. Hardcore pornography playing on the TV in front of me as I sit with my new roommates.

"Shit, sorry!" Trent laughs loudly and frantically starts pressing more buttons on the remote but only succeeds in turning the volume up when Chalice tries to grab it from his hand.

"Who left that in there!" Chalice screams above the sounds.

"I don't know, maybe Kevin?" Trent yells back, his five tails spin behind him, and I narrowly avoid being smacked by one. "Probably during the party last week!"

The sounds of moaning, grinding, and hair pulling surround us while the two of them fumble with the remote till it flies from their hands, and I somehow catch it mid-flight.

It takes me a second to find the right button to turn the DVD player off and only a second more to gently place the remote onto the coffee table.

The three of us stand in awkward silence until I clear my throat and get up.

"Um, thanks for the pizza. I'm kinda tired from moving all day so I'm going to get to bed."

"No worries," Trent says, grabbing another slice of pizza. "See you tomorrow. Sorry about the porn."

"Sweet dreams, Julie," Chalice says with a smile. I don't reply as I bolt from the room and scurry to my bedroom.

As soon as I close and lock my door behind me, I find I am actually exhausted. I'm able to sink into bed and let this eventful day finally come to an end. I don't even have the energy to make a dash for the bathroom to brush my teeth; I'm just too drained from the emotional day.

I do, however, have enough power left in my system to change into a nightshirt and remove my CPAP machine from the drawer so I can set it up on my bedside table.

Then as soon as I slip my mask over my face and turn off the light, I fall into a deep, deep sleep.

I wake up a few hours later with the incredible urge to pee. A quick look at my phone tells me it's two in the morning and judging from the quietness surrounding me, Trent and Chalice must be done watching porn and in bed.

The image of the blond Minotaur from the video is hot on my mind as I pull CPAP mask away from my face and sit up in bed. While it was a rather startling way to begin my first night within my new home, it also left my body feeling restless and agitated. It didn't help seeing the absolute plowing that busty Minotaur was receiving from both ends as I sat sandwiched between two of the hottest creatures I've ever known.

I've never been so hot and bothered in my life before.

Creeping slowly from my warm bed, I make my way out of my bedroom and toward the bathroom I now share with Chalice. Light streams from under his door, but I don't hang around in case he'll notice me and dart quickly into the bathroom to take care of business.

With an empty bladder and freshly brushed teeth, I click off the light and open the door as quietly as possible so I don't disturb my new roommates, but as soon as I step barefoot into the hallway, I can see that Chalice's door is cracked open.

Light beams from it to the floor in a contained ray of gold, and in the still night, I can hear heavy breathing drifting through the quiet house. Tiptoeing toward my room, I can't help but lean in to see the cause of the grunting and straining sounds.

Shit, he's jerking off!

I'm both too stunned and too excited to look away. It's not like he's given me permission to watch him, but I just can't glance away from the way his hands glide up and down his massive golden cock. The muscles in his arms bunch and tense when his head tips back, and I pull away in case he sees me and dash inside my room, closing the door nosily behind me.

Once I'm in bed, I fold the sheets over my face because even though no one can see me, I'm still embarrassed for embarrassed sake. And now I'm even more hot and bothered than before! That golden cock was, for lack of better words, magnificent.

I'm just starting to drift off once again when my cell phone chimes to life, and I look down to see a text message from Trent.

Trent: I saw you. Naughty little human.

I want to pull the covers back over my head and never come out again, but Chalice's straining muscles and Trent's words keep swimming through my head, and instead of slipping my mask back on and going back to sleep, I reach into my nightstand for my vibrator.

Pressing it between my legs with one hand and holding a pillow over my mouth with the other, I'm able to coax out a frenzied orgasm that has my whole body clenching and waiting for something more substantial.

But that will have to wait until another day because I think I'm now finally feeling relaxed enough to sleep.

Sort of.

CHAPTER FIVE

I t's been over a week since moving into the house with Chalice and Trent, and I've finally stopped sulking silently into my pillow—thinking of my old home every night. In this time, my parents have sent the obligatory text messages asking how I'm doing and if I'm enjoying my new life. It's nice of them to reach out, but it's hard to gauge how much they really care. It's in their nature to think I'm a big girl who doesn't need them, which is true in most ways, but they tend to 'act human' for me when it crosses their minds.

Getting back into my old routine of volunteer work and working at Candle Love has helped me feel somewhat normal again. Well, that and constant masturbation to keep me from dry humping my hot roommates.

It's nice to be at work today, though, and not hanging around at the house with nothing but my thoughts. Even if my coworkers are a mixed bunch, this still feels like a second home when I'm here, and today is no exception as I sit in the back room waiting for my shift to begin.

The door swings open and Eddie, a human and demon hybrid Demonnie, barges into the backroom of Candle Love. He dramatically gasps for air and waves one gray-toned hand in front of his nose and clutches the other to his chest above his heart.

"Fuck! That one Fox lady is back at it with all the room sprays. I tried pretending to restock in that corner area and thought I blocked her, but she somehow shimmied around and took them straight out of the box. She sprayed them everywhere. Every. Fucking. Where."

Eddie spins dramatically, purposely bumping into me and letting his hand linger on my shoulder for moment before gagging and pretending to faint on one of the two chairs we have. His large bronze colored wings fall behind him to the floor as he sighs loudly. The plastic chair scrapes against the smooth tiles and bends dangerously beneath his weight. He then squeezes his eyes shut and holds his breath.

"Watch it, Eddie," hisses Portia, a way-too-pretty Fox Folk with nine tails. She has to side step his wings and maneuver around his prone body. "We're running out of chairs back here because your big ass keeps breaking them."

"Not my fault I was blessed with such an amazing body in addition to astonishing good looks. But I guess that means there's just more of me to love." He opens his eyes to wink at her and she bares her teeth in a sneer. "Besides, maybe if we break them all, Marilyn will have to buy us new ones."

"Fat chance of that happening. Marilyn probably used the store's chair money on her most recent plastic surgery."

"Careful, Portia, you don't want to get caught talking shit again. Aren't you already on a final warning for your potty mouth?" Eddie grins at her.

She bares a set of perfectly white and straight teeth at him and disappears out the side door to go back to the front portion of the store.

Portia is one of the few nine-tailed Fox Folks I've ever known to hold a part-time job. Most of them come from rich families, so you don't see anyone with nine tails working in any place requiring you to wear a uniform. It's normally just the Runts, those born with less than nine tails, who take on jobs to prove something to themselves or their families.

Rumor has it that she got into some trouble with her family and they made her get a job to learn how to earn her own money. Though I'm not sure if it's working because she seems to do less around here than Eddie. But at least she makes really nice displays out of our product launches. It's probably the only reason she's still employed because she is always getting herself into trouble around here.

"How can Portia work under these conditions?" Eddie furrows his brows and glares after her. "I literally can't breathe out there."

"Stop being so dramatic." I swat his shoulder and laugh. "It's part of the job and you should be used to it by now. Anyway, I bet if you went out there and flirted with spray lady, you could get her to stop or at least browse a different section of the store."

"Even I have my limits, little one." Eddie stands and stretches his wings, making me have to dodge quickly out of the way. "But I appreciate your healthy dose of respect for one such as me."

"Goddess . . ."

"You mean 'God,' Julie. Get it right." He smiles down at me and laughs. "I only go by 'Goddess' on the weekends."

"I'll try to remember that."

I've always liked Eddie. While I've had lots of interactions with Dragoons, he was one of the first Demonnie I ever got to know on a somewhat personal level. Sure, we're probably more "work friends" than actual friends, but when you spend a lot of time with someone at a job, a close relationship just sort of evolves.

He's super tall and attractive, with thick dark hair and wings the color of shiny new pennies. But I long ago decided that I never stood a chance with him. Besides, I don't think I could put up his lifestyle outside of work. A different night club every weekend? No thanks. That's just not my scene. I'll take a quiet coffee shop with very few creatures inside or a nice evening at home with pizza and video games over all the glitz and glamour of any nightlife in New California or even New Las Vegas.

Eddie is also a really big flirt, which is probably why he's such a good salesman when he's actually working and selling candles up front. The older woman, in particular, absolutely eat him up.

We're just too different and could never work.

"Hey, did you see the bulletin board today?" Eddie asks after tossing me a clean blue apron from the communal bin. It still smells like the roses and lavender scented soap we use to clean them. (We also sell the same exact soap if anyone asks.)

"No, why?" I glance over at the cork board set on the wall by the small office in the backroom's corner. Management uses it for anything work related, and we use it to post silly photos of ourselves. It looks the same as it did yesterday except for a pretty blue poster board attached front and center.

"Design contest," says Eddie. "They're looking for entries from employees to design the labels for one of the next product line launches. Aren't you into that art stuff?"

"Oh, um, I sort of am."

He only knows because he caught me drawing on napkins once on break time.

Eddie's face brightens, and he gestures to the sign with a genuine smile on his face.

"You should submit something."

"Well . . ."

"Would you two get out on the fucking floor and actually start your shifts. I'd like to go home eventually," the high-pitched whine of Portia's annoyance rings through the backroom and startles both of us. It's followed by her stomping over with her nine tails an irritated flurry of movement behind her. It's a wonder she has such control over them that they don't knock anything over.

"On my way right now," Eddie says smoothly, breezing past her and narrowly avoiding being hit by her tawny brown tails. "Just going over the bulletin board updates before starting my shift."

"Sorry, Portia," I mumble, ducking around her and hurtling out the door behind Eddie. She may not be my favorite creature, but I probably should get to work.

Coming out into Candle Love is like entering a portal to another world, and it takes my eyes a moment to focus on the brightness of the store. The backroom is cool and dark, and surprisingly doesn't smell very strongly of one thing or another. Out here, though, is an entirely different matter.

I can see why Eddie was so upset because I'm hit immediately by a wall of room spray smells, all mixing with each other and combining into what I can only describe as a sunset on a beach while drinking a margarita as you're baking chocolate cookies inside a pile of fall leaves. Even the other customers seem to be keeping their distance as the lady continues to spray, sniff, and repeat on every spray lining the shelves.

"See?" Eddie mutters to me as he walks by to help someone else as far away from her as possible.

"It's not so bad once you get used to it," the sing-song voice of Rose floats by me, and I turn to look at the rose gold Dragoon beside one of the registers. "I imagine it as the scent of an older couple married for fifty years, sitting on their terrace overlooking the ocean, sipping drinks as the world drifts into autumn around them."

She sighs dreamily and stares off into . . . well, nothing.

"I think I can imagine that," I say.

"Of course you can, dear, you've an artsy mind. Thick with paper flowers, creative juices, and the milk of inspiration."

"I, um . . . thanks Rose." She smiles sweetly and continues to rearrange Portia's hand sanitizer and lip balm display.

Rose is gorgeous for a Dragoon and dresses like modern day witch with long, flowing skirts and kimono jackets, and she's always adorned with colorful jewelry.

She's very sweet, but she also tends to have her head in the clouds most days. A lot of customers really fall head over heels in love with the dreamy and romantic stories she makes up, and I think she's our top candle seller. Even better than Eddie.

I'm probably the worst because sometimes I just hide behind displays and hope no one asks me any questions.

"Rose," Portia whines, running over and snatching the items from Rose's long fingernails. "I just set this up. Leave it alone."

"Portia . . ." Rose sighs and flicks a lip balm back into place. "Your aura seems off today. Are you feeling well?"

"You do look kind of sweaty," I unhelpfully add.

Portia's tails spin wildly and one actually flicks me in the face, which is very unlike her. She may be a bitch sometimes (well, all of the time really) but I've never seen her this worked up about one of her displays. I can even see a bead of sweat dripping down her forehead.

"Mind your own fucking business," she snaps. She pauses to take a very long and noisy drink from a soda she has hidden beneath the front counter. "I'm just not feeling like myself today. It's a good thing I'm off duty in a few minutes."

If I didn't know any better, I'd say she was about to start her heat, which happens with mature Fox Folk women every other month. I don't know much about it, only the stuff Frankie has told me about, but most of them take suppressants to curb the side effects. Apparently not Portia, though, so I guess she's running on a frightening mix of hormones and diet soda.

I spy Eddie coming over with a concerned look on his face and watch as Portia takes several steps back as he approaches. Her eyes go wide when her back unexpectedly bumps into one of the displays. Rose and I jump forward to steady the table and prevent any of the candles from falling, but it doesn't do any good and one smashes onto the ground in a flurry of lavender scented glass shards.

"Oh, Goddess, I'm . . . why was that there anyway?" Portia's nine tails stand straight behind her, and her ears flatten against her skull. "Honestly, this store is a mess. Why aren't you doing your job, Julie, and keeping this shit organized?"

"Are you okay?" I try to approach her like an injured bird, but she jumps away and hurries toward the backroom.

"Its fine, I'm fine . . . I'll see you guys tomorrow!" She calls over her shoulder while making a hasty retreat.

Rose grabs a broom and dust pan which she hands over to me, and together, we start to clean up the shattered candle.

"What do you think that was about?" I ask out loud.

"If I didn't know any better, I'd say she was going into her heat. She's being a bigger snob than normal." Eddie laughs nervously and rubs at one of his bronze wings. "I thought she was on suppressants."

"We shouldn't be talking about her like that, not behind her back," I whisper, and Rose nods before looking pointedly at Eddie as he throws his hands up defensively and backs away.

I may think nasty thoughts about Portia because she's mean to me most of the time. But saying stuff like that out loud seems . . . wrong. I mean, we all have our secrets and stuff we want to keep private.

I should know.

"Fine, fine," Eddie calls over his shoulder, crossing his arms over his broad chest and walking backward looking at us. "Forget I said anything."

Rose hums in response and continues to tidy up.

"So are you going to enter that design contest?"

"Well, I, hmm . . . I don't know. Maybe?" I try to keep busy as I absentmindedly rotate a few out of place candles so their labels are all facing the exact same direction. "I'm not that good."

"You don't have to be good to put love into your work," she responds and pats my back with her extra-long tail.

"Uh, thank you?"

Was that even a compliment? I can't tell with her sometimes.

The rest of my shift continues in a blur. The only reminder that it's about time to go home is when Eddie's stomach growls so loudly that several customers standing by the cash register take notice, and I look out to see that the vibrant day has turned to night.

The problem with working in a place with barely any windows is that you can lose track of the time of day very quickly. You can only tell what time it might be based on how hungry you are.

I bet they don't have this problem across the parking lot at the Burger Bliss. They're probably always eating free burgers over there. In fact . . . that sounds like the perfect dinner for this evening.

So as soon as I'm clocked out and Eddie and Rose are left behind to close up the store, I get in my car and drive the short distance through the parking lot to join the very long drive through lane.

A juicy burger will get my mind off stupid things like art contests and the two cute guys waiting for me at home.

The drive through line at Burger Bliss always moves incredibly slow. I suppose it's because they make everything fresh to order, but I would think they would have to have some sort of better system in place to speed things up. Maybe, Candle Love has more in common with them than I think, and they also deal with their share of customer related slowdowns.

The Minotaur in the car ahead of me in line has already honked his car horn several times and tilted his massive head from his window to tell the person ahead of him to hurry up and pull forward in line. Then, following the curve of the line, he turns his car widely and runs over a few plants along the side of the lane before sticking his head out again to yell at nothing but the crushed bushes.

I'm so absorbed in watching him that when the drive through lane speaker crackles to life beside me, I nearly jump from my seat.

"Hi there! What can we make for you today?" It's the chipper voice of a Mousequeek, the mouse human hybrids of our world. They have slightly high-pitched voices and always seem to be in a good mood. Maybe it's because they can eat whatever they want and never gain a pound, unlike my own stumpy human body.

"Uh, can I get a double burger—hold the cheese—wrapped in lettuce with a side of potato fries?"

"Of course! Anything to drink? We have really good lemonade!"

I can hear her just fine, but I can also hear a lot of background noise. It must be busy inside their restaurant, even though it's pushing nine thirty at night right now. Another reason I would never work here is because I would hate getting home after midnight.

"A diet please . . . oh wait. I mean, just a cup of water."

"You got it! One double-burger-no-cheese-on-lettuce, fries, and a diet water!"

"Thanks," I mutter and pull forward a few feet after she recites my total.

The sky is nothing but black tonight, and I can't make out any stars when I look up through my windshield. It's probably because there's so much light pollution from the blinding bright lights beaming from the restaurant's windows like cones of tractor beams from an alien ship.

I've always been interested in astronomy and wanted to be an astronaut when I was a kid. I took all the University classes I could on the topic until I decided to take a break from school, though how I'll ever turn an interest like that into a career is beyond me. Stargazing as a hobby might be as far as I'll ever get to actually being in space.

"Oh, hi Julie!" A very recognizable voice breaks into my thoughts, and I look up at Burger Bliss's drive through hand-out window to see none other than Chalice poking his golden flecked face out and waving at me.

I swallow hard. At least he's at work, and I'm sure our interaction won't be very long. As long as I'm not too awkward, this should be fine.

"Look Trent, it's Julie!" Chalice calls over his shoulder and just as I'm approaching the window, I see Trent leaning across the counter from the customer's side of the restaurant and giving me a wide mouthed grin.

I spend a little too much time making sure to align my car perfectly at the hand-out window before looking up at him from my lower angle.

"Hi Chalice, I, uh, didn't realize you worked today."

He smiles and flashes a grin as Trent makes a comment I can't hear.

"I'm actually leaving in a few minutes, did you want to hang out? Trent and I were going to go get some food."

"Oh, no. Well, I'm getting food here, so . . . um, maybe another time?"

"That's too bad," Chalice says, taking my card to pay for the meal. "I would love to hang out with you sometime."

"Yeah, I'd like that. Hanging out is fun." I accidentally let my foot slip from the brake pedal and my car lurches forward before I slam my foot down again.

Smooth, Julie, smooth.

Chalice looks nervously at my car and then back over his shoulder when a pretty Fox Folk Runt waves her arms at the window. She's obviously trying to tell him to move the line along, and I don't blame her.

He holds my food out to me, and I snatch the bag ungracefully from his hand. There is a small moment where our fingers brush ever so slightly and the seriously small contact makes me let out a small gasp at the tingle I feel afterward.

"I'll see you later, Chalice," I say, forcing what I hope is a cute smile on my face as I get out of there as fast as I can carefully drive out of the lane to get away from the sultry eyes of my two hot roommates.

Once I'm on the road, I have to make a few U-turns and turn down an unfamiliar street all because I accidentally start driving toward my family's home. Well, former home.

Then, it's only when I'm collapsing on my bed that I realize I didn't stick around long enough to get my water from Chalice. Luckily, it's just water, and I make a mad dash out of my room to fill a cup before once again sequestering myself and my now cold dinner in my room.

But every fry I eat seems to remind me of Chalice's golden tone scales, and every bite of burger reminds me of his smile as he handed my food out to me. Even Trent's sly grin makes an appearance in my horny mind.

Ugh. I don't know why I'm hung up on either of them. Sure, they're both hot, like seriously hot, but it's not like I'd have a chance with creatures like that. Besides, since we're roommates, I don't want to make things weird.

At least . . . that's what I'm going to keep telling myself.

CHAPTER SIX

"**G**oddess, Julie, did you even sleep last night? That's the third largest yawn I've ever seen." Rose peers closely at my sleep-deprived face and squints her eyes. "I have a special tea I can give you if you need some energy, or if you'd prefer, I have a different one that will knock you right out."

I don't feel like explaining that—even though my CPAP machine was working hard to make me sleep, my wicked mind could not stop thinking about the feel of Chalice's fingers touching mine.

It feels so chaste, thinking about just his fingertips. But his short nails were the first thing I noticed about him, well, besides his golden ass running out of the front yard. Maybe that's why just the thought of those fingers and hands running over my body is making me all squirmy, fidgety, and sleep deprived.

And that's just Chalice; thoughts of Trent with his lazy smile and twitching white-tipped black tails is a whole different problem. We still haven't said a word to each other about me spying on Chalice jerking off in his room.

Being this tired is going to make it a long night because I'm headed to my volunteer job at the New Harvest Food Bank after work. I'll barely have time to eat something before I begin my shift later this evening.

"I'd stay away from Rose's teas." Eddie laughs from his position on the floor under a nearby display. He closes the bottom drawer, now packed full of overstock candles and looks up at us. "Most of them are highly illegal."

"The majority of them aren't widely accepted by the general populace, but they've been used for countless generations. And, they're grown in my grandmother's garden. No one is going to arrest a sweet old creature in her eighties, even if she is growing questionable crops in her backyard." Rose flips her tail at Eddie, and he topples on his ass trying to bat it away from his face. He starts laughing on the floor.

"But they also taste bad!"

It makes Rose laugh as well, and Portia rolls her eyes at us from across the room.

"Would you three stop wasting time?" She whisks by in a flurry of tails, her eyes scanning the large windows and glass door at the front of our store. "It's just past lunch and you know we get busy."

She looks slightly more pulled together today. Not that she isn't always the best dressed, most polished creature that works here, but she isn't sweaty and only half as irritable as usual.

"Ah yes, the afternoon Burger Bliss rush," Eddie chuckles, hopping up and stretching his wings. It makes a nearby Demonnie woman—probably in her sixties—giggle, and he winks at her, walking over and spewing some lines about our newest body care line.

"Have you given any thought to the contest?" Rose asks after Eddie leaves, and we begin taking a lap around the displays making sure everything is perfectly tidy.

"No, not really. I got kind of distracted last night."

I let out another undignified yawn to hide the fact that I'm clearly lying. Yes, I thought about it, but Chalice and Trent sort of consumed my thoughts and made it impossible to come to a decision about anything.

"You really should enter, I think you'd . . ."

Rose is still talking, but her voice suddenly fades to nonexistence when I happen to look over at the doors and see my two extremely hot roommates, golden Chalice and sexy Trent, waltzing into the store.

Trent's wearing one of his normal frayed band shirts, but Chalice is wearing a formfitting, pale blue top that skims over his slender, highly toned frame. It brings out the hazel color of his eyes.

When he locks eyes with me and smiles, everything in the world stops like an old-fashioned romance movie. Only instead of suspended rose petals flying through the air, it's just their fragrance and the reflective artwork of a thousand glass candle jars creating a million small rainbows in lieu of flowers.

"Hey Julie," he says, coming up to Rose and me. "You showed up at my work last night, so I thought we'd show up at yours."

"Cha-Chalice," I squeak in surprise, running my hands down my work apron. "Hi there."

"Nice to see you, too, Trent. Why, thank you, Julie. I'm glad I could make it as well." Trent steps up next to Chalice, swinging his five black and white tails behind him in a slow and seductive wave. He gives me a wink and pretends to be interested in smelling a forest green candle called "Enchanted Dew Drops."

"Hi Trent," I say, rubbing my hand over my face to hide my blush before looking at Rose. "Oh, uh, this is Rose."

She looks at both of them up and down, and with a raised eyebrow, she gives me a bemused, rosy gold smile.

"Charmed."

"Oh, are we making new friends?" Eddie walks over to us, ignoring a customer trying to get his attention.

"Eddie, these are my, um, new roommates, Chalice and Trent," I stammer.

Eddie gawks at them and stands up straight. He slicks back his hair and slightly extends his bronze wings so they halo round his broad shoulders.

"Julie, you didn't tell me you live with two literal sex gods."

I start choking on my own salvia, and Rose pats my back as Portia saunters over with wide eyes and flared nostrils.

"Keep it in your pants, Eddie, or at least in the back room," she says, but turns her eyes toward my roommates with her own critical and calculating look.

The change in her demeanor is instant and I watch in horror as the normally up-tight Portia melts into a drooling kitten. Her nine brown tails swing together in perfect harmony, and I swear she smells like she's been using the lilac scented hand cream we have on display up front. The smell is overpowering.

"Julie hasn't told me a thing about you two." She leans against one of her own candle displays and nearly knocks over a pearly white candle holder in the shape of a heart. Rose catches it at the last moment, but Portia's eyes never leave Chalice's face, even when Trent flicks his tail at Chalice in thought. He catches his eye, and they exchange a look with each other. Portia, on the other hand, sneers at me.

"There isn't much to tell. We're Julie's roommates." Chalice takes a step back from Portia and holds up a greasy bag up to me. "I brought you a snack, do you have a break coming up?"

"Yes. Yes she does." Rose pushes me forward, and I nearly lose my balance. Chalice reaches out with one of his big arms, and I latch onto it, feeling his muscles beneath my fingertips.

"Fuck. That. I wanted to go on a break and . . ." Portia begins, but Trent drums a finger on a nearby display and gives her a forced smile. His five tails twitch limply behind him when he turns to look at her.

"I was hoping you could," he pauses to sigh, "show me your favorite candle?"

Portia huffs, but takes the bait as she switches her focus to Trent's five tails. I sense the smallest movement of her eyebrows as she scans over his Runt status, but she thankfully keeps her mouth shut and follows him across the store to a wall of pretty pastel candles and body care.

I'm not surprised that nine-tailed Portia would look at him like that; she's a very traditional Fox Folk, and they typically take little notice of anyone with less than the nine required tails. But I am surprised at her very obvious flirtation with Chalice.

Not surprised at her doing it, I kind of expected that, but that it made my blood simmer to see her batting her fake eyelashes and pushing out her chest toward him. Even the fact that Trent walked away with her is stirring feelings inside me.

Am I . . . jealous?

No, I can't be. These are my new roommates, and while I think we should all be friends and on good terms, I should not be fucking my roommates . . . right?

Frankie would be so disappointed in me again.

Then again, who said anything about fucking? I'm just going out to Chalice's truck to eat some food. That's not fucking. Maybe I'm jumping to conclusions and thinking too far ahead. Besides, I really doubt if I would ever have a chance with either of them anyway, so a little hanging out isn't going to change much in our current relationships.

Both are way too hot for me, and if Portia is any indication, Chalice is definitely not lacking for attention. The three of us are just roommates and probably won't ever be anything more.

"What do you say, Julie?" Chalice asks again, but I'm already taking off my apron and clocking myself out using the register terminal.

"Yeah, let's get out of here."

At least this is something Frankie would approve of.

As I walk out the front doors with Chalice, I can feel everyone's eyes on my back, but none more so than Portia's. I make the mistake of looking back at her and not even the devastatingly good looks of Trent can pull her attention away from glaring at me.

Oh well, it's not like she ever liked me before this anyway.

"I thought we could sit in the back of my truck," Chalice says, leading me to a very old-looking blue truck taking up two parking spaces in the middle of the parking lot. He must see me raise an eyebrow at his parking job because he sheepishly rubs the back of his neck and looks at me.

"I didn't want anyone parking close to me."

"I see." The paint on his truck is old and chipped that I wonder if he would even notice if anyone dinged that vintage thing.

He flips the tailgate down and hops up effortlessly. The truck bed sags under his weight as I weigh my options on how to get up there without looking like a complete idiot. But before I can come up with a plan, I feel Chalice's golden hands grab me under my armpits and haul my body upward in one giant swing.

Gasping from surprise I nearly fall backward into him when my feet touch down on the truck bed. Luckily his tail helps to hold him steady and we stay upright until taking a seat on opposite sides facing each other.

Tucking into his embrace for that small moment made me realize he smells better than any candle the Candle Love company has ever sold in its entire lifetime as a company. I can't even describe it, it's . . . magnetic.

My eyes lock with his as he gives me another gold-tinged grin that causes my stomach to flutter.

"You're so light, I bet I could toss you around anywhere."

Um, yes please . . . geez, Julie, keep it together! Everyone is probably watching you from the windows. A quick look back at

Candle Love confirms this when I get a glimpse of bronze wings ducking into a corner when I glance over.

Trent is there too, with Portia rambling about something by his side, but I can tell his icy blue stare is on Chalice's truck.

"Ye-yeah." I squeeze my legs together thinking about the other night when Trent caught me spying on Chalice.

Now I think I've suddenly forgotten how to sit like a normal human and awkwardly fumble around my legs and arms until I think I look cute and comfortable. Well, as comfortable as one can be sitting in the back of a truck.

"I wasn't sure what you normally order, so I have a few things in here." Chalice opens the bag and hands me a wrapped burger. "Not sure which one this is, but we can switch if you don't like it."

I laugh and take the handout.

"I'm not too picky when it comes to burgers," I tell him, and his face brightens.

"Neither am I, but then I do cook them for a living and have probably gone immune to them at some point."

Under the wrapper is a veggie burger with cheese, lettuce, and dressing, and I find my stomach pinch in hunger just looking at it. If Chalice and Trent hadn't shown up, I probably would have run over to the sandwich place on the other side of the shopping center. You can get your food pretty quickly, so you don't have to take the gamble on a place like Burger Bliss which is known to be super busy all the time.

I take a big bite and sigh in pleasure.

"Good burger?" he asks, and I have to take some time chewing before I can answer him.

"It's hitting the spot right now." I accept a napkin that he hands to me and wipe my mouth carefully before continuing. "Thanks for, um, bringing it over."

"Anything for a roommate," he says with a silly, lopsided grin. "I used to bring Trent home burgers all the time until he told me to stop because he thought all the grease was giving him acne."

Oh, that's how it is. He just brought me food because we're roommates now. Suddenly, my burger doesn't taste as good as it did a few minutes ago.

"Are you off work right now?" I ask, trying to change the subject.

"No, I've still got a few hours, you?"

"Same."

We sit in silence chewing our food, and I'm at a complete loss at what to say to him next. The minutes of my lunch break are ticking by, and I feel like I may be wasting his time.

"Do you like working there?" I finally ask.

"I do! It's a lot of fun and seriously fast paced, uh, unlike . . . here."

I laugh as he gestures vaguely toward Candle Love. He's right, of course, the two places are night and day.

"I like it slow. It gives you a chance to breathe once in a while and not have to be around a shit-ton of people. I can get . . ."

My words trail off. He doesn't need to know these personal things about me, not yet at least. I'm sure he'll find out, but the desire to overshare with him is strong, and maybe it's because I feel so comfortable with him.

"There are a shit-ton of people there!" He tilts his head back when he laughs and I think I see the inking of a black-lined tattoo climbing around his collarbone, but it's gone in a flash as he continues to eat his burger. It calls attention to another part of him that I've been dying to ask about. And I guess this is as good a time as ever.

"So, I, um . . . please stop me if this is too personal, but I was wondering why you keep your nails so short. Most of my family, my adopted family that is, all kept their nails really long and I noticed your sister did as well. I thought that was a Dragoon thing?"

Chalice goes quiet as he studies his fingers, curling them in and inspecting his short nails. He looks up at me through those thick eyelashes some boys have that girls can only dream about and flashes me a devious smile.

"If you're a good roommate, maybe I'll tell you someday."

My face heats up, and I try to hide it by taking another bite of burger, though I can think of a whole list of ways I can be a good girl, I mean roommate, to him.

"What are you up to after work?" Chalice asks suddenly, and I have to pull my mind from the gutter and focus on the real thing in font of me.

Fuck, one of the two nights a week I'm busy. Though maybe it's a good thing, as much as my body wants to throw itself at this golden-assed-god, it probably wouldn't be the best idea. Even if Frankie would say otherwise.

"On Thursday and Friday nights, I volunteer at the New Harvest Food Bank, so I'm headed there right after work."

"Fuck, that's kind awesome of you, Julie!"

I take another bite of burger because I feel the blush creeping back.

"Just something I've been doing since middle school. I like it there. There's a lot of volunteers, but we're pretty spread out and the work is really easy because it's mostly just separating things into boxes. Occasionally they ask us to hand stuff out, but I prefer the back room jobs."

"I was going to ask if you wanted to hang out later, but it sounds like you're busy. Still, that's really cool of you to give back like that."

"Um, you can come with me if you want."

Oh Goddess, why did I ask that? This is a bad idea, Julie. Bad, bad, bad! I want to be on good terms with my roommates, but the more time I spend with them . . . the more I want them both.

This is bad.

"Can I? They'll let us come by and help?"

"Us?"

"Oh yeah, I'm sure Trent will want to come if that's okay."

Fuck.

"Yeah, you can come as my guests tonight, but if you make it a habit, then you'll have to fill out paperwork."

"I hate paperwork."

"Don't we all?"

"But I'd do it for you. I'd love to come help out tonight and see what it's all about. It's just off the main road, right? The big building with all the paintings on the walls? We can meet you in the parking lot."

"That's the one, we'd love to have the help," I respond and force a smile on my face, but the smile he responds with is full of the golden flare that attracts me to him.

Even sitting down, he looks tall and imposing. And the hints of his tattoo against the thin dusting of gold scales crossing his neck makes a beautiful contrast. I hope he'll show me the whole thing one day.

Am I falling for this guy? Ugh, this isn't good.

I feel like I may be digging myself into hole by doing this. A super sexy hole, but a hole none-the-less. If things don't work out in the long run, it's going to make living together complicated if not impossible.

And if that happens, I'll have nowhere to go.

CHAPTER SEVEN

The New Harvest Food Bank isn't far from Candle Love, but it is in the direction of my family's old home. The familiar buildings and shops that line the road bring a pang a longing to my stomach, though they quickly turn to butterflies when I pull into the expansive parking lot in the back.

Before me is a large concrete warehouse that someone has gone to great lengths to make beautiful by painting the outside walls. I'd say the job was mostly successful if you like gigantic murals of grassy fields, cows and chickens, but maybe that's the art snob that secretly lives inside me. I think I could have done better.

However, the walls have seen much better days and no one even remembers who created them in the first place. It's entirely possible they're leftover from what this place was before it became The New Harvest Food Bank: an animal meat processing plant. It went defunct years ago when most of society switched to primarily plant-based diets and New Harvest moved it. So now the murals are old, chipped, and fading.

Maybe someone will redo the outer walls or paint something new on top of the old scenes, but who knows when that could happen. The creatures we help through here, though, seem to like them, and that's what really counts in the end. It also helps to make the place easy to spot from the streets and highway.

I can see Chalice's blue truck in front of building and park next to him. He moves out of the way as I pull up, and I see that Trent is nearby, leaning against the building and watching me.

"Hey, Julie." Trent is the first to speak as he walks over to meet me at my car. Then, before I even have a chance to open the door, Chalice runs over and does it for me, offering a hand to help me out. Kinda unnecessarily, but I appreciate the gesture.

"Hey, um, looks like you guys found the place okay."

"Of course," Chalice says in an easy, relaxed tone. "I didn't realize it before, but I've passed by here a bunch of times. The walls are very memorable."

There may have been a very small part of me that hoped they'd get lost and head back home after an apologetic text message. The fact that they're here with me now means I'm going to have to spend time with both of them outside of the house. The thought of which fills me with a kind of embarrassed and tingly feeling.

Oh Goddess, it's like I'm a ten year old with a crush.

Or more appropriately, two crushes.

One of Trent's tails flicks behind my calves, and I feel the tip tickling just behind my knee. I take a step nervously forward, even though all I want is to stand there and let him tickle me anywhere he wants.

Trent and Chalice couldn't be anymore different, but they're both stirring up some major feelings in me. While Chalice is large and golden like the sun, Trent is like the moon with his five black tails ending in their white, starlight tips. His eyes are deep and mysterious, and those . . .

Not now, Julie! You're here to volunteer, not sex up your room-mates in the parking lot!

"Follow me. I'll show you inside where you can get some shirts and vests. You have to wear a reflective safety vest inside, but the matching shirts are just for show. Tom, the, uh, head of the organization, is always out and about taking pictures for his blog and likes to keep things looking professional."

"Makes sense," murmurs Trent as he takes in the big murals. Chalice takes a step back to admire them as well.

"These are impressive, but it makes it look like you give out cows and chickens," says Chalice. "Someone should really paint over them."

Trent picks at some loose paint flaking off the wall closest to us. He catches my eye and I'm caught in his blue stare for a moment before he winks and looks away.

"Yeah, probably." I shuffle my feet. "But we should get inside now."

"Lead the way, Diamond," Trent says, waving a hand toward the building.

"Diamond?"

"Yup. Julie, Jules, Jewel, Diamond." Trent's tails wave slowly behind him. "A precious stone."

Chalice rolls his eyes at him, and I turn away so he can't see how red my face turns.

"Thought we decided on waiting till the one month mark before picking a nick-name for her?"

"What can I say? It came to me in a moment of brilliance." Trent slaps him on the back. "Besides, you're welcome to think of your own name for her if you want. I don't mind."

They lock eyes for a moment, and I swear they must be having some sort of telepathic conversation again. These two must be really good friends if they can read each other's thoughts like this.

And "Diamond?" What was that all about?

Oh no, they're both looking at me and waiting for something. Goddess, that's right, I need to bring them inside, but what do I say about this new nick-name? Quick, Julie, think of something to say!

"I like it, um, Slim."

Oh.

My.

Goddess.

Fuck.

Trent laughs and gently pushes Chalice and me toward the warehouse's back door, which someone has propped open with an empty tomato crate. They're standing on either side of me and I can feel Chalice's warm and tall presence on my left and Trent's slow tail flicking on my right.

"Slim, huh? I think you can do better than that," he teases gently and the lightness of his voice makes me laugh.

He's right, I probably can, but now isn't the time for that. Later tonight when I can't sleep because my thoughts are too consumed by their hotness will be perfect.

After taking a deep breath that I hope neither of them notices, I lead the way into the warehouse. It's a typical Thursday night here, which means the place is packed with volunteers. I usually only come here Thursday and Friday nights and as you can imagine, Friday is much slower because who, besides someone like me with little to no social life, would choose to volunteer Friday nights. It's usually filled with just a few couples who would be spending their time together anyway.

"Julie!" The chipper voice of Tony echoes around the high ceiling as the facility's human director dashes to me with his abnormally positive attitude.

It took me some time to get used to his outgoing personality, and he can still be a little too much to handle at times, but he's grown on me. Probably because I know he really wants to do his part to help anyone dealing with food insecurities. So I like him, even if his loud voice, wild gesturing arms and super hyped personality makes me want to hide in a hole.

"Tom, these are the guys I live with, um, roommates, er . . . friends."

Smooth Julie strikes again.

"Nice to meet you, Tom. I'm Chalice and this is Trent. Julie invited us to come along and help out tonight if that's okay?"

"Of course!" Tom's loud reply hurts my ears. "You're so very welcome to help out! Head over to that bin over there and grab a shirt and vest. I'm afraid we're running a little low on them, though. It's a busy night tonight so you'll have to dig around to find your size."

"We'll make it work." Trent grins at me and drags Chalice along with him to the shirt and vest bins.

Tom turns toward me with a raised eyebrow.

"Roommate friends you live with?"

"Uh, yeah." I give a stuttering laugh and point awkwardly over my shoulder at the bins. "I better go get a vest."

Tom chuckles but doesn't pry, another reason I've grown to like him. He respects my personal space.

"Thanks for stopping by and spreading the joy of The New Harvest Food Bank!" He claps my back with a swift pat and skips off to a group of volunteers just entering the warehouse. I use it as my chance to bolt over to the bins.

"You know, Julie, if you wanted to see me in a teeny tiny shirt, you only needed to ask." Chalice does a spin before me, and he's now wearing an extremely ill-fitting New Harvest Food Bank shirt. It's almost long enough to cover his middle and the thin fabric clings to his biceps and chest as if he were shirtless. When he raises his arms, most of his rock hard abs are on display.

Trent, on the other hand, has won out and found himself a ratty, old shirt that has definitely seen better days. It fits much better, but the logo is so indistinguishable that it might as well be some unknown punk rock band rather than a non-profit food bank.

I swallow back a lump in my throat before replying.

"Yeah, you get a shirt when you go through the process of singing up fully. Guests, uh, have to take from the cast off pile." I hand them a few neon green and yellow safety vests, which thankfully fit better and at least cover a little more of Chalice's body.

"I kinda like mine," says Trent. He slips his vest over his head and gestures for me to turn around so he can help adjust some of the loose straps on the one I put on.

His long fingers graze my waist and press against me for a small moment and my body instinctively leans into his touch. I have to stop myself before pressing too far and I hope he doesn't notice.

Why did I even say anything about coming here tonight? This could have been a normal Thursday night, but no, I had to say something about it and now I'm going to be spending time with both Trent and Chalice, working hard and possibly sweating next to each other. Just these two hunky creatures and I sweating next to each other for hours . . .

Oh Goddess, it's going to be a long night.

Work at The New Harvest Food Bank isn't hard, but it can be . . . gross. Mostly it's fine, you just sort through bags and boxes of food stuff donated from local grocery stores, but when you do come across something inedible, you have to discard it right away.

Chalice learns this the hard way when he opens a bag of bell peppers and an overly ripe one literally melts in his hand. Trent and I are quick with the paper towels, but he excuses himself afterward and he doesn't see him for almost ten minutes.

"Food waste is such a crime," Trent murmurs to me when we're alone. "I'm glad the big chains are at least doing something with all this and its going to a good cause. But I feel like we can do better."

"Agreed, food insecurity is a real thing. Most of the creatures I know didn't grow up with it, at least not to my knowledge, but it's much more common than you'd think. Food can get expensive, especially when you're feeding a big family."

Trent swishes his tails in thought, and we're quiet for a few minutes as we sort through a big crate of cereals. Someone must have packed them in too tightly at the store, and most of the boxes look bent inwards, but while they may not be great looking, they're still perfectly usable.

"Food is expensive," he finally says.

"I guess you would know, you're working on becoming a chef, right?"

I actually catch Trent's face flush red for the first time since I've met him. Becoming a chef isn't a secret, right? Misty said it so casually when she gave me the house tour, and the amount of fancy cheese and jam in our fridge at home could be considered a giveaway.

"It's a tough business to break into, but I'm working on it. It's hard since I'm still working full-time as a consultant." He hands me the last cereal box and winks. "Are you asking because you'd like me to cook for you sometime?"

Now it's my turn to blush.

"I don't think I could turn down a free meal, but, uh, don't feel like you have to just because we live together."

Trent chuckles softly.

"Yeah, just because we live together."

Our conversation dies off, but Chalice arrives soon afterward with freshly washed hands, and we're quickly diverted into a conversation about what type of breakfast cereal is the best.

Even though I'm sandwiched between two extremely attractive creatures all night, the work flies by, and when Tom comes by to take our picture, I'm taken aback when he mentions the time.

"Wait, it's already past ten?" I wipe the sweat from my forehead and take my phone out to double check.

"It's not that late." Chalice chuckles by my side, but Trent looks over with a furrowed brow. His big ears twitch backward at an angle as he frowns.

"Sorry, Diamond, I thought you knew it was getting late. Chalice and I are used to staying up till dawn sometimes, but it doesn't seem that way for you."

"That's the understatement of the year." I sigh and stretch my arms above my head. "I guess I was just having a good time. Well, as good a time as you can have volunteering at a food bank."

"You're doing work for a good cause, I don't mind if you have fun while you do it," says Tom. "Anyways! One last picture of my late night working crew, then it's out the door with you three so I can close up shop for the night."

Before I can say anything, Chalice's arm whips out and curls around my waist, hugging me into his side. I'm dwarfed by his presence, and his amber and ginger smell overwhelms me in a good way. Trent leans in next, tilting his head so it's pressed against the side of mine. The softness of his ears tickle a little but not as much as one of his tails flicking between my legs from behind.

"Say 'cheese!' Tom snaps the picture on his phone and grins at us. "This'll be perfect for the blog. Thanks guys, now get out of here!"

He doesn't need to tell me twice, my exhaustion is hard to ignore, and I'm a little stunned as to how I made it through this entire day without passing out. I don't even know if tonight will be any better; being this close to both of my roommates all evening is bound to make sleep impossible. Tonight is going to be all I'm going to think about. Hopefully my dead-ass tired body will win out over my horny thoughts, but that's probably wishful thinking.

I stretch my arms over my head as I step out of their embraces and turn to face them. "Thanks for coming to help tonight."

"Of course, I had a good time." Chalice's smile is wide as we walk back toward the bins to drop off our shirts and vests.

"You come here every week?" asks Trent.

"Every Thursday and Friday."

"Every Friday night? Really? Don't you ever . . ." Chalice is silenced by a stern look from Trent and trails off before finishing, but I already know what he's alluding to.

"Yeah, well, I don't really have too much of a life." I laugh like it's a joke when, in fact, it's probably true. "So it's not like I'm sacrificing much."

It must work, though, because they both laugh.

"You're a better person than I am," Trent says as he opens the door for me and the three of us step out into the cool, dark night. "I don't know about giving up such a fun night of the week, even for a good cause."

"I guess they don't really need me to come here on Fridays, I just never . . ."

I stop myself before saying too much. I'm sure my new roomies will notice that I have little to no social life outside of Frankie, but I don't have to explain that to them in detail. They can find out on their own.

"Never want?" Chalice playfully nudges my side with a thick elbow. "Never had two fine pieces of ass like us to spend your weekends with?"

I almost stumble on my own feet, but Trent presses a hand to the small of my back to keep me upright.

"I think what my dear friend is trying to say is that we're surprised you don't have one or two or three creatures fawning at your feet trying to show you the time of your life every Friday."

"Well, no, I don't. And for the record, there's more than one day of the week, and I am available the other six."

As soon as the words come spilling from my mouth, I wish I could take them back. Sure, Frankie would be proud, but at what cost? I sound much braver than I actually am, and besides, it's not like I would even have a chance with these two. They are way out of my league.

Oh, and they're also my roommates.

"Why all the interest in spending Friday nights here? Did you want to come again tomorrow?" I ask in an attempt to steer the conversation away from my personal life.

That seems to get their attention, and they glance at each other. A secretive look is exchanged between them, but I'm not familiar enough with either to determine if the look is good or bad. Finally, Chalice breaks the silence with his usual carefree and loud laugh.

"Wish we could, but we've already made a few plans."

Trent levels a look at him, and when Chalice stares back with a completely oblivious look, he sighs and runs a hand through his hair.

"We, uh, invited some people over to the house tomorrow night. Should just be a little get together, but you're welcome to join us."

Spending my Friday evening trying to make small talk with creatures I don't know sounds like a horrible idea, so I shake my head and force a smile on my face.

"That's okay. I already have a commitment to come here. If they're still around when I get back, though, I might spend some time outside my room."

Another look exchanged between them and hopefully not about my obvious lie. There's no way I'm going to stick around and talk to people I don't know. I'm going to hide in my room.

"I'm sure we'll still be awake," Trent says kindly. He opens my car door for me. "You okay to drive home? You look tired."

"No, this is just how I normally look." I try to hide my grimace as I get into my car. Why did my brain choose that as a response? These two must think I'm so lame.

Trent smiles and flicks a tail lightly at my face before closing the door.

"See you at home, Julie!" Chalice calls out, rapping his knuckles on the window to get my attention and offering a dazzling smile. I wave back and watch as they make their way to Chalice's truck.

Damn, they have cute asses.

Ugh, what is wrong with me? These two are completely off limits, and besides, I don't even think I could choose between them anyway.

I take a deep, deep breath as I start my car and pull out of my parking space.

Everything is going to be okay. As long as I stay level headed about this situation and control my horniness, everything will be fine.

I hope.

CHAPTER EIGHT

Maybe I am lame. No, that can't be it. I'm not the most interesting human in New California, but I suppose I have a surprising number of positive traits someone would look for in a friend or a significant other. At least I think I do.

Though, I'll admit that earlier this Friday evening really seemed to test that theory. Everyone at New Harvest was paired up tonight, and even those not on a date or with their partners, had their entire families complete with children. I've never felt more single and alone in my entire life. Even Tom commented on it, which was enough for me to make up some (lame) excuse and leave early.

Now it's past nine in the evening, and I'm driving down Cumberbatch Way noticing far too many cars parked up and down the street. Someone nearby must be having a party and the lack of street parking is really getting on my nerves.

Then, the realization that creeps up my spine when I pull into our driveway and find that the party is being held at my house turns to pure horror. And the fact that none of the party guests have left me, someone who actually lives here, a place to park is the last straw.

I circle back and find parking two blocks away and stomp down the sidewalks toward the house with my purse slung over my shoulder and a scowl on my face. Even though I'm fuming mad, the moment I open the front door, all the fight leeches from my false bravado, and I stand motionless in front of swirling sea of noise and bodies in front of me.

It's too much.

There are too many people, and I really, really don't like it.

The need to escape and hide floods my system, causing every pore to leak sweat and my vision to blur. Luckily, there is a wall beside me, and I reach out and place a calming palm on the smooth surface. Taking a few breaths in and out, I finally summon enough courage to reach behind me and close the front door.

Just as I'm doing so, I hear a loud and familiar voice chanting from the living room and my feet take me in his direction. Perhaps the golden-assed Chalice can answer for this 'little get together' he and Trent promised last night.

Speaking of which, I don't see Trent anywhere, but I hear the faint sounds of a guitar streaming from behind the door to the garage and assume he must be in there.

I'm deciding if he might be the easier option to yell at when Chalice slams a heavy hand on my shoulder.

"Hiya, roomie! Glad you could make it!"

"Well," I pause to remove his hand, "I live here."

He blinks as if the thoughts aren't exactly registering in his brain and then runs a hand through his gleaming hair. Loud music is making my ears throb as I look up at him and notice the slight pink tint to his cheeks.

Goddess, he's drunk.

"That tracks," he finally says before grabbing my hands and hauling me along with him. My purse begins to slip from my shoulder, and I make a hasty grab to keep it secure. There's no way I'm losing track of it with all these creatures around.

"Chalice," I try to get his attention, but he's still pulling me along with him. Grinding my heels into the carpet, I force us to stop. "Chalice!"

He doesn't seem to hear me over the music, and before long, he's brought us to the living room and positioned me in front of the TV. Someone boos and throws a beer can that narrowly misses my head, but his grip on me is strong, and I can't get away.

"This, everyone, is the beautiful roommate I was telling you about. Isn't she something?"

Someone whistles loudly.

"Take it off!" Someone else yells.

"Chalice . . ." I squirm, and instead of letting me go, he spins me around to face him. His eyes are bright and beautiful in the dim light.

"You're gorgeous, Julie," he murmurs and brings his face close to mine. His breath smells like some kind of fancy liquor that seems familiar but I can't place. "Kiss me, please? I really want you to kiss me, Julie."

"Chalice, why are . . ."

"Kiss him!" Someone screams and someone else laughs.

It's hard to focus on much else with the literal golden sun in my face, even the obvious fact that he's drunk feels miles away. It's just me and him, and his hands pressing into my shoulders are warm and comforting. Then, when he moves his body close to mine and I feel his hardness between us, a thirsting need comes violently upon me, and I can't help but close the distance between our lips.

For being so large and intimidating, Chalice has a comforting mouth that pushes warmly against mine and when I feel the softness of his tongue probe against my lips, I open to accept him without question. But the sharpness of mixed alcohol hits hard and I pull away, turning my head and fighting the urge to spit out the taste.

The kiss feels wrong on so many levels, but also right in some kind of horrible way, and gets over so quickly that I couldn't even say it actually happened. The only proof being the hooting and hollering of the audience aligned before us on the couch.

But when he dips his head in for another, I pull back even further. I place a hand on his chest and lightly push him back. Not wanting to make a big deal about everything and throw the whole room into an uproar. I give him a lying, coy smile and causally lean up and tap his nose.

"Later, Big Boy, I need to pee."

For once, my awkwardness pays off and the whole room erupts into cheers and laughter, and I use it to make my escape, dodging bodies, tails, and wings as I scurry from the room.

My face feels hot from the anger since he put me into a position like that. It's enough to override my annoyance at the house party raging around me, and it carries me through the kitchen to grab a snack before heading to my room.

The fridge is packed full of beer and fruit juice, but I successfully pry out some of Trent's fancy cheese and am looking for some crackers in one of the cupboards when a familiar laugh carries with the music and into my ears.

Of all the creatures in the world, I'm horrified to see Portia and two of her nine-tailed friends standing close behind her. All three of them look uncomfortable and appear like they're dressed way too nice for a house party like this. But something about the way

Portia's nostrils flare whenever some male walks by tells me she's not here to play beer pong.

"Nice party," she says and flips her tails behind her in a slow dance. "I'd love to let the host know. Do you know where Chalice is?"

"I . . . uh."

Just then, the full-bodied laughter of the big golden Dragoon rings through the kitchen and the gleam in Portia's eyes matches with that of Chalice's gold colored ass.

"Portia," one of her friends whines. "Sounds like he's over there, can you just go talk to him already? This place smells, and I want to get out of here."

I cram a cracker in my mouth and watch her friends squirm in discomfort.

"Better get going before things get really wild." I say, grabbing a single beer from the fridge. It pops open with a loud crack.

"Ugh, fine."

I have to swing it away when Portia, her tails, and her entourage push by me.

"Bye, Julie," she calls mockingly over her shoulder. "See you at work!"

Her friends don't even bother saying anything to me, and I watch in silence as the three of them wander off toward Chalice and his captive audience.

I take another swig of my beer and eat cracker with some cheese.

Why is she even here? Did she only come to hit on Chalice? Is he going to kiss her too?

"Better slow down on that, don't want to get too drunk before the cops show up."

I look over to see Trent leaning against the counter. He's wearing slender jeans and a tattered shirt that looks purposely ripped to show off his defined shoulders and abs. After scrutinizing his expression, I determine quickly that he is not nearly as drunk as Chalice.

Still, I'm mad as hell and slightly buzzed from drinking my beer so quickly. So instead of answering him, I punch him in the shoulder and scowl just before downing the rest of the can.

"This is not a 'little get together,' this is a fucking house party!" Spit flies from my mouth, but I try not to care.

I push the remains of my cheese and crackers into his chest and slam my now empty beer can on the counter next to him.

"Sorry, Julie, we . . ."

"Ugh, save it," I grumble, turning on my heels and walking swiftly through the house toward my room.

It's still too loud and way too chaotic, but the sounds muffle as I walk down the hallway. The all consuming need to hide and get away from the sea of people behind me is overwhelming, and my mind is a hazy, milky blur.

I just need some time to myself, and I'll be okay.

Everything is going to be okay.

But when I open the door and find, to my absolute and disgusted horror, a Demonnie and a Fox Folk Runt making out in my room, I loose my fucking shit.

"Get out!" I've never screamed louder in my entire life, and I feel the words scraping through my throat like razor blades. Trouble is that the music that follows me inside muffles the worst of it, and I'm not sure how much they can even make out.

The Fox Folk Runt looks too stunned to move and the Demonnie she's with drags her out with a quick muffled apology, but I still spin on them with the intent of hurling more sharpened words in their direction until I'm met head on with Trent's body when he pushes his way into my room and slams the door behind him.

I give him a scathing look and turn my back as I survey my room for any damage. I don't dare open the drawer my CPAP machine is store in, but the area around the bed looks undisturbed. I must have arrived just in time.

"We really should get you a new lock for your door," mutters Trent.

"Oh yeah? Does this happen often? I wasn't aware . . ." I pause and take a deep breath.

With the door now closed, the music is finally muted enough for me to form clear thoughts, but I still want to choose my words carefully. When you're this angry, sometimes it's easy to say things you can't take back.

"Julie, I . . ." Trent makes a move forward in my direction, but the way his body sways under him causes two of his tails to smash into a stack of boxes I'd purposely left near my dresser. One of them topples over and several sheets of my artwork spill out and flutter to the floor. He hiccups loudly and swears under his breath.

"Ugh, you're drunk too." I run a hand down my face and push him out of the way so I can pick up the pages.

Trent kneels next to me, using his tails for extra support, and collects one of them for me.

"Only a little," he confirms. "One of us tries to stay somewhat sober when there's a party happening."

I snatch the paper from his hands.

"You mean your 'small get together?' "

He winces.

"I'm sorry, Julie. Really. I . . . we . . . well, Chalice and I didn't want to make a big deal about it because we didn't want Misty to find out. We didn't think you would mind."

I let out a big sigh.

"I have every right to be upset about this. There were strangers in my room, and if I had known about it, I could have, I don't know, prepared for it."

"Prepared?"

"Yeah . . . I, well, it helps to know about things like this so I can make a plan of action in case, uh, it gets overwhelming. It's just something that . . . helps."

Trent nods and sits on my bed.

"Is there anything I can do to help with that?"

I shuffle from one foot to the other, but eventually sit beside him on my bed.

"I appreciate the thought, but I don't know. It helps being in here, though. It was getting really loud out there."

He nods again and turns a thoughtful look at my door.

"I think I know how you feel. Well, I take that back, everyone is unique in their feelings. But I can empathize a bit at least."

"Sure."

"No, really. I imagine it's a little like preforming in front of a bunch of creatures. I once got this gig at a coffee shop, you know, like in movies and stuff. I was up there on this little stage, singing my little heart out and playing my little guitar, but . . . all I could think about was getting the fuck out of there. All those eyes on me? Creatures pointing and whispering to each other? I mean, fuck, what were they even saying?"

Trent runs a hand through his hair and lies backward in my bed next to me. I notice he tucks his tails beneath him and to the side. One of them flips out and onto my lap.

"I guess it's kind of like that, but I don't know if social anxiety is the same as stage fright."

"Stage fright?" He chuckles lowly. "You make me sound like a kit, no, it was more like being stuck in a corner with everyone laughing because you peed your pants or something. Like everyone talking shit about you but you can't do anything about it. At least that's how I can be sometimes, again, I know it isn't exactly the same.

I can't help myself, but I reach out and run my fingers through the white tipped fur of the tail idly twitching in my lap.

"I don't know if I'm necessarily looking for someone to empathize with me, but in any case, thank you for sharing with me. I know it's, uh, hard to open about things like that."

"Are you feeling better now?"

"Yeah, it's nice being away from the crowd outside."

I lay backward next to him, and we stare at the ceiling in silence. His tail slides from my hands as he rolls over to lay on his side to look at me.

"Diamond, can I kiss you right now?"

"Wait, what?"

"Can I kiss you?" He asks again.

Maybe it's the beer buzz, or the dimly lit room, or the music thumping in the background, but something in me says I should let him. That kissing him couldn't possibly have any sort of repercussion, which I know—deep in my mind—is utterly false. Of course it will. I shouldn't be making out with both of my hot roommates on the same day, especially while we're all not thinking clearly.

But . . .

That something brewing in my mind, causing me to both overthink and not think at the same time says this should happen, despite what tomorrow may bring.

"Why would you want to kiss me?"

"Because it feels right in this moment."

"Um, okay, sure."

A second later, he's on me, rolling over on the bed and trapping my body beneath his own. He doesn't start with my lips, but instead nuzzles his face into my neck, letting his mouth hover above my skin so that I can feel the warmth of his breath wash over me. My hands fly out, desperate to grasp some part of him, and pull him closer as his lower body presses into mine.

"Julie," he whispers into my ear and the huskiness of his voice make my toes curl.

I'm caged beneath his arms as he pushes himself forward, rubbing the hardness straining against his pants between my legs. A moan escapes my mouth at the rythmic motion of his hips and the fluttering of his lips against my skin.

"I thought you were going to kiss me?" I whisper.

"I want to do more than that." His mouth moves upward from my neck, drawing a slobbering line with his tongue. Then his lips are against mine, soft and gentle despite the desperateness between our bodies grinding together.

It quickly turns into a drunken, slobbering kiss that has us breaking apart for air every so often, but the breaks are quick because we join back together quickly as if the air in our lungs requires each other to function. His tongue dips in deeply and my own meets his in its own greedy dance while the pace of his hips rubbing against my body intensifies to a hurried frenzy.

His muscles beneath my palms become tense and he lets out a rumbling moan that verges on being a deep throated purring sound, but then suddenly pulls back from me.

Our lips break apart from each other with a mutual gasp, and I stare upward at him. His arms stiffen beneath him and he pulls up to look down at me with wide, horror-filled eyes.

That's when I realize the wetness soaking between us.

Oh, Goddess . . . he just came in his pants on top of me.

We lock eyes, but I don't have much time to soak in the complex mix of emotions running through his expression before there is a pounding on my door.

"Julie!" A voice screams from my doorway. "Are you in there? Can I come in?"

My head whips to the side, looking first at the door and then back at Trent who looks too stunned to move off me. While she's hard to hear, I know that voice belongs to none other than Frankie.

"Wait!" I yell out. "Just a second!"

The spell breaks from Trent, and he jumps up from the bed. He looks down at the wet stain against his jeans, back up at me, back to the jeans, and then back to me again.

"Julie!" Frankie calls again.

Shit, I need to do something.

I snatch a sweater from my closet and toss it at Trent before pushing him toward the door, which opens seconds before my palm touches the knob.

"Julie?" Frankie asks, but any concern that might have been etched on her features is long gone when she sees Trent clutching my sweater to his pants and stumbling past her into the hallway. He turns to look back at me, but neither of us seems to know what to say.

"Uh, should I come back later?" Frankie asks with a snicker.

I grab her arm and pull Frankie into my room before turning to face Trent again. He tries to say something but closes his mouth tight with a worried, panicked look in his blue eyes. To his credit, he refuses to look down at his jeans. I suddenly remember his cocky smile when Frankie and I first met his naked ass out on the front lawn and realize this version of Trent is something I've never seen before.

And I really don't know how to handle it.

"Uh, goodnight! See you at, um, breakfast!" I scream and shut the door in his face.

CHAPTER NINE

F rankie takes a very exaggerated whiff of the air around her before slinging her full backpack onto my bed. She then flexes her wings and grins. It's that wide, feral grin that I've seen from her when she feels like she's been let in on some big secret.

"It smells like sex in here!" she proclaims, loudly.

"Sort of," I mumble, turning back toward my closed door and making sure it's closed tight. I feel a little bad for kicking Trent out so quickly, but his room is next door so at least he can go change.

Fuck. I should have said something to him before he left. It would have at least given me a chance to see his reaction. I can't imagine what he's thinking right now.

Him or Chalice.

Frankie hums for my attention and points a long fingernail at my crotch.

"Got a little jizz on you, darling."

I look down and notice the front of my pants where Trent had been grinding is soaked through. Feeling my face begin to flush, I turn from her and start rummaging around in my drawers for something to change into. While I do that, Frankie breaks into laughter on my bed. The noise rivals the music still coming from behind my door, but is short lived when she sees the expression on my face.

That feral grin is still there, though.

"Fuck, girl, you must have some powers I don't know about because I have never had a guy that turned on to where he literally closes out the venue before his pants come off."

I find an old pair of leggings and tug them on as I turn to roll my eyes at her. She giggles and sits up on the bed.

"No powers that I'm aware of. It was hot and all, but I truthfully didn't see that coming."

"No pun intended." She snickers again. "Still, I'm impressed. I came to check up on you, but it clearly seems you're doing okay on your own."

I sit down beside her and tuck my feet beneath me. I've always felt safe with Frankie and not just because she's much taller than I am, but because she's my best friend and always has my back. Talking to her is usually easy, but for some reason, it takes me a moment to find the right words for her now.

My mind clings to the fading clouds of lust from my encounter with Trent, but that annoyingly sensible side of me knows that I just made a huge mistake. Two big and sexy mistakes.

"Frankie, I did something bad," I tell her, and she circles a wing around my shoulder.

"Something or someone?" she asks.

"Something, but almost someone, and someone else. Earlier, Chalice kissed me in front of a whole room full of creatures and then, well, you saw what I just did with Trent in here. All in the span of ten minutes, tops."

"But did you get anything out of it? Wanna jump their bones even more now?" She waggles her eyebrows.

"Trent asked if he could kiss me, and I said he could. And this was just minutes after I practically made out with Chalice! I mean, how could I be this stupid? This is going to make living here impossible. I'm going to be houseless soon because there is no way I'll be able to show my face to either of them. I can't tell them . . . oh Goddess, what if they tell each other? What are they going to think of me?"

Frankie has kept quiet, listening to me, but at my last comment, she presses a long finger against my lips.

"Shush, everything is going to be fine. So you kissed them, big deal. You're allowed to do whatever you want, and if someone wants to slap a label on you for it, then it's their problem and not yours. Besides, it seems to me that something must be brewing between you three if you're all getting down and dirty this early on. Did you like kissing them?"

"I . . . think so? It all feels like it happens so quickly, but I'm pretty sure I did."

"Then if I were you, I'd just relax and enjoy the ride."

"Yeah, but I'm not you. You're, like, cool and collected. I'm a freak who can't breathe on her own at night and hides in dark corners to get away from everyone. How am I supposed to relax during something like this?"

I rub my arms and feel goose pimples prickling my flesh despite the warmth of my room. The buzz from my beer has all worn off, and I'm left simmering in nothing but my worrying thoughts.

I can't believe I let myself get this carried away and made out with not one but both of my male roommates tonight. It's a good thing Misty isn't here because with the way things are going, I might as well kiss her too.

No, as pretty as she is, I don't think I'd be into that. It's the two male creatures living under the same roof that have been giving me all sorts of sexual frustration. Even thinking of them now calls up all sorts of sexy thoughts into my mind, and I give my head a shake to get rid of the dirty images.

"Julie." I hear Frankie through my thoughts and look at her. "Nothing is going to get solved tonight. They're both drunk, one of them al

ready got off tonight, and you're not thinking too clearly yourself. There is nothing more you can do tonight."

In my heart, I know she's right. Yet while the swirling emotions inside me beg to differ, I let out a big sigh and attempt to put my trust into her words.

"You're right. You always are."

"Of course I am! That's because I'm the intellectual one of this relationship and you're the creative one."

"Wait, wait, wait . . . I'm the smart one and you're the artsy one! You live in an artist loft above what I think is a nude body painting class masquerading as a pottery studio."

"How are you the smart one, huh? I'm the one who Mrs. Bell gave a perfect score on that science project in middle school."

I burst into laughter as memories from our childhood slowly push aside my anxiety.

"You are never going to let me live that one down! I had the flu, anyone could have done what I did up on that stage. Besides, it added to the authenticity of my volcano."

"That's not how I remember it," Frankie laughs. "I remember you being all nervous and throwing up inside the thing before it 'blew.' I felt really bad for you, but that sure was a memorable day. King of smelly though."

"I remember it being one of the first times I really felt how, um, difficult it was to be in a room with that many people. Especially with everyone looking in my direction when I was up on stage."

"Yeah, I know." Frankie reaches over and gives me a proper hug. "That's why I came by tonight, uninvited by the way. Friend of a friend of a friend got a text about it, and since I hadn't heard anything from you about having a house party, I figured you didn't know it was even happening. I was worried."

"Thank you." I hug my best friend back fiercely. "You're right, they didn't tell me."

"I'm sorry."

"It's okay, but I'm glad you got here when you did. Couple of minutes earlier would have been better, though. Would have saved me from," I gesture toward my damp pants crumpled on the floor, "getting to that point."

"You'll look back and laugh at it one day." Frankie shrugs. "But let's get your mind off kissing boys and crunchy pant. That party is still raging outside, but I brought my laptop and two pairs of headphones. Wanna catch up on the latest episode of *Love Isle*?"

"Yeah, that sounds good. I could use a distraction. It's been a long night."

Frankie dives into her bag and rummages around for her headphone and laptop. While she sets everything up, I can't help but let my eyesight linger on the doorway.

As much as I want to drift away in the nonsense that is reality television, I can't help but fantasize about either Chalice or Trent knocking on my door. They could come inside and either drop to their knees in forgiveness or carry me off to their rooms.

But I guess that would only create more chaos. It's going to be weird enough having to see them tomorrow and although I really want to put some thought into how that'll go, I don't think I can muster enough brain power tonight.

All I can do now is sit back, relax and laugh along with Frankie while watching crappy TV.

When I wake up the next morning, it's extremely obvious that Frankie spent the night. My floor is a mess of blankets and several pillows, and there are two empty bags of chips stuffed into the small waste basket I keep in here. She's nowhere to be seen, but her bag of stuff is still leaning against the bed so she must be around somewhere.

Dragging myself from bed a light headache ascends upon me and I realize I must have taken off my CPAP mask at some point at night and fallen asleep without wearing it. The mask lies discarded on my nightstand staring back up at me, and I drop it into the nightstand drawer with a tired sigh. No wonder I feel like shit this morning.

I want nothing more than to stay in bed and never come out of my room. Walking out there will mean I'll have to face both Chalice and Trent, and I'm not sure if I'm ready for that.

A stomach ache begins to form inside me as the anxious feelings manifest themselves into something tangible, and I suddenly wish I never moved here. Why couldn't my parents have given me one more year? Maybe even a month longer at my old home might have shifted destiny just enough to not bring me to this house.

I wipe away a few frustrated tears from my face.

Ugh, I can't blame them. I have only myself to blame for putting myself into this position. Well, maybe I couldn't have prevented Chalice from kissing me in front of all his friends, but I could have reacted differently. I could have said something. And I certainly could have kicked Trent out of my room before things got too hot and heavy.

I let out a heavy sigh and look for a change of clothes. I have to leave for work soon and sitting here stewing on my thoughts isn't going to make anything better today. Eventually, I'll have to leave this room and face my choices.

Dressed for the day with my purse tucked under my arm, I take a big breath and put my hand on the doorknob to let myself out. But just as I do, a stream of piercing curses filters through the air of the house.

I hurry through the hall, narrowly avoiding a pile of smelly alcohol-infused vomit on the floor, toward the sounds of Frankie loudly telling off Chalice and Trent, as well as some random Demonnie guy with extra long horns who looks like he passed out on the couch and got caught in the crossfire.

"What were you two thinking, hmm? You don't just throw ragers like this without telling all your roommates. How could you not tell her about it? That was so fucked!"

"Well, I . . ." stammers Chalice.

"Shut the fuck up, I don't want to hear excuses." Frankie crosses her arms and levels a look at both of them. She's tall but not nearly as tall as Chalice, and even Trent has about an inch on her, but the way she spreads her wings and broadens her shoulders makes her looking both terrifying and inspiring.

I'm glad to have her on my side and pity anyone who gets on her nerves.

"Um, I'm just going to go . . ." The Demonnie on the couch starts to creep away and Frankie turns to look his way.

When he moves, I notice the coffee table is littered with empty and half-full cups, someone has spilled more beer on the couch, and there are about twenty paper taco wrappers strewn about all over the floor. The whole house also still smells strongly of bodies, sweat, and beer.

"Who are you?" Frankie asks him with a snarl.

"Ted," he squeaks.

"Well, Ted, better get the fuck out of here before I . . ."

"Frankie," I call to her softly from the hallway, and she spins to look at me. Her face softens immediately, and she grins.

"Morning, Julie! I was just having a conversation with your new roomies. I think they have something to say to you."

She turns a feral eye back to both of them and lets loose the smallest trail of smoke from between her teeth. Chalice shrinks backward and Trent adverts his eyes.

"I'm really sorry we didn't tell you about the party, Diamond," says Trent. "I promise it won't happen again."

"Yeah, me too, Julie." Chalice shuffles his feet, but he looks up at my face and catches my eye. The sparkling hazel orbs remind me of last night's drunken kiss and my body tingles remembering the feel of him pressed against me.

But when I look next to him and see Trent, my memory goes back to making out with him on my bed. The grinding of our bodies together being enough to set him off and how, even though I really want to deny it, I was about ready to go myself.

My stomach cramps together as my mind whirls in thought, going back to blaming my parents for moving away. I think again about how I could still be living at home and not be in a situation where I'm making out with everyone and enduring so many people in my personal space.

It hits me, not the churning indecisiveness but the anger stemming from the knowledge that these two invaded my space by planning a big party without my permission and are also somehow weaving even closer to my heart by asking me to kiss them.

I'm not blameless in this, but wow, I sure want to blame them.

"This place is still a mess," I say loudly, tearing my eyes away from both their apologetic faces and attractive God-like bodies. "I want you to know that I am in no way cleaning any of this up."

"We'll clean it," Chalice says quickly.

"It'll be like nothing ever happened," says Trent, and I hope he doesn't catch me wincing at his choice of words.

"I'll help too, I swear it, Julie!" adds Ted, and we all turn to look at him in surprise. Even the corner of Frankie's lip twitches in a small grin.

I sigh and adjust my purse around my shoulder as Frankie gives one last, hard look at the three stunned faces before her. She then pulls out her phone to check the time.

"Goddess, Julie, I'm sorry. I didn't realize it's so late. You're going to be late for work!" Frankie waves her phone in front of my face so I can see that she's right.

"It that really the time? Fuck." I run my hands over my face and look at Chalice and Trent (and apparently Ted) one last time. "Just clean this place up, okay?"

All three of them give enthusiastic nods as Frankie links her arm with mine.

"Come on, darling, I'll ride to work with you and keep you company. Let's leave these guys behind to take care of things here."

"Yes, let's do that."

Frankie narrows her eyes at both Chalice and Trent as she leads me to the door, and I turn to sarcastically wave at them.

Trent nervously rubs the back of his neck, but avoids making eye contact with me (I don't really blame him). Chalice, on the other hand, looks at me with all his golden goodness, and I can tell he's sorry for what happened. I can forgive them, that's easy enough, but they don't need to know that.

"By the way," I say before leaving, "someone threw up in the hallway, and it smells. You might want to get that first."

"You got it, Julie!" calls Ted.

"Who is that?" Frankie whispers to me as we walk out of the house.

"No idea," I respond with a laugh. And it's true, I have no idea but hope the guy will at least help out like he said he would. Chalice and Trent are going to need all the help they can get.

It's a beautiful day outside and the tension inside me seems to lighten as soon as I step away from the house and feel the sun on my face. Crisp, fresh air feeds into my lungs and brings forth a sense of renewal.

"Where's your car?" Frankie asks, looking around with a puzzled expression.

"Fuck, I forgot. It was packed here last night, and I'm parked a few blocks down. I had to walk all the way back here in the dark."

Frankie looks about ready to charge back inside, but I grab her sleeve and drag her with me toward the sidewalk.

"I plan on forgiving them," I tell her, stroking her arm to calm her down. "Goddess knows they'll have to forgive me when they find out I made out with both of them last night. Come on, while we walk, we can think of ways to get them back for the party."

"Oh, I can think of a couple ways to 'get them back.'"

I smile at her and give her arm a squeeze. I love having Frankie as a best friend.

CHAPTER TEN

I t's been three days since Chalice and Trent's party and I've successfully dodged them both every one. It wasn't easy, but once I learned their patterns, I was able to avoid Chalice's early morning showers and Trent's late night cooking experiments all while making sure I ate every meal inside my room and only emerge for quick bathroom breaks.

Maybe it's wrong to avoid them. Actually, I know it's wrong. I should face my fears and talk to them about what happened that night, but the truth is that I haven't even fully processed it myself. I'm still adjusting to living outside of the home life I grew up in, and throwing in some complicated feelings for two of my three roommates isn't something I currently have the bandwidth for—which is partly why I'm so excited to have today off from work. It's sunny and warm, and I've decided that it's the perfect day to try out the backyard pool. As soon as Chalice leaves for work and Trent leaves for whatever computer consultant-based work he set for up the day, I'll have the whole place to myself and will be able to enjoy the weather in peace and quiet.

Frankie is driving to New Las Vegas for an art convention, otherwise I'd invite her over, but she has a long car ride ahead of her and made me promise to call later and check in. Though she probably just wants to know if I've talked to Chalice and Trent yet.

In preparation for my hopefully relaxing day, I hurry to the kitchen to start gathering snacks. I thought I'd be fine and not run into either of the hotties, but as soon as my feet skid into the kitchen, I have to stumble backward to avoid stepping on one of the white-tipped black tails sticking out of the fridge.

Trent leans out from the fridge holding a carton of milk and wearing nothing but a pair of black boxer briefs. He takes a long swig and grins at me. There's a thin line of milk above his lip, and he licks it off slowly.

"Hi, Diamond." The confident Trent I remember meeting when I first moved in comes out in his voice. It's not the confused and embarrassed version I saw the other night in my room when he . . .

I feel my face flush as I remember the wet spot between us, and how just by making out with him, he somehow came in his pants in a matter of minutes.

He must remember the same thing, because the smile falters, and we're left standing there looking at each other in silence. That is, until the refrigerator starts beeping loudly from the door being left wide open. Trent shuts it quickly, but the jarring 'beeps' seem to do the trick and break the spell between us.

"So, got any plans today?" I ask, turning around and pretending to rummage for some cereal in a nearby cupboard. I'm not really that hungry, but it seems like the best thing to do at the moment. I find some corn flakes and fill a bowl with some.

"Just a meeting with a new company," he replies.

"Cool."

"Yup, just a new consulting gig I'm looking into."

I poke at my dry cereal and realize I'm going to have to ask him for the milk he's still clutching in his hands. Putting it off, I take my time picking through spoons in the cutlery drawer.

"Well, I, uh, hope they like you."

He chuckles lowly, and I hear a little of the cocky Trent come out.

"Doesn't matter if they like me, it all depends on if I like them or not. That's the fun about being an in-demand consultant. You can choose who you get to work with."

I nod like I have any idea what that's like. That kind of freedom seems out of my league right now. Maybe someday when I've graduated or entered a different kind of employment that doesn't involve selling candles, I'd like to be my own boss. Or at least follow my passion and be brave enough to do something with my art.

"Then I hope you like them," I tell him, and he smirks.

His tails lash about behind him, and I do my very best to keep my eyes above his waist. It's probably best that I do not focus on the fact that he's only in his underwear.

"Things aren't looking too good for them right now. They've already rescheduled this meeting twice. But I'm trying to be fair and reserve judgement for when we actually meet in person."

I nod again.

"How about you? Whatcha got going on for today?"

"Oh, I don't know. It's my day off, so I'm just going to relax, I think. Maybe go in the pool. Hey, um, can I have some of that milk?"

Trent startles when I reach out toward him, but he recovers quickly and places the carton on the counter before sliding it over to me like a bartender at a night club.

As I pour the milk into my bowl of cereal, I wonder if he's feeling just as awkward and embarrassed as I am right now. Not sure I can really tell because he does a fairly good job at playing it cool, which is so unlike me.

I want to talk to him about the other night, but I also . . . don't. Maybe if we both pretend it never happened, then we can go about our lives as if nothing ever happened between us.

But then there's Chalice, does he know I also kissed him? Has Trent told Chalice about what happened? Are they waiting for me to do it? To talk to them, or tell the other what happened? Goddess, am I overthinking this?

"Uh, I think that's enough milk." Trent's voice breaks my train of thought and I suddenly realize I've overfilled my bowl and the milk has sloshed over the sides of the bowl and onto the counter. Little flakes of cereal ride the waves across the counter toward Trent, and he looks down at them with a furrowed brow.

"Hey, um, did you want to maybe talk in private? I could . . ."

"Nope! I'm good." I slam the milk carton down and hastily lift the bowl to drink some of the milk so it doesn't continue to spill over the side. I miss my mouth, and it cascades down my shirt, dribbling down my chin like I'm a child.

Trent cracks a smile and lifts an eyebrow at me.

"Well, I'm always available if . . ."

"We're good! We're good? Yes, I mean, we're good!" I laugh nervously and slide the back of my hand over my mouth. "Have a good time at the meeting!"

I slam the bowl of messy cereal into the sink and bolt from the kitchen, heading quickly in the direction of the hallway and my room. I'm so busy with wiping milk from my mouth and neck, that I don't notice Chalice in the hallway until it's too late.

"Good morning, Julie!" He rumbles and the scent of dark, smokey amber unapologetically hits my nostrils.

"Good morning . . ." I stop speaking when I notice he's only wearing a towel draped around his waist.

He must have just come out of the shower because his golden skin glistens with moisture and his matching hair has been slicked back against his head. Water drips from his huge biceps as he rubs a stray droplet from his eyes and looks down at me.

"Is Trent in the kitchen? I need to ask if I can borrow some of his lotion," he starts, and I blink a few times before answering.

"Um, ye-yeah. He's in there."

"And, oh, I noticed you're about . . . out of toothpaste."

I have to laugh at that, and it distracts me from staring at his body.

"Why were you looking at my toothpaste?" I ask and he shrugs.

"It's right next to mine. Anyway, I can pick you some up after work if you want."

"Only if you're going to the store anyway, I can pay you back later."

"Don't worry about it, it'll be my treat." He adjusts the towel handing off his hips, and I almost, but not quite, get a glimpse of everything hiding underneath. It makes my breath catch for a second.

Deep breaths, Julie, you got this. You can handle two attractive, half-naked men. Still, I better get out of here before I do or say something I'll regret.

"Anything for you, roomie," he says and smiles. "Hey, um, if you're not busy later, did you maybe want to . . ."

"Busy all day, but ask me later!" I let out an ear-piercing and awkward laugh and then duck under his arms. I nearly trip over his tail as I scurry past him and toward my bedroom door.

"Okay, no worries, I'll text you later," he calls after me.

"Sounds good," I grab at the doorknob, miss it because my eyes are on that thin towel wrapped around his rock hard stomach, and have to grab for it again.

I can see the corner of his mouth lift up in a wry smile, but I don't stick around any longer than I need to and quickly dash into the safety of my bedroom.

Why aren't the men of this household wearing any clothes to-day? There is seriously only so much a girl can handle!

It isn't long until I hear Chalice's truck pull out from our dri-veway and the sound of Trent's motorcycle roaring to life from the garage. I'll finally have the whole house to myself in just a few minutes.

I decide to keep with my original plan of basking outside in the sun (with plenty of sunscreen), splashing around in the cool water of the pool, and soaking in complete luxury in the hot tub.

But before anything happens, I need to give Frankie my promised phone call.

I'm only a little surprised when she picks up on the first ring. She must be at a rest stop.

"Goddess, finally," she cackles over the phone. "I'm so bored!"

"Regretting your choices already?"

"It's a long trip and there is nothing, literally nothing, around here for miles. I swear I was looking at the same species of cactus for over two hours. It must be the only thing that grows around here! Ugh, at least I'm halfway there."

"Where are you now? It doesn't sound like you're driving."

"Rest stop for some tacos, I'm starving and need that sweet taco heat for the rest of the drive to New Las Vegas."

There's a lot of noise behind her, and I have a feeling she's at one of those tourist-trap places off the highway. Those kinds of places are always packed with people and just thinking about being around so many strangers somewhere in the middle of nowhere makes my skin crawl. However, from my experience, they tend to have the cleanest restrooms because they're so popular and are the best places to pee.

I wonder if she's at the same place I ran into Tandi, the Mousequeek girl from University, that let me know about this house. Kind of wished she would have warned me then about the creatures I'd be living with!

"So anyway," continues Frankie, "did you do it with either of your roomies yet?"

"No."

"Have you at least talked to them?

"Also, no."

"Come on, Julie, you're going to have to at some point. I'm sure they want to talk to you, in fact, I bet they want to do more than just talk!"

She laughs loudly and I wonder how many creatures are giving her looks. Not that she would care if they were.

"I just, well, I don't even know what I'd say. I haven't decided if I like-like either of them. This whole thing could just be a matter of misplaced attraction. Besides, sleeping with either could make things even more awkward between all of us."

"Well, you know what I think?"

"What's that?"

"You just gotta fuck both of them, then pick whichever one you like the best!"

"That's so one-sided, Frankie. I mean, they're good friends, wouldn't that be weird?"

"Not if they're that good of friends. You know, the kind that like to share, so maybe a threesome is in your future! Just follow your gut, or heart, or body, or whatever, and do what feels right in the moment. You have good instincts; just remember how awesome you are!"

"Goddess, Frankie. Okay, I'll 'follow my gut.' Sound good?"

"That'll do for now, but hey, I need to get back on the road. Call or text me later with all the details!"

"I promise I will."

"Looking forward to it!" She cackles in laughter before the line goes dead.

As soon as I'm off the phone with Frankie, I change quickly into a yellow bikini I've had forever and a pair of soft grey shorts. I don't bother taking my phone with me or even putting on shoes, and just sling my old beach towel over my shoulder.

Looking both ways down the hallway, I determine that I'm still alone in the house and let out a sigh of relief. I didn't realize it before, but I've been really tense these last few days and the thought of relaxing out by the pool sounds super appealing.

I have to walk through the kitchen on my way outside, but when I do, I notice someone has left a small plate with three cookies on the counter. A note says they're for me and made by Trent using a recipe from his Auntie.

I feel bad for eating some, like it's a confirmation of all my feelings in a single bite of sugary goodness, but they smell too good to resist. I eat all three and try not to feel weird about it.

The weather outside is still very nice, even if it's a little later in the day than I'd like. I quickly turn on the heating system for the hot tub, and deposit my towel on a nearby chair.

Sunlight sparkles on the water and when I tentatively dip my toes in, the ripples look like glittering silky sheets of blue and gold. I slip under its covers and let the water surround me, enveloping me like I'm sinking into a bed made of liquid clouds.

After floating in the water for some time, I try swimming a few laps just to burn off some of the jittery energy still left inside me. I'm not the best swimmer and even though there is no one else around, I still stop after two rounds just in case someone catches me floundering about.

Finally, when I'm tired out and over being in the cool water, I pull myself out of the pool and make my way to the now steaming hot tub. The surface inside is black, giving this water a much different look than the pool, but when I turn the jets on, the frothy white bubbles hide it all and I can't even see my own feet in front of me.

It's very nice and totally relaxing, but just as I'm laying my head back against the side, I hear a door open behind me. A shadow falls over my body, and I jerk forward in the tub, scrambling to the opposite side to look at my visitor.

It's Chalice, and he's standing there staring at me.

"Um, hi, Chalice," I mutter, moving my arms under water and shrinking down so that all he can see of me is my head popping out above the bubbles.

"Oh, hi, Julie. Want some company? I got off work early today, and it looks like we both had the same idea."

I notice he's wearing a pair of loose board shorts and holds his own towel in front of him. It looks like he's ready to get in and it'd be rude to turn him away. I'd be in my every right to do so, I got here first and have a right to privacy, but . . . Frankie did say I need to "follow my gut," and right now, my gut is saying I should let the hot guy in the water.

"Yeah, that'd be fine."

My eyes are wide as he lowers himself into the water, and I watch as his golden skin disappears beneath the bubbles. Since he's so much taller than I am, his chest easily rises above the water line, and he can easily drape his arms around the tub's sides. He then lets out a pleasurable sigh that I can't help but blush at.

"Room for one more?"

I tear my eyes away from the Golden God and see that Trent has now appeared in the doorway. He's still dressed nicely in slender grey slacks, a white-collared shirt and thin black tie. Looking at it over the bubbles makes the whole outfit seem out of place.

"I thought you had a meeting?" I ask, and he grins at me while loosening his tie.

"They postponed again, so I told them I wasn't interested," he answers and slides his tie off from around his neck. He drops it on the ground before Chalice and me, and then proceeds to take off the rest of his clothes.

Chalice rolls his eyes at him and turns his vision upward at the wooden terrace just above our heads. I watch silently as Trent strips off his shirt and jeans, and then feel Chalice move over so he's sitting next to me. His arms remain rested against the tub behind me and are dangerously close to my skin.

"Leave your underwear on at least," he mutters to Trent, who turns and winks at him.

"Anything for you, Big Boy," he laughs.

I let out a nervous giggle so I don't feel left out.

Before long, Trent has taken off all his clothing except the tiny pair of black boxer briefs I saw him in this morning. He crawls into the tub with much less splashing than Chalice and takes a seat on my other side.

So now I'm sandwiched between my two sexy roommates in the hot tub. One is in his underwear and then other has fingers that are brushing against the skin of the back of my neck.

Fuck.

CHAPTER ELEVEN

This new house I'm living in has a very nice backyard. It's the kind that makes property value increase tremendously due to the size as well as the tall fence lining the entire thing. It's the perfect height to hide every single thing you could possibly do in your own backyard with your own private pool and jacuzzi. And by every single thing, I mainly mean sex. You could do sex here and your neighbors would never know.

Unless, you're loud, I guess.

Wow, my mind has really gone straight to the gutter, but it's hard not to think about things like that considering I'm wedged between the two hottest guys I've ever seen.

The water of the tub covers most of my body with only the top of my breasts barely visible above the line of bubbles. Chalice and Trent are taller, so the water hits them much lower on their bodies, but that only provides a better look at both their bare chests.

Okay, I've got to get these thoughts under control, time to make some conversation . . .

"So, uh, Chalice, what's your favorite food?"

His body rumbles next to me as he laughs.

"Good question, I don't think I've ever really thought about that. I guess, potatoes."

Trent laughs next, but he stretches under the water before he answers, and I feel one of his tails brush against calf. It sends a ticklish jolt up my leg and into my chest.

"That's actually a pretty good answer, you can make all sorts of stuff with the humble potato."

"Like fries," responds Chalice, following Trent's example and stretching his legs under the water. When he does so, he has to extend his arms further along the sides of the tub for a better grip, and his fingers brush against the nape of my neck giving me goosebumps despite the warm water.

"Fries are amazing, how about you, Trent?" I ask.

"Tough question, but I'd have to go with pumpkin muffins. We have an old family recipe, which isn't so much an actual recipe as it is something someone saw in a magazine ad once, but I've been eating pumpkin muffins since I was a kit. I'll make you a batch someday."

"You're welcome to make me food anytime you'd like," I say with a laugh.

"Okay, my turn now." Chalice turns slightly so he can look down at me. "I don't think I'm wrong here, but you're single, right Julie?"

I feel the heat from more than just the Jacuzzi water rush to my face. I guess I should tell the truth here.

"Ye-yeah, single. For a long while now, actually."

Goddess, why did I add that last part?

"Ah, makes sense," rumbles Chalice.

"Whoa, whoa, whoa, what do you mean by that?" I splash some water at his face, and he grins mischievously.

"Only that I haven't seen anyone coming or going from your room, so I had a hunch. Are you looking for anyone right now?"

"Well, uh, I'm not sure what I'm looking for if I'm being honest. Boyfriends just sort of appear in my life."

Trent scoffs.

"That popular, huh?"

I glance over at him in horror, but immediately tell from his expression that he is only teasing. Well, his expression, and the fact that one of his tail tips accidentally brushes against my upper thigh at the very same time we make eye contact.

When I look back at Chalice, I see him making some sort of gesture with his eyebrows and mouthing something I can't quite make out. The look is gone as soon as he catches my eye, but I wonder what they're silently communicating between each other.

He looks so sexy sitting there among the bubbles and rippling water. While Trent is totally gorgeous as well, he's got the whole fur thing going on, and those tails—when they get out of the water—are going to be a dripping mess. But Chalice . . .

The water drops scattered across the thin sheen of golden scales along his jawline sparkle like opals, each radiating their own tiny rainbows. And I can easily imagine the powerful looking arms he has, extending across the tub's edge being used to pin me against a wall or bed.

Something brushes my leg from the side and from the feel of it, it's one of Trent's tails. It drags lazily up my leg, dances across my thigh and with the lightest flick between my legs, it disappears as Trent lets out a loud sigh.

"Alright, that's enough hot water for the day. I'll see you two later." He catches my eye and winks just as one last tail flick provides a final stroke up my thighs, lingering for a moment, pressing against the yellow of my bikini and dangerously close to my covered clit. It's just enough pressure to make me gasp.

Out of the corner of my eye, I catch Chalice rolling his eyes as Trent pulls himself out of the tub. I don't even have time to see how drenched his five tails have become because I'm too busy staring at the thin, wet cloth of his boxer briefs and how they do not leave anything to the imagination.

A pair of golden fingers with short finger nails caresses my chin and pulls my line of vision toward Chalice.

"Hi Julie," he says with a cocky grin. "Has anyone told you today how awesome you are?"

"Just one, Frankie, but I generally average three on a good day."

My response takes him off guard, and he lets out a loud laugh.

"Fuck, that was my best pick up line."

"Your best? Oh dear . . ."

He splashes me with a little water, but I answer with an even bigger splash that has us both laughing and slapping at the churning water like children.

"Well, I'm serious," he finally says, rubbing his hand down his dripping face and shaking water from his golden blonde hair. "You're smart, you donate your Friday nights, you're funny and fucking gorgeous."

"How do you know I'm smart?"

"To be honest, I think most creatures are smarter than I am, so it's not a stretch to believe that you are as well."

"You shouldn't sell yourself short like that. It's not like you're dumb. I've seen actual dumb and cruel creatures before, and you are not one of them."

"I don't like the sound of that." He settles down next to me. This time, I can obviously feel his short finger nails trailing along the top of my shoulder.

"I don't like to talk about it a lot, but I had . . . a pretty bad boyfriend in the past. It was a long time ago, and I'm very over it, but he was someone cruel and dumb. You, Chalice, are the exact opposite of him in every way."

"Well, I'm glad you're free of him," says Chalice. He then moves to the opposite side of the tub so that he can face me. Water splashes over the sides as he moves, and although he's not sitting beside me anymore, this feels much closer and much, much more intimate.

He's a fairly large guy and the tub we're sitting in, while big, still doesn't have a whole lot of room. He leans back against the side and stretches his long legs out so that they extend to the ledge I'm sitting on. He's slouched in the water, sitting on the base of his tail that I can feel sweeping the tub's floor between my feet. He's effectively trapped me between his legs while leaving enough room so its not too awkward.

"Julie?" He asks in a low, husky voice that makes my legs tremble under the water. I'm grateful for the bubbles concealing my clenched fists. I'm aching to run my fingers up and down the muscles of his calves or tickle his tail with my toes.

There's also an incredible urge to start touching myself while replying to the mostly naked Golden God before me.

"Mmm, yeah?"

"I picked up your toothpaste and left it on the bathroom counter."

The pop of deflated energy between my legs feels so obvious to me that I'd be surprised if he couldn't feel something snap between us.

What am I even doing? Thinking about launching myself the short distance to sit on this guy's lap? Well, yes, I am thinking about it, but thinking and acting are two very different things. If I stay here any longer, I'm going to get myself into trouble and not the good kind of trouble that may include a spanking from this hunk, but the kind of trouble that would make living here even more awkward than it already is.

"Oh, um, thanks! You know, I really should go brush my teeth again. There wasn't much left this morning so I'm feeling not so fresh right now. Then I'm also going to take a uh long shower."

Great cover story, Julie. Another Oscar worthy performance for the ages.

"Gotcha," Chalice responds, moving his huge body so I can maneuver easily out of the tub. "I'll see you in a bit?"

"Yup!" I scurry ungracefully out of the tub and snatch up my towel before wrapping it securely around my waist and hurrying inside. There's a tightness in my chest and I feel the hitch in my breath coming upon me again. I need to get inside and be alone with my thoughts as fast as I can.

From the corner of my vision, I think he's watching. But I can't see whatever expression is on his face as I disappear into the house. Fuck, I don't even know what he thinks about me!

I can still hear the sounds of the water jets as I rush through the kitchen and down the hallway, but they soon become quiet when I get inside the hallway bathroom.

Stripping myself of my wet bikini, I stand naked in front of the mirror and can't help the ambush of emotions in my mind.

I've always been more quiet and reserved than Frankie and my family members. Whether that's a trait of being human versus a Dragoon or not, I can't say for sure, but I've always thought my personality has some sort of defect in it that zaps my confidence and causes me to overthink.

Thinking, thinking . . . so much thinking. When I'm surrounded by too many people, I feel an overwhelming sense of dread and panic. When I'm alone, it's a quiet overthinking situation that involves just me, myself, and I. The emotional tide of intrusive thoughts that I think others are thinking that suddenly comes home to where it belongs: my own mind.

I don't know if I'm "awesome" or "gorgeous." In fact, I'd probably say I'm neither of those things, so hearing someone compliment me about them feels strange. Maybe not from Frankie because she's said them a million times, but coming from Chalice spins my mind out of control.

Deep breaths, Julie, deep breaths.

I concentrate first on what just happened:

I was minding my own business in a tub full of hot water, and my two roommates showed up and got in with me, one of whom was only wearing his underwear. Fuck, that sounds like the start to one of the porn movies out by the TV.

Okay, but besides the fact that we're all barely wearing any clothes, was there anything else? I guess there really wasn't; of course they sat next to me and maybe some of their body parts brushed up against my body parts, but that's what happens in hot tubs . . . right?

RIGHT?!

Whew, I need to calm down. Nothing happened; it's not like either of them asked me to have sex with them, which is only a little disappointing.

No. I cannot go down that train of thought.

Deep breaths.

We were in the water and then Trent left and Chalice said he picked up toothpaste for me and put it in the bathroom. I can see it right now on the counter. It's the exact same brand and the exact same flavor as the one I had before, and my heart melts that he would do something so, well, mundane for me.

But I guess we're roommates after all. I suppose I'd be expected to do the same thing for him if I notice he's running out of something hygiene related. We share this bathroom after all. I probably wouldn't have done that for my own brother when we shared a bathroom.

I take another deep breath and start the shower.

Once the warm water washes over my skin, I feel myself begin to relax. Muscle by muscle, the tension eases a bit and I can divert my mind from things other than, well, sex. The distraction goes well until, amongst the rushing of water in my ears, I think I hear someone knocking on the door.

That's strange. Chalice knows I'm in here. Why would someone be knocking?

I turn the water off and stick my head out from the shower door. "Yeah?"

"Hey, Julie, I know you're taking a shower, but I really need to grab something from under the sink," Chalice calls back. "Do you mind if I come in really quickly? I promise to keep my eyes closed!"

My thoughts swirl. Sure, it's kinda weird that he wants to come in while I'm naked in here, but I'm in the shower. With the steam and closed door, it's not like he'll be able to see me. Though, a secret and deep down part wishes he could. It's a sexy thought if I'm being honest.

"Uh, yeah, sure!" I turn the water back on, but stand near the steamy door so that I can watch him come inside.

The bathroom door opens quickly, closing just as fast after the large golden form of Chalice stumbles inside. He keeps one hand held tight over his face while the other gropes blindly in front of him as he looks for the sink counter's edge. While he has his hands under control, his long tail flips behind him dangerously and I watch as it whacks against the wall and nearby toilet with some solid and painful sounds.

He turns and bends over but his tail, clearly out of control now, sweeps across the counter and scatters several things across the bathroom floor. I can't help but snicker at the big guy turning in their direction and looking down while still keeping his hand glued across his eyes.

"Uh, sorry about that."

I take a deep breath.

"It's fine, you can open your eyes," I respond and step back further behind the foggy glass of the shower door. "It's not like you can see anything from out there anyway."

"Are you sure?"

I detect both an eagerness and hesitation in his voice.

"I wouldn't say you could if I wasn't," I reply, watching his misty form through the glass door. I can't make out much more than a golden blob with a tail.

"Thanks, um, is everything okay? You kind of rushed out of the tub earlier. I didn't say anything stupid, did I?"

I put some of my fruity scented soap on a washcloth and absentmindedly rub my arms down with the suds. I feel the honesty begging to spill out from me, probably from the intimacy of the shower, or that I think he might just deserve the truth. It feels much easier to explain things from the safety of the steam.

"It was just getting a little too, um, stimulating being in there."

"Oh yeah? Was it my stimulating conversation or something else that had you running to the hills?"

I'm not sure, but I think he's leaning against the wall beside the shower now. His face is still obscured by the foggy glass, but I can definitely make out his large frame. The presence of him combined with the vulnerability of being naked makes me shudder.

"I wouldn't say I 'ran for the hills,' I just . . . I don't know, had second thoughts. I needed to get away before I did something dumb."

He's silent for a moment, but I can tell by the golden shadow that he's moved closer to the shower door.

"Well, in the tub, you said I wasn't dumb. So if you did me, you wouldn't be doing anything dumb."

Something shifts inside me, as if my very being is an endless playlist of songs, and I've just skipped to a new track. Everything I had been thinking about, the pros and the cons, of my new roommates suddenly becomes obsolete when the new lyrics take over, and I can think of nothing but submitting to my body's desires.

I don't know if I opened the shower door or if Chalice did, but steam begins pooling out in a grey cloud just as cold air hits my skin, making my nipples pucker in protest.

The shower space, big even by Dragoon standards, is more than enough to hold our two bodies, and Chalice has no problem slipping inside with me and shutting the door behind him. The hot water soaks the shorts he's still wearing until they are nothing more than a second skin, leaving a clear and bulging outline of his growing cock.

He closes the distance between us and takes my hands, all while never looking down at my naked body. He places my hands on the edge of his swim trunks and looks down at me.

"I just want to make sure you're okay with this." He looks into my eyes. "Believe me, this is something I've been thinking about for a while now, but only if you're into it. I will leave right now if you ask me to. I need to know if you want this."

I dip my fingers below the waistband of his shorts, tugging them down a few inches. He brings his own hands up to thread them through my wet hair and I lean upward to kiss him.

"I want this," I say with shower water spraying into my eyes, and with a low groan, he responds by kissing me.

CHAPTER TWELVE

C halice tastes so much better this time. The sticky sensation of mixed alcohol is a thing of the past, and there is nothing left but the soft taste of peppermint, as if he recently chewed gum.

With his fingers wrapped in my hair and his palms gently pressing against the sides of my head, he's able to control our kiss, making it long, lingering, and needy. His tongue flicks against my lips, dipping inside my mouth with urgency as if, truly, this has been on his mind for a while now.

We finally break apart for air.

"Are you cold?" he asks. "I think I'm blocking most of the water from you."

He's right, his large body stands between me and the shower head, so I barely feel a drop, but I'm far from being cold and shake my head.

"Not with you here." I give his shorts another soft tug, which makes him groan and push his hips forward into my touch. It causes my fingers to graze the hardness beneath the wet fabric and I gasp at the first indication of his engorged size. He kisses me again, and I crack my eyes open to watch the bulge in his short twitch with pleasure.

Chalice grabs my hands again and directs them back to his waist band and, without breaking our kiss, our fingers make quick work of the strings to his board shorts. With my hands assisting, they fall from his hips to a wet puddle on the shower floor. He flicks them away from the drain using his long, golden tail and pulls me close.

There is a built in seat toward the back of the long, rectangular shower. I think it's probably built for a large Dragoon to hoist a leg up for better cleaning, but it acts like a chair for my more human stature. Chalice uses his body to back me up toward it and braces his arms on the wall to either side of my head when I sit down.

His cock, level now with my face, is enormous. That's to be expected, he's a big guy, but the sheer golden hue to the taught skin combined with the shower water makes it practically sparkle.

Imagine that if you will, a giant sparkling dong.

I try to reach out for it, but he moves too fast, and I miss my chance. He kneels before me and spreads my legs with a gentle push of his hands. The shower sprays the back of his head with water and what misses him, covers me in a fine mist as he positions me to the very edge of the seat. His fingers knead and tickle my thighs as he looks up at me.

"Comfortable?"

"Yes," I respond, but I'm not sure he can even hear me above the sounds of the shower, and I'm too engulfed in sensation to attempt raising my voice. I nod just in case and chew my lower lip.

"Good," he murmurs, leaning forward and dragging a hand toward my waiting and expectant core. His other hand circles around my ass and holds me steady after I squirm from the stimulating touch between my legs.

His body presses against mine as he tilts his head into the crook of my neck and breathes deeply. I tighten my arms around his shoulders at the same time he inserts one of his long fingers into my warmth. He's gentle and probing, as if assessing me from the inside.

A low purr of contentment rumbles from his chest.

"A little tight, but deep. I think you'd fit me just fine."

I let out a mewling gasp in reply because while he's talking, he's also pumping that finger inside me and using his other hand to guide my lower body at a steady, maddening rhythm. His thumb finds my clit and effectively cuts off my communication skills altogether, and I'm left with nothing more than letting my head fall back with a moan of pleasure.

"Goddess you sound so hot when you moan like that." He slows his hand, but I hear his breath hitch as he moves to my shoulder and grazes my skin with his teeth. The hand beneath me moves to under my breasts and he brings a nipple to his mouth.

He suckles deeply, and it's my turn to let out a contented purr. The feeling of receiving pleasure from his hands along with the way he possessively leans into me is driving me over the edge.

"Oh . . . wow, I'm going to . . ." I can't get my words out, and he chuckles as the pace his thumb is pressing and circling against my clit increases.

"Going to come for me, gorgeous? Because I want you to."

He doesn't have to ask twice, as I heed his throaty words and let myself go against his hand. He must sense my body tensing between us because as soon as I let loose, the hand not between my legs, grabs me in a close, protective embrace.

A powerful, jolting orgasm rocks through my body and makes my back arch against him. The sheer intensity of it, along with the dull ache it leaves afterward, lets me know it's been a while since someone has made me feel this good.

Even if the guy to provide me with this happiness also happens to be my new roommate. Fuck it. I'm already this far in, might as well continue to enjoy myself. I may have to face the consequences of my actions later, but at least Frankie will be proud of me.

When my body stills, I feel Chalice stroking my wet hair and gazing at me with lust-filled, big hazel eyes. I give him a coy smile and stand on shaking legs before him. This close, and also this naked, really reminds me of how short I am, and I'll definitely need him down on my level if I'm going to do what I want with him.

I slip around him, pressing my back against the slick shower wall until I'm the one standing in the hot stream of water. I then give him a gentle push so that he's the one sitting down on the chair. He barely fits after he shifts his tail around, but there's just enough room for me to drop to my knees in front of him.

His cock stands at attention in his lap and I marvel again at the sparkling, huge appendage. Sure it's in line with his large body, but I've only seen a handful of cocks in my life and they were just that, handfuls. Chalice is a definitely a two hander.

Briefly, a thought drifts through my mind and I wonder if Trent is a similar size. It almost seemed that way from what I felt and could see the other night in my room. He is slimmer than Chalice, but just as tall, so it's possible. He probably doesn't glimmer like a gold brick though.

"You don't have to do that if I'm too big," Chalice says, bending over and smoothing my wet hair from my face. "Don't get me wrong, I want to be inside you in every way, but I might be a little awkward for your mouth."

I look up at him from my position between his legs and place my palms on either side of his head so I can look into his eyes.

"Then why don't you help me with it."

His eyebrows raise up in question as I take his hands and place them one atop of the other along the upright shaft of his cock.

Cupping my own hands over them, I then lean down and take the head of his cock into my mouth.

Chalice lets out a hiss of pleasure that leaves behind the faintest smell of smoke. He must have let loose a little stream of fire so I assume I'm doing a good job at this.

The silky skin has been washed away of any precum that may have been, but I feel him start to let out some more in my mouth as my tongue swirls along the head and the few inches below that I can easily reach.

I use my hands to control his movements so I can coordinate the stroking sensation with my mouth. Chalice really seems to like this, and I look up to catch him with head rolled back, mouth open, and eyes closed. I remove my hands and let him move on his own while my mouth takes in as much as I dare.

"Fuck, Julie." I feel him twitching against my cheeks. "Your mouth feels incredible."

"I think I like watching you jerk off," I tease.

He chuckles lowly, opening his eyes and looking down at me. He removes one hand and lifts my chin up toward him. The other hand continues to move rapidly along his cock.

"I'll let you watch me jerk off anytime you want, but right now, I want to fuck you." He takes his other hand away from himself. "Please."

My toes curl beneath me in pleasure, and I stand up to allow him to get off the chair. I'm pushed back under the water, but only for a second because as soon as he rises, he tilts down, grabs my thighs and hoists me up with my back against the wall. I feel myself hovering over the enticing slickness of the head of his cock, and I wrap my arms around his shoulders for support.

He breathes another hiss of pleasure into my ear.

"I'll go slow, but let me know if its too much." He pauses, still easily holding me up. "Are you, um, on any . . . protection? I can get a . . ."

I tighten my grip, lean my head into him and kiss the golden scales along his cheeks.

"I'm on the pill," I answer and feel a small release of tension from his body next to mine.

"Got it, just wanted to make sure. Though if you're okay with it," he pauses again, but this time to start lowering me onto him, "I want to come all over your body after I get a good taste of what it's like inside you."

I tilt my head back so I can catch his eye.

"I had no idea you were so dirty, Chalice. I like it."

I don't get a response because he's concentrating on lowering me as slow as possible onto him. It's both slow and torturous and absolutely amazing to feel him sliding fully into me, filling me so completely that even I find myself amazed at what my body can handle.

"There, you see? A tight fit, but you fit my length wonderfully."

I gasp when he shifts his hips and slides out slightly before slowly pushing back into me.

"Goddess." I feel my fingernails digging into his skin, the light covering of scales hardly holding up to the way I cling to his massive body. "You feel . . . so good. Fuck."

I feel the tension building in my body once more and even though I sense a slight discomfort from the shower wall grinding into my back, the way Chalice's cock fills me makes me think of little else. My body wraps easily around him, adjusting to his size and girth, but still leaves me with a tight, full feeling inside as we pulse together again and again.

He lets out another rumbling laugh and increases his pace until I hear his breathing becoming staggered and erratic, which tells me he's close. I am too.

"Chalice," I whimper into his ear. "I'm going to come soon, put me on the bench."

He gives my right ear a playful nip just before extracting himself with a deep groan. The coolness of the shower chair is shocking as he sets me down on it but is short lived as I have much better things to pay attention to.

Chalice leans over me, bracing one hand on the shower wall behind me, leaning forward and stroking his cock just above my collarbone. In turn, I reach down between my legs and rub my clit, which only needs a few firm strokes before sending my body down its second joyful current of pleasure.

Watching with hooded eyes, Chalice has only a few more strokes before he lets out a shuddering moan and releases on top of me. His come streams out, mostly covering my chests in streaks of creamy white that drips between my tits and collects all the way down between my legs.

He lets out a sigh of warm breath and braces his other hand on the wall above me, panting hard with closed eyes. After a minute, he opens them and looks down at me.

"Goddess, you're perfect. Fucking perfect in every way."

"That was . . ." I struggle to find my breath. "Really good."

"Just good?" He raises an eyebrow at me and chuckles.

"More than good, really. I don't even know if I'll be able to walk out of here."

Chalice bends down further and kisses my cheek.

"Then rest now, I'll take care of you."

He steps back so that some of the shower water, which thankfully has not gone cold yet, begins to stream on me. It washes most of what Chalice has left on me away, but what remains is quickly wiped up by a soft washcloth he runs over my skin. When I try to take it from him and clean myself, he pushes my hand away.

"I got it, gorgeous."

With gentle administration, he cleans every bit of my body with a minty smelling soap, and even massages a sweet smelling shampoo into my hair. He then helps me to stand and wash away the suds. He makes quick work of washing himself down, and we both finally step out of the shower into the steamy bathroom.

We don't speak. Maybe that's a good thing or maybe it's not. We're either both comfortable in what just happened, or we're both considering the ramifications of our actions. Either way, there are no words exchanged as we both grab towels and dry off.

Chalice ties one securely around his waist before turning toward me and scratching the back of his neck.

"So, uh, can you walk now?"

I let out a small laugh.

"I, uh, think so?"

"Okay, well, just in case . . ." He crosses the bathroom in two big steps and picks me up in his arms, cradling me towel and all, into his chest as he steps out into the hallway.

I suddenly feel really sleepy, possibly from all the hot water, but maybe also from the proximity to this gentle giant who just, uh, fucked me nearly senseless.

He takes me down the hallways toward his room, but just before he kicks his door open, I hear the sound of Trent strumming away at his guitar from the garage. He's singing something as well, but I can't understand the lyrics and the sounds cut off dramatically when Chalice closes his bedroom door behind us.

Yawning, he lays me down on his enormous and unmade bed, then curls up behind me. I'm being spooned by the Golden God himself.

I know I need to stay awake; there's no way I'll be able to sleep here without the aid of my CPAP machine, but it's just too difficult.

There are a million things going through my mind right now, but because there are too many and I'm just so tired, none of the thoughts complete themselves. They leave my mind hazy, which combined with Chalice's soft breathing behind my head and the soft bed sheets, make me fall right to sleep.

I snort myself awake soon afterward and curse myself for falling asleep in Chalice's room. There's no way I can sleep very long without using my CPAP machine to help keep me breathing. I have to take a moment to steady my racing heart from being jolted awake so suddenly and in that amount of time, I'm able to realize that both our towels have fallen off and we've been wrapped to-gether naked since the time we both passed out.

It's dark in his room and judging by the view from his window, it must be just well past evening. There's just enough ambient light, though, to look down and see Chalice sprawled out on the bed, naked and golden. His cock, even unaroused, looks impressive and I impulsively chew my bottom lip just looking at it and remember-ing what we did together in the shower.

But I need to leave now, I don't want Trent to notice me coming out of Chalice's room wearing nothing but a towel. And I don't want Chalice waking up and wanting to talk . . . about things.

But why is that?

Why do I care that Trent knows I fucked Chalice?

Why don't I want to talk to Chalice now?

As much as I know it's going to complicate my life beyond all reason, I don't think I regret doing it. But have I now blown my chances with Trent by hooking up with Chalice? Fuck, what is wrong with me? I knew I should have stayed away from both of them. Now I've just gone and complicated things.

I get up slowly so I don't disturb him and carefully rewrap the towel around myself. His room is about the same size as mine, but his massive bed seems to take up the entirety of the space. It makes it hard to maneuver quietly around to the bedroom door.

Just before leaving, I turn back to look at him. He's still asleep
and very, very naked. Goddess, he's good looking, sweet, funny,
and caring. He also seems to have a thing for me. But I don't know
if it's a good idea to do this again.

Besides, there's Trent . . .

If that's even still an option anymore.

Also, what if I make everything so awkward that I have to move
away?

I make my way into the hallway and the whole house is silent.
The sound of Trent's guitar in the garage is gone, and there is no
light from under his door. He must have gone out.

My stomach growls as soon as Chalice's door is shut behind me,
and I realize that it's well past dinner. I'll need to get something to
eat if I plan on hiding in my room for the rest of the night, so after
taking another look at Trent's darkened doorway, I decide to take
a quick trip to the kitchen for a snack. Even if I'm only wearing a
towel. No one should be around to see me.

But just as I enter the brightly lit room, I see Trent standing
beside the counter eating half a sandwich. We stare at each other
for what feels like forever, and I clutch my towel to my chest.

"Oh, um, hi. I didn't think you were home."

He nods but doesn't make any eye contact.

"Yeah, no plans tonight. Are you hungry? Want half of my
sandwich?"

"Depends on what kind of sandwich it is," I reply, walking closer to him. When I get close, I notice his nostrils flare and each of his five tails begin to slowly twitch behind him.

"Does it matter? I'm sure you need to replenish some calories after all that . . . swimming."

I take a step back, but he slides the plate toward me along the counter. It looks like a standard ham and Swiss cheese, and I'm monetarily surprised he's eating something so basic.

"Excuse me?" I blurt out, a little horrified by his hostility. I may deserve it, but it still takes a moment to process his reaction.

I don't have long, though, before he lets out a long sigh.

"I'm sorry, I didn't mean anything by it," he gives me a long look. There's no anger to it, only a mournful looking pain.

"That's all . . . it just happened. I wasn't planning on . . ."

"Just eat the sandwich, Julie. You don't owe me any explanation as to why you chose him first."

"I still feel like I need to explain. I think. I don't know. I just want you to know that I also . . ."

Trent lets out a throaty growl and begins to stalk out of the kitchen. I attempt to stop him by placing a hand on his shoulder, but my towel becomes loose and I have to hastily grab it instead so it doesn't fall off.

"It's a good thing." Trent eyes my exposed skin as he talks. "He can give you much more than I can anyway, what someone like you deserves."

"What do you mean by that?"

"Nothing," he says with another sigh. "Just eat the fucking sandwich, Julie."

I watch in silence as he leaves in a flurry of white-tipped tails. One of them brushes against my arm and another flips across my bare shoulders. Both small touches make me shudder in pleasure, leaving me astonished that I could still be left wanting after receiving more than I needed from Chalice.

After he leaves, a heaviness sits firmly on my chest, and I place my palm over the exposed skin touched by his tails.

Have I just ruined everything?

CHAPTER THIRTEEN

The walk back to my room is quiet and dark, but my mind is loud with thoughts as I stew on Trent's cryptic words and attitude. It makes the half sandwich sit like a rock in my stomach. A constant reminder of him.

My bare feet are cold against the floor as I hurry into my room, so I can change into pajamas and get in bed. Once there, I notice a text from my parents saying "hello" without any of their typical questions, so I ignore it. It's nice of them to reach out, but I have other things currently on my mind and just want to sleep away my thoughts.

Yet sleep proves itself an impossible dream as I lay in bed for an hour tossing and turning. I eventually kick the covers to the floor, fling off my CPAP mask aside and stare at the ceiling debating on what to do. While I've been beyond satisfied from my encounter with Chalice, I finally decide to use my vibrator in a desperate attempt to calm my mind, but am quickly interrupted by a soft tapping at my door.

"Julie? Are you still awake?" the soft whisper of Trent wanders in.

I creep across the floor and open the door for him. He's changed since I last saw him and has on a simple white shirt and black shorts that may or may not be his underwear. Even in the ambient light of night, I can make out a few of his tattoos snaking up his arms and stare at one of a whisk in a bowl of batter as he starts talking.

When I finally look up at him, I'm momentarily lost in his blue eyes.

"I, uh, want to apologize for snapping at you," he says quietly. "You didn't deserve that."

"Well, I'd like to think I'm old enough to know what I do or do not deserve, but I appreciate the apology."

"Yeah," he murmurs and rubs the back of his neck. "Do you have a minute to talk?"

I do really like the fact that he came to me to apologize, but now I'm really not going to sleep tonight.

He doesn't elaborate so I leave the door open for him and sit on my bed. Trent takes the hint, closes the door gently behind him and sits beside me.

"You know, the last time we sat together like this, things got, um, a little steamy," I say, trying to keep things light.

Even after Chalice rocked my world earlier, I feel my body responding to Trent's closeness. There is something warm and comforting about him. You'd think that would be something from Chalice, since he's so big and protective, but there's something else about Trent. Something magnetic.

"I remember," he sighs. "It's what I wanted to talk to you about."

"Oh?"

He takes a deep, deep breath.

"I, um, have an issue with that. With controlling myself."

"You mean . . . you just let loose?"

Even in the dark room, I can see him give me a wry look and raise an eyebrow.

"Let loose? Is that what the kids are calling it these days?"

"Goddess, you know what I mean." I turn slightly so I can face him. "Just confirming what I think you're trying to tell me."

"I get too excited too fast and, well, you experienced it first hand during the party. I have a bad habit of creaming my pants way too quickly. It's a flaw. You deserve better than someone who can't control themselves all that well."

"I'm sorry you think it's a flaw, you shouldn't. I don't think its anything to be ashamed of, and I'll be the judge on what I think I deserve or not."

"I am ashamed, though. It's made it hard for me to establish any kind of relationship or even . . . never mind." He lays back on my bed, making himself comfortable. I can't help but glance at his lean, muscular legs and the tight little shorts that don't leave much to the imagination.

"I have something like that too. A 'flaw,' I guess. It's also made it hard to get into any long-term relationships."

"You don't have to tell me anything, it's not a contest," he says, shifting to his side so he can see me better.

I make a sudden decision to come clean. About the CPAP machine, not anything about him or Chalice. I'm not ready to go there just yet.

"I know, but it's something I've been hiding and, seeing that we live together, it'd be better to have it out in the open. You'd probably find out sooner or later."

"Now I'm intrigued." His eyes bore into mine.

I sigh deeply and rise from the bed to kneel in front of the nightstand. It may be nighttime in my room, but there's enough light coming from the window to easily see what I'm doing as I open the drawer and take out my CPAP machine.

Trent is right that it's not a contest about sharing the most embarrassing secret, but its hard not to look at it that way. Almost like a transaction. But while that may be the case, this also feels like the right thing to do.

I never thought I'd be able to share this secret with a guy, even though I had a feeling that I would eventually share if I ever wanted to marry or be with someone long-term. There is just something about Trent that makes it feel natural. That makes it feel okay.

I set the base machine, which is not much more than a black box about the size and shape of a shoebox and top it with the corresponding headgear and long, plastic tubing that connects them.

"Ta-da!"

Trent is silent as he gets up again to take a better look at the CPAP machine in all its glory. I can't even tell if he knows what it is or not. It's not like he would recognize the brand, and there isn't anything obvious about machine itself. If you didn't look at the mask and make the connection that it would fit over someone's nose and mouth, it might just remind you of something from an old sci-fi movie.

"Is that what I think it is?" he asks.

"Depends what you think it is."

"I had an uncle who used one, but I only ever saw it a few times when I was a kit. He used to snore like crazy until my auntie had him do a sleep study and they found he had breathing problems at night. It changed his life. This looks much sleeker than the one he had though. This is your 'flaw'?"

"Yeah, I suppose. It's kind of embarrassing, at least to me. Think about it, you get very close to a guy, things get hot and heavy, and he wants you to spend the night afterward. You'd be left with making an excuse or sneaking out of there, or you would have to bust this bad boy out and connect yourself to it as you two spoon in bed."

"Ah, I get it." He pauses and gives the machine a long, calculating look. "But it hardly seems like a deal-breaker, especially if you really like someone. And besides, if anyone, one-night stand or long-term boyfriend, had a problem with something like this, then they're obviously not the right choice and you could do better."

"Eh, maybe. I don't know. Even without this thing, I'm sure I'm not anyone's first choice. It's been ages since I've had a boyfriend."

Trent reaches other and cups his hands around my face so that I can't look away from him.

"Hey, you were able to charm Chalice into fucking you senseless in the shower. I think you're doing pretty well for yourself."

I force out a nervous chuckle and try to pull away, but Trent leans in and kisses my forehead. The smell of him clouds my senses and is a mix of musk and cinnamon. The kiss itself is slow and tender, and the soft feeling of his lips lingers long after he pulls away and embraces me in a warm hug.

"Sorry," he murmurs into my hair. "That was a little crude of me. I'll leave you alone so you can sleep, it's late. But just so you know, I wouldn't mind you using your CPAP next to me in bed. You're welcome to anytime."

It's much colder when Trent rises from the bed and looks down at me. I suddenly want nothing more than to grab his hands and pull him back down and against me. To entangle our bodies together and let him prematurely come on me as many times as he wants, provided he can at least assist me in coming a few times too.

For a moment, I think he may be feeling the same way because he leans in and slowly kisses my lips this time. But there is a well controlled restraint when he does so and from the tenseness I see in his posture, I already know he's not going to stay.

"Goodnight," I whisper as he pulls away.

"Night, Diamond," he whispers back.

As soon as Trent leaves and the door closes securely behind him, my fingers start to itch in a familiar way as the urge to paint or draw something falls over me.

I wait a few moments until I know Trent is back in the master bedroom and leap from my bed to find a fresh pad of paper. At some point in the evening, the moon aligned herself perfectly with my window and everything is illuminated in her glow.

Smoothing out the crisp pages of my art journal, I begin to draw. Long lines and short lines, shadows and smudges, I go through colored pencils and different watercolors until I've taken the images from my mind and pressed them on the pages before me.

I'm not even sure what I'm drawing until the icy blue eyes of Trent peer upward at me from a sea of golden, shimmering scales. Then I realize I've created some sort of hybrid between my two beautiful roommates surrounded by roses. They are the same pale purple color from the neighbor's yard back at my family's former home. The ones I saw everyday of my former life.

Satisfied, I slam the journal shut and tuck it safely under my bed. It's late and I'm tired. There will be plenty of time tomorrow to sort through this emotional onslaught of fragmented feelings. They certainly aren't going anywhere anytime soon.

The morning finds me stumbling half asleep into the kitchen. I've never been a morning person. While it may be great to wake up early and get more accomplished in the day, my mind always seems to want to sleep in. So it takes a moment for my sleep-addled brain to remember yesterday's events while the dull ache in my body reminds me of Chalice's big cock.

Oh, that's right. I fucked one of my roomies last night and nearly fucked the other one.

Goddess, what am I going to say or do when I see Chalice again today? I don't know if I should play it cool and pretend like it's no big deal or if I should say something. Maybe I'll just keep my mouth shut and wait to see how he responds.

But judging by how quiet the house feels around me, he must have already left for work. I'm not even sure if Trent's around because it looks like he's taken his lunch out from the fridge. Doesn't look like I'll have to face anyone in person just yet.

I hurry and make coffee, then grab a packaged toaster pastry before heading out the door. It's a beautiful day, but there's a crispness to the air that reminds me of the changing seasons. The main holidays may be a few months away, but when you work in the candle industry, your holidays are always on a different schedule than everyone else. We celebrate much, much, MUCH, earlier.

Thinking about work makes the candle design contest pop into my head, and before I leave, I grab my newest art piece from my bedroom. Blue eyes, golden scales, and light purple flowers stare at me from the page. *It's very pretty and would look great as a candle*, I think. Well, probably. I guess we'll see what Candle Love Corporate thinks.

Maybe I could enter securely into the contest? That way no one will know if I don't win, and by the slim, nearly impossible chance that I do have, no one will know I even entered. I just won't put my name on it. With the decision made to enter regardless, I grab the paper, stuff it into an empty folder, and hurry out the door.

Candle Love is part of a large outdoor shopping center, so our front doors are open to the vast parking lot we all share. We're also located on a corner lot that juts out into one of the turn-in lanes leading you along the different store fronts. It can be dangerous when drivers aren't paying attention, and a few of us, included me, know to look both ways before crossing the lot to get to the store. We've had a couple of close calls in the past.

If you don't take the time to look, you run the risk of a car having to swerve out of the way before hitting you. Or worse, actually hitting you. But even with my mind muddled and confused from my roommate situation, I still remember to watch the road before making my way up to the front doors because it's that important.

We don't open until ten in the morning, but the employees get to work far earlier to stock the store. I've never been in a place with more hidden storage than the main floor of Candle Love. There are hidden areas under just about every well-crafted display station. And someone needs to keep the products rotated every single day.

I never thought about it until I started working here, but there is a lot, and I mean a fucking lot, of prep work that goes on before the doors are unlocked for the public.

Speaking of locked doors, only a few of us have keys to this place, and I am not one of them. Which means I actually begin each of my shifts standing behind the big glass windows, trying to get the attention of whoever is here before me.

Today it only takes me a few minutes and a couple of not-so-discreet knocks on the door to get Eddie's attention.

"Welcome, foolish little mortal." He bows deeply and spreads his wings out dramatically and carefully among the stacks of half-finished candle displays. "So good of you to grace me with your presence."

"Uh huh." I shrug off my sweater and brush past him. I head toward the backroom to get my work apron on and store my purse, but have to stop short when a mountain of brown packing boxes blocks my way.

"Are you ready for a fun-filled morning of opening boxes with me?" Eddie leans casually against the stack, which by the way, is taller than he is.

"Good Goddess, why are there so many?" I have to shimmy by the stacks to access the backroom and barely make it to my small personal locker in the back.

"Upcoming Candle Love Member's only sales," he says, tapping a box. "Well, the ones with the black and white tape are. The yellow tapping is for mid-summer restocks, the orange for late-summer restocks, and blue is for fall or winter, I can't remember. No clue what the black tape ones are for."

"I'm not ready for this." I gaze at the mountain of boxes and brightly colored packaging tape. Inside them are carefully wrapped candles, body care products and various items used to enhance their displays in our store. We'll need to unpack and sort through all of it. Normally, everything is packaged perfectly, but occasionally we receive slightly damaged goods, nothing too bad, but poor enough to warrant a rejection. Those items get placed in the "employee sale" bins, which also contain a random assortment of out of season products.

In my first few weeks of working here, I went a little mad with purchasing as much as I could because of the great prices, but I ended up with too much and eventually had to purge my home inventory. Besides, I get enough of the smells and lotions when I'm here working all day.

"I can see the excitement on your face." Eddie flashes me the same kind of grin he uses on customers when he wants them to buy whatever he's showing them.

"I don't believe you." I roll my eyes but still secure my work apron around my waist and set the folder containing the Trent/Chalice art on top of the nearest stack.

"Oh, what's that?" Eddie's eyes stare at the folder, and I can tell from the twitch of his bronze-colored wings that he's interested. I snatch it back quickly.

"It's, um, my entry for the contest."

"No shit! You're actually going to enter? I'm so proud of you!" He throws an arm around my shoulders in a half hug. "Can I see it?

"Um, no."

If I didn't know any better, I'd say he looks hurt.

"Aww . . . please?"

"I wasn't going to tell anyone about it; it's embarrassing, and what if I don't win? You don't need to see someone's failed piece of artwork."

"Can you describe it for me?" he asks.

"Um, it's some eyes, some gold and some purple flowers. Please promise you won't tell anyone."

"Only if you promise you'll tell me if you actually win the thing." Eddie moves out of the way and points to the small office space we have. "Better store it in there so it won't get ruined or something."

"Fine, but only if you keep it a secret!"

He pretends to lock his lips and throw away the key.

After stowing the folder safely away on our Manager Marilyn's desk, Eddie and I continue with our product unboxing.

It's the kind of work that takes just enough brain power to make you stay focused but leaves just enough room for your mind to wander. So in between opening boxes and storing candles, body care, hand soaps and various display props, I find myself thinking of both Trent and Chalice.

The golden wax of a particular candle reminds me of Chalice's jawline and the crystal blue liquid of the next body wash is reminiscent of Trent's eyes, and so on and so forth. My imagination doesn't leave me alone until I get to a particularly dark purple candle that reminds me of Frankie and even smells like her sage-infused apartment. At least it's enough of a change to get my head back in the moment, and I shift my focus back to my job.

Eventually, I find something missing from one of the boxes and look over to ask Eddie about it only to find him staring at me. He looks away quickly, and I think I detect a small blush to his grey skin.

"What?" I ask him. "Do I have packing tape on my face?"

"No." He laughs softly. "You look fine. I was just thinking about something."

"And what's that?"

"Just that I'm excited for another thrilling day at Candle Love with you!"

I laugh and pull off some stuck packing tape from my arm. Eddie flashes a big smile as I turn around and stick in on his shoulder.

"Oh please, you know nothing thrilling or exciting ever happens around here."

CHAPTER FOURTEEN

After more than an hour of unboxing and cart loading madness, I hear a distinctive tapping on the front door and know that Portia, and hopefully Rose, have arrived for their shifts. Eddie runs off to let them inside, and I take the time to stretch my back and arms. Stocking shelves and unpacking candles is a lot of work. It's also really gross. My fingers are tacky from the glue they use for the color-coordinated taping, and all the boxes shed an enormous amount of small brown particles that stick to everything.

With Eddie gone, I make my way to the employee bathroom and find an out of season Yule soap that smells like peppermint candy and scrub away at my cuticles and fingertips.

"Yeah, she totally did!" I hear Eddie explain excitedly and Rose's amused laugh.

"I'm so glad she did," she says. "I've been trying to tell her to enter."

"Enter what?" Portia's voice echoes from further away.

"The contest!" Eddie answers to the accompanying sound of his wings banging into our leftover mountain of boxes.

I jump from the bathroom, a paper towel still in my hands as I dry off.

"Eddie, that was a secret!" I hiss, and he turns to look at me with the most innocent expression ever. He slicks back his dark hair and grins. The guy is pretty but clueless sometimes.

"Sorry, I totally forgot."

"Goddess," I mumble and turn away from him. There goes keeping my entry private.

Pointing at the loaded carts full of fruity-smelling candles and spicy-scented lotions, I look toward Portia. "Here's the stuff for the displays. The fixture packet for them should be tucked in there too."

"I never look at the instructions." She waves her tails absently. "Where is this art Eddie was telling us about?"

"Oh. I, uh, already put it in Marilyn's office. Sorry."

It's probably not hard to believe that I'm actually NOT sorry. While I wouldn't mind showing Rose, sharing something deeply personal with Portia makes my skin crawl.

Her ears twitch as if she would flatten them in anger, but she recovers quickly and drifts by me to the bathroom.

"Well, I for one, am glad you entered," says Rose. "The world needs more beauty, and artists brave enough to share their souls are especially valued."

I look away so she can't see my face turn red at her comment. I'm not a real artist. Sure, I've been drawing and painting my whole life, but it's just for fun. Never something I thought I would put my very soul into.

But her words do give me a pause.

I think of my most recent art piece that is laying in the office. Was I so consumed with thoughts of Chalice and Trent that part of my . . . soul wanted to reflect that and, ugh, share it with the world? That's certainly something I'm going to have to think about later!

"Julie?" Portia has emerged from the restroom looking flushed. She wipes her hand across her forehead in a gesture worthy of a regency romance. "Can we switch duties today? I have a massive headache."

"Don't you hate backroom work?" asks Eddie.

Portia shoots him a look.

"Don't you need to take a break or perhaps mind your own business?" she spits back.

Eddie throws his hands up in defense.

"I don't care what you do, but I do care about missing breakfast and morning coffee. Anyone want anything? My treat."

"I'm good, I brought some of my tea for Julie and me to share today," says Rose, placing a rosy hand on my shoulder. "You're going to love this batch. I made it especially with you in mind."

Eddie and I exchange a look.

"I'll, um, grab you a latte just in case," he whispers before leaving.

"Well, Julie? Can we switch?" Portia's nine, fluffy tails swirl behind her as she watches me closely for an answer.

She's not taller than I am, but she's much thinner and her skin is like caramel-colored porcelain. With a coating of berry-colored lipstick and her perfect features, she makes me feel rather insignificant. The beauty and confidence in her actions make her a pretty intimidating sight. I almost see why nine tails would be the preferred number because they only add to her mysterious allure.

But I would take Trent and his five tails over her any day. I think most creatures would.

"Yeah, I guess," I tell her, and Rose claps her hands in delight behind me.

"Fabulous!" I turn to see her pouring something pungent and bright purple into an extra mug. She holds it out to me.

"So, uh, what is this exactly?" I ask, taking the mug and smelling it. It smells like, well, a candle I once found in the discount bin.

"Secret sauce," she giggles, clinking the side of her cup against mine. "Trust me, you'll like it."

She's actually, weirdly, right about that. The dark liquid goes down smooth and tastes much better than it smells, even if it leaves me wondering what exactly it's doing to my insides.

Rose and I each push out a full cart of merchandise to the front of the store and get to work dismantling an older display there. We're going to replace it with Yule items even though it's hot enough today for the beach, but like I said, seasons and holidays have no meaning when you work in a store that specializes in seasonal scents.

We work in silence for about ten minutes, which is enough time for Eddie to return with a few extra coffees that he stashes in the back room *just in case* anyone needs more caffeine. But Rose isn't one to work in silence for too long; besides, talking makes work go faster.

"You look like you have something on your mind," she says kindly, fixing a candle that I have placed backward on a nearby shelf, something that would never fly at Candle Love. We're all about perfection here!

"Sorry about that, I guess my heads are just in the clouds today."

"My head is always there, I'll keep you company, but you look like something is bothering you." She flips her hair back over her shoulder, and I catch a glimpse of her pinkish-red scales along her neck. She's really pretty too, more than Portia and much more than me.

Ugh, why is everyone here making me feel so inferior today? What is wrong with me? All the doubt about my feelings, as well as Trent and Chalice's feelings, plus the anxiety of everyone knowing I entered the contest is making my confidence really low right now. But I don't know if I want to bring all that up to Rose, even though I have a suspicion she can probably read my mind. She's weird like that.

"Just boy problems," I answer simply. I take a moment to open one of the new body soaps and sniff it. I have to put it back immediately because it smells way too much like Chalice's body soap. It must have the same scent notes.

"I see," she says, her voice soft. "You're such a pretty thing, you must have your choice of mates out there. I wouldn't worry about things."

"That's just the thing; there are too many options and I can't decide," I blurt out before hiding myself in the fixture magazine and attempting to study the intricate woodland display we're trying to put together with pieces of colorful plastic and fake pinecones.

Rose giggles.

"See, pretty thing, the creatures flock to you."

"It's been ages since I've had a boyfriend, so I doubt I'm that much of a find." One of the pinecones rolls away, and I have to jog across the floor to retrieve it.

"Drink your tea," she tells me, and I raise an eyebrow at her.

"Why?"

"Because," she says and waves her hand mysteriously at me as I come back over to the display. "It'll help."

"It will help me find a boyfriend?"

"Better." She waggles her eyebrows at me and gestures for me to take a sip.

"What's in here again? It tastes like . . ."

But I don't get to finish my sentence because there is a sudden, terrible screeching sound outside the store. Rose and I stand transfixed as we both look toward the commotion, staring in horror at the car hurtling toward us from the parking lot.

It feels like it is happening slowly. As if I'm watching a movie and the frame rate has slowed to a crawl, so the audience has time to see the car's tires fighting for control, the way the windows burst into glittering fragments, and the look of sheer panic in the human driver's eyes.

But once the car makes contact with the heavy, but mostly glass, doors of Candle Love, time catches back up with a defending crunching sound that sends Rose and me stumbling back and attempting to shield ourselves from airborne glass, soaps, lotions and candles that come careening toward us.

Then comes the silence as the scents of cranberry, vanilla, pine tree, scorched rubber, and car fluids leech into the air. It's enough to make me feel bile rising in my throat, which could be from the smell or pure fear making its way through my body.

And in the quiet, Rose and I rise from our hiding space and look up at the car that just drove through the front of our store.

"Julie!" Rose's voice breaks the silence, and she clutches my arm. "You're bleeding!"

I touch my forehead gingerly and poke at a small cut above my eyebrow. My finger comes away bloody, but a quick scan of my arms and legs proves I've been spared from any other wounds. A glance at Rose says she looks about the same, though her arm seems to be forming a bruise the size of an orange.

"I don't think it's bad." My voice is shaky and uncertain as I attempt to stand up on quivering legs and look around the demolished front of Candle Love. I stumble and Rose catches me.

"Rose! Julie!" Eddie's voice screams from somewhere beyond. He sounds stricken with worry. "Please say you two are alright!"

I stand with Rose's assistance, and we glance back at Eddie standing before the door to the backroom. His face is pale, and I can tell from the agitated twitch of his wings that he's on edge.

"We're okay!" Rose calls back, pulling something out of her hair that looks like a piece of glass.

"Julie? Are you hurt?" he calls out.

"No, I'm fine."

"Thank the Goddess, what about the driver?" Eddie asks, making his way carefully over to where we stand. He arrives and puts a hand protectively around my shoulders. All three of us look over at the front of the red, shiny car parked literally inside our store.

I'm relieved when I hear the human driver before seeing them. Even though he's letting out a string of loud swears, they're all aimed at the stunned Demonnie passenger in his car. If he's well enough to scream all those "fucks" at the top of his lungs, he's probably not too seriously injured.

I feel Eddie's hand on my back and look up at him as he folds his wings protectively around Rose and me. I'm almost lost in their big bodies, but it's warm and comforting between them.

"Do we even have protocol for when something like this happens?" Rose asks.

"Fuck if I know, but I bet we can take the rest of the day off." He sighs. "I'll call Marilyn and let her know."

"Good, I can do with a day off." Portia saunters out of the backroom, brushes by us and the absolute mess of crushed glass as if it were only fall leaves, and begins to walk out the front door . . . well, what's left of it. I guess there isn't really a door or wall there anymore. It's just a big hole now.

"Portia! Wait, you can't just leave!" Eddie snaps at her, but she flicks her nine tails at him, turns her head and waves.

"Sure I can, watch me. There's no way I'm sticking around here now, but I did you a favor and called emergency services. Bye!"

None of us can think of something to say to her as she leaves. We're too stunned.

Even the car's driver and passenger watch her as she carefully exits the demolished area with her designer shoes. I have to admit at being a little impressed that she's so able to delicately and carefully navigate around the damaged floor. None of her furry tails so much as touch anything around her.

After a moment of silence, Rose clears her throat.

"Alrighty then, let's get outside and make some phone calls."

"You two go." Eddie refolds his wings and looks at the car. "I'll check in on those two, and I'll meet you out front."

We nod and watch as he makes his way to the red car, and then Rose and I take a deep breath before carefully picking our way out of the debris and to the front of the store. We grip tightly each other's hands to make sure we don't trip because we're not sure footed Fox Folk like Portia. I nearly fall trying to avoid a cluster of smashed hand soaps and Rose almost slips in a puddle of spill lotion.

I've never seen so much broken glass. Glass from the windows, glass from the big doors and countless glass candles litter the ground in a rainbow of fractured light and colorful wax. It's both beautiful, dangerous, and exceptionally fragrant.

Thank Goddess we didn't have any customers in here yet, or this accident could have ended much differently. I can't imagine what carnage could have been inflicted if this happened on a busy afternoon. It sends a shiver down my spine just thinking about it.

Outside we find a small crowd gathering, mostly employees from our neighbor stores, a sporting goods place and a store that specializes in charcuterie and chocolate. I can even make out some of the Burger Bliss employees standing outside their location and looking over.

"Are you girls okay?" asks the huge Minotaur manager of Flicker's Sporting Goods. His worried expression scans over Rose; then he casts a quick glance in my direction.

"Yeah, I think I just need to sit," I respond, and Rose squeezes my hand.

"Me too," she says before turning to the Minotaur. "Someone already called emergency services, Roy. I think we just need to sit down."

He nods, but looks reluctant to let us, or rather Rose, out of his sight.

"I'll be nearby if you need me," he tells her firmly, and with a stiff nod in my direction, he hurries over to help Eddie and the creatures still sitting in their car amid the wreckage of Candle Love.

We walk over to a small bench outside the charcuterie and chocolate place and sit. I don't think I've ever been more grateful to sit in my entire life, and my legs practically give out as soon as my ass hits the cold metal of the bench. A minute of silence goes by while we try to absorb what just happened.

"Well," Rose starts, "This is not how I saw my day going."

"Me neither." I sigh. "I'm just glad we weren't open yet. How do you think that happened anyway with the driver?"

Rose gestures with her pink-scaled head toward the road in front of our store. There are black tire marks clearly swirled into the road and a damaged tree off to the side.

"Either the driver failed to see the posted speed limit or they had to swerve to avoid hitting something or someone. Either way, someone out there wasn't paying attention."

"Julie!" I hear someone screaming my name and look up to see Chalice racing across the parking lot toward us. He must have been at work because he's still wearing his uniform of black pants and blue apron. There's even a spatula still in his hand.

He skids a halt in front of Rose and me, drops to his knees and throws his arms around my neck.

"Are you okay?" he whispers into my ear as one of his hands creeps up and threads through the back of my hair.

"I'm okay," I whisper back.

When he pulls away, he cups my head in his hands and examines my face.

"Fuck, you're bleeding," he says hoarsely, and I think his eyes may be misting over.

"It's nothing, just a little scratch. It could have been much worse."

I pull back gently from Chalice and look toward Rose.

"Hey, is your arm okay?" I ask.

"I think so." She stretches it out, and Chalice and I look at the deep purple bruising along her forearm. It almost blends in with her rosy complexion, but it still looks nasty.

"Goddess, if you two had been standing any closer, you could have been hit." Chalice's face is etched with anger. "I'm going to have a word with the driver of that car."

He gets up to leave, but my hand whips out to grab his and hold him back. I can see the angry flush rising up amongst his golden scales and a stream of smoke drifts from his snarling mouth.

"Don't, I'm sure it was an accident,"I tell him.

"But you could have been killed," he insists, but holds back from running off.

"But that didn't happen," I respond, placing my hands along his cheeks in the same fashion and smiling. "I'm okay. Just stay here with us."

"Fine, but you probably should text Trent and tell him you're okay." His eyes narrow as he looks back at Candle Love and sees the driver and his passenger being led out by Eddie and Roy.

"Right now?" I tug at Chalice's arm to get his attention again.

"Yeah, I texted him before running over here and told him you were involved in a big accident. I, uh, didn't really give any details."

"Shit, my phone is in the backroom."

"And mine is back at Bliss," he replies slowly.

Rose giggles beside me, and I turn to catch her bemused expression as she stares off into the parking lot.

"I don't think that will be a problem," she says, pointing at the gathering crowd of creatures. Stones from her many rings catch the light and glitter as I look in the direction she's pointing. I can see several emergency services vehicles pulling up and the crowd parting for them, but what's also obvious is an agitated Fox Folk Runt with black and white tails sprinting through the crowd in our direction.

Trent skids to a halt in front of me, nearly barreling Chalice out of the way, and we embrace in a fierce hug that verges on being uncomfortable.

"Careful, Trent, she's been through a lot," Chalice lays a hand gently on Trent's shoulder to pull him back, but my own arms cling too tightly to let him move.

"Julie," he breathes into my ear. "What happened?"

"Car smashed into the store," I tell him and feel his spine stiffen at my response. He pulls back to examine my face, running a finger over the slight cut above my eye.

"Did anyone get hurt?"

"I don't think so," Rose answers for me. "I saw the driver and his passenger walking away at least. Candle Love on the other hand . . ."

All four of us turn and glance back at the scene of destruction. Several Demonnie in emergency service vests are putting up caution tape around the gaping hole left by the vehicle, and it looks like Marilyn has arrived and is talking with a few of them.

"Julie, we should go let her know we have some personal effects inside the store and ask if we can get them," Rose says, and I nod in agreement, clutching her hand again as we stand up from the bench.

"I'll drive you both home afterward," says Trent.

"I can drive myself . . ."

"Out of the question," he responds firmly, and Chalice nods.

"Your cars will be fine, I used to leave mine in this parking lot all the time."

"Okay," I whisper, and Rose squeezes my hand.

"Thank you," she says quietly. "We'll be right back." She then pulls me with her toward Marilyn.

Once we're a few paces away, Rose leans in and whispers in my ear. She smells just like her teas—sweet, earthy, and mysterious.

"Boy problems, huh?" She lets out a loud giggle, and I marvel at how calm she is after just having a near-death experience.

"See," I sigh and poke at my cut. "Too many options."

"Why not just take them both?"

"I don't know if they'd be cool with that." I laugh nervously and look over my shoulder at Trent and Chalice. They're still at the bench and look like they're bickering about something.

"Have you asked?"

"Well, no . . ."

"Just talk to them." Rose gives me an encouraging smile as we near Marilyn, who ushers a few of the emergency techs over to us. One of them grips a medical kit and frowns at me.

"Are you sure?"

"You never know what they might say," she replies with a grin. "You just never know sometimes."

CHAPTER FIFTEEN

The techs make a quick work of Rose and me, and we're released after making brief statements of our experiences. There isn't much to say, only that we are standing there doing our job when a car suddenly appears, but I get that it's their job to ask questions. They even call Eddie over to record what he witnessed, or rather heard, of the accident.

Both the driver and his passenger were taken away in an ambulance, but I'm sure they're receiving the same treatment. Maybe a little worse because they were technically the cause of this whole ordeal. I still don't know exactly what happened, but I think it had something to do with the way the two of them were arguing with each other. I could hear them all the way across the parking lot as techs were checking them out.

The only one of us that didn't have to deal with the aftermath is Portia, who was able to get out before anyone's arrival. Tech after tech ask to question her, and we tell each one that she walked out on her own accord, so she couldn't have been injured or upset about what happened. Maybe she had the right idea, though, because I started to get irritated by all their questions. I hold on for longer than I thought possible, but by the time they are done with us, I am agitated and sweaty.

Luckily, as soon as they leave us alone and Marilyn secures our purses and cell phones, Chalice and Trent comes over and ushers Rose and me toward Trent's sleek, black car.

Once I'm seated in comfortable leather seats, the tension in my body becomes obvious, as if my whole body suddenly shrinks into itself like a deflated balloon. My legs and arms turn to jelly, and a heavy, dull weight lodges inside my head. I can barely keep my eyes open. Rose, on the other hand, stays alert enough to text a few people before climbing in beside me, allowing my head to lean on her shoulder.

I turn to stare out the window, but my brain barely seems to register the outside world as it drifts by. I'm too consumed with thoughts on how things could have ended much differently had I been standing anywhere else in Candle Love. I could have been standing by the glass doors in the direct path of the speeding, out-of-control car. I could be . . . seriously hurt or worse.

Feeling grateful for being spared, my mind skims the other, more practical, outcome of today's events, which is that Candle Love itself is going to be under some serious construction if it's ever going to be ready to accept customers again. The Candle Love I grew to know and love is forever gone, and anything new they build will never be exactly the same. I'll have to get used to a brand-new store. That is, if they even rebuild, which is something I don't want to think about right now.

Rose doesn't live far away, and no sooner have my eyes closed than I'm woken up by her gently repositioning my body so that she can get out of the car.

"I think we may be bonded for life now, Julie," she says.

"Near-death experience sisters?"

"You bet!" She leans back into the car and gives me a hug.

Maybe it's because of my upbringing and having an all Dragoon family, but her hug is so comforting that I have to wipe away a tear from my face when she pulls away. Luckily, after escorting her to the front door, Chalice stuffs his massive body into the back seat and I have his familiar presence wrapped around me.

"Shouldn't you be at work?" I murmur when he pulls me into his arms and lets my head rest on his broad chest.

"Yes, but they let me go early. We were a little overstaffed anyway."

I nod absently and yawn. I both want to get home so I can jump into my own bed, and want the ride to last as long as possible so I can keep cuddling with Chalice.

"You should text your family and let them know you're safe, maybe Frankie too. Word travels fast, and you should beat the news so they don't worry."

"That's a good idea," I say, taking my phone out and typing out a quick message to Frankie and not even a second later, my phone begins to vibrate from her immediate callback. She'll only keep calling until she talks to me, so I answer it right away.

"I'm okay," I say in lieu of a greeting.

"Are you sure? What if you have micro cuts too small to be seen by the naked eye? That store is practically made of glass, there must have been shards everywhere."

I laugh lightly.

"Yes, there were shards everywhere, but I was far enough back that not very much hit me at all. Besides, the emergency techs cleared me to go home."

"I see . . . were any of them hot at least? Did you mention you have a hot friend who's been on the hunt for some new meat?"

"Goddess, Frankie!" I laugh a little too loudly, and both Chalice and Trent glance at me with worried expressions. "It's good to know you have my best interests at heart."

"I always do! And while I trust you're okay because you say you are, I'm still coming over tonight to check on you in person."

"Okay, but I may be asleep when you get there."

"That's fine, I'll wake you up with food. How are . . . your other two problems?"

"We'll, uh, talk later about that. I promise."

"Hmm, okay, but I want details. Like, all the details."

"Fine, but hey, we're almost home now and I gotta run. I'll see you later though."

"See you tonight, beautiful!"

After speaking with Frankie, I text my parents letting them know about the accident and that I'm okay. Better they hear it from me and not on the news or through a friend still in town. They text back right away and say to let them know if I need anything.

Then, I bury my phone in my purse in case Frankie follows up our conversation with her usual incriminating text messages. I'm still wrapped in Chalice's arms, so there's no way I could hide anything she sends over. And knowing her, she's sending over eggplant emojis and hearts. Besides, we're pulling into the driveway now, and I can always check my phone from the safety of my bedroom.

Trent rushes over to open the door for me and extends a hand to help me out. I take it and let my palms linger in the warmth of his grip as I hold on, unable to let him go even after my feet hits the ground. My legs still feel weak, the adrenaline from the day's events starting to take its toll on my body, and I feel completely sapped of all energy. I begin to feel wobbly, the world spinning as my legs threaten to give out completely and send me crashing to the driveway. But Chalice flies out from the car and picks me up like I'm nothing more than a doll. He then nuzzles his face into the side of my head.

"You look a little shaky. Is it okay for me to carry you to your room?" he whispers.

I nod and snuggle closer to him, breathing in his spicy amber scent. I lose my grip on Trent's hand, but Chalice brings his own kind of comfort with him. And that's okay right now.

From the corner of my eye, I can see Trent shutting the car door behind us and hurrying along to keep pace with Chalice as he takes me inside.

It takes the big guy no time at all to get to my room and lay me down on the bed. I'm still fully clothed, but I don't even care because I'm so very tired. It's like every muscle and bone just suddenly gives up as soon as my body hits the sheets.

"Julie, Chalice and I will be right outside if you need anything," says Trent, leaning down and kissing my forehead.

"Anything at all," echoes Chalice, giving my hand a squeeze.

I murmur in response, which I hope they'll be able to understand. My body has decided to quietly shut down and take a nap now, and forming actual words feels like a distant dream. Luckily, they must have understood my mumbles because they both leave after Chalice tugs my shoes off and Trent drapes a blanket around my body.

Once the door is closed, I force myself to get back up and set up my CPAP machine and put my mask on so I can breathe while after I dose off.

Then, finally, everything goes black and my body relaxes into a deep, dreamless sleep.

I wake up to the sound of Frankie arguing outside my room. It sounds like she's trying to come inside but someone, or rather two someones, are keeping her from entering. It prompts me to rip off my mask and drag myself out of bed and open the door to the three frowning faces looking down at me.

I've never felt so small and fragile in my whole life.

"Julie!" Frankie cries, throwing her arms around my neck. I hug her back just as hard, but pull away when I notice she's carrying a large plastic bag full of warm containers.

"Oh, did you bring me dinner?" I ask, realizing just how hungry I am when my stomach asks her the same question.

"I did, nothing but the best for my bestie," she says, holding up the bag. "And I brought enough to share."

Frankie's wings shuffle behind her as she scans over Trent and Chalice, who have taken a step back from her. She's still shorter than both of them, but Frankie has always had this aura about her. It's like something powerful or magnetic, which has always given her a commanding presence. It's probably why we became such good friends; she has what I don't.

"What did you bring?" Trent's nostrils flare as he eyes the large bag in Frankie's hands.

"Smells good!" says Chalice, nudging Trent out of the way and offering to take the bag from Frankie. "I can get us set up in the kitchen.

Frankie gives them both a wicked smile.

"Thank you," she says sweetly, earning her a narrow-eyed look from Trent.

"So, what is it then?" he asks.

"Only my favorite tacos in the whole of New California. Trust me, you're going to love them." She turns and gives me an exaggerated wink as I stare back at her in horror because I know exactly what she has planned.

"Hmm. Sounds like a challenge." Trent's five tails swish behind him but still as he turns to look at me. "Julie, how are you feeling? Can I do anything for you?"

"I can list a few things you could do to her," Frankie says under her breath. I nudge her hard in the ribs, and she cackles.

"I'm good, thanks. I'm just going to change, and I'll meet you guys in the kitchen."

"Alright," he says. For a moment, I think he might reach out and touch me, but he instead turns on his heels and heads toward the kitchen.

"Frankie," I start as soon as he's gone, "Did you go back to that one taco place again? The one on First Street?"

"I think you already know the answer to that. Besides, don't you want me to give my seal of approval for both of them? Seems to me that you aren't going to just pick one."

"Yes, I mean, no. I do want your approval for, well, both . . .I think."

"Hey, don't worry so much. I'm definitely not the one to judge a happy throuple, if that's indeed what this is turning into. I just want to make sure you're happy and that you're doing okay. You've had a rough day."

Frankie actually reaches out and embraces me in a softer hug this time. She wraps her wings around me like she would do when we were kids and I was feeling low for one reason or another. She has always been there for me and I can't think of anyone better to be here with me tonight as I sort through my feelings.

"Thanks Frankie," I murmur into her hair.

"Don't thank me just yet, thank me after dinner."

"I can't believe you brought THOSE tacos. They are going to hate you," I chide her, but she blows a raspberry through her deeply colored lips.

"It'll be worth it. Earn my approval; trust me."

Frankie gives me another wicked smile, and I hurry back to my room to change into a pair of sweatpants and grab a preemptive antacid. Why, you ask? Because those tacos Frankie brought us are some of the spiciest things I have ever, and I mean fucking ever, put in my mouth.

In Frankie's opinion, eating spicy food is a form of bonding. It's something her family did on a regular basis, and while many Dragoons have a fairly high tolerance for high spice levels, her very human friend, I, does not. Whenever I went to her house for dinner, her dad would have to make a separate dish for me that didn't include the various hot peppers and spices her family loved. Once we had pizza delivered, and I saw her cover it in an entire bottle of hot sauce. The. Entire. Bottle.

I learned very quickly never to share food from my best friend's plate. While our coffee orders may be similar, our taste buds couldn't be more different.

She also has this fascination with watching other creatures try her favorite spice levels and swears to me that you can tell a lot about an individual by the way they handle their reactions. So I'm not surprised in the slightest that she brought over THOSE tacos for dinner tonight.

I'll be safe as she always brings a separate mild dish for me, but I am interested in how my new roommates will react to her way of getting to know them.

When I finally make it out to the kitchen, Chalice has already set up four black containers on the main counter, each containing an assortment of small tacos. They're made with some sort of mystery meat inside, wrapped in a double layer of corn tortillas, and each have a different layering of onions, cilantro, pineapple, tomatoes, corn chips, and lime-colored cream.

They're fairly small, and if you were brave enough, you could probably eat them in two to three bites, maybe less if you're big like some Dragoon, Demonnie, and Minotaur.

What you can't tell from looking at them is that they each have a hidden layer of different sauces piped on under the toppings. That is what you have to look out for, and if you don't know which is which, you could be in for a world of hurt. The trick is knowing the topping combinations.

Trent eyes them suspiciously and looks to Frankie.

"Where did you say you got these from?" he asks.

"A lady never reveals her secrets." She bats her eyelashes at him and snickers. "Let's just say I'm close personal friends with the owner of a taco shop on First Street."

Trent stares at the tacos like they could be talking to him while Chalice sets out a few paper plates. They look like leftovers from Yule again, but the accompanying napkins are just plain white. He starts to dip a hand into one of the boxes, but Frankie slaps it away.

"Hold on, Golden Boy, I have to tell you more. These are no ordinary tacos." She gestures her hands over them. "I need to give you a fair warning before you dig in. Liability reasons and all that, you know."

Trent takes a deep breath.

"I thought I smelled something suspicious about them." He leans against the counter and catches my eye. "A chef friend of mine told me about a place on First that does a sort of . . . challenge."

Frankie snaps her fingers at him.

"Don't give away my secrets!" She pulls out two plump tacos and places them on a plate that she slides over to me.

"Thank you," I respond primly, taking a seat at one of the counter-height chairs and tucking a napkin over my lap.

Frankie's idea of bringing the tacos over is brilliant. I feel so much better than I did earlier. The fogginess in my mind plus the tension from today's events eases a little more as every minute passes. I know it's thanks to the doting care of my best friend, but also to the two roommates who immediately came to my aid. It makes my heart warm with happiness . . . and possible as warm as their mouths are going to be when Frankie's tacos are done with them.

"These are some of the spiciest tacos in New California." She waves her hands dramatically over them again, pointing at the box closest to her. "The ones closest to me are more on the mild side and as they go further down," she gestures toward the last box, "they get hotter."

"So you brought us spicy food?" Chalice asks, lifting an eyebrow at her. "I've had spicy food before."

"But I feel like there's a catch here," Trent chimes in.

"Indeed." Frankie gives him a sagely nod. "I will only allow my best friend to consort with someone of my equal. Which means, Golden Boy, that if either of you want to be associated with Julie in anyway, you'll have to eat most, if not all, of these tacos."

"How come Julie has her own plate?" Chalice eyes my two tacos, and I hold them close.

"Nope, these are mine." I laugh and take a big bite of the first one. I swallow quickly and pretend to fan my mouth afterward. The taco is, of course, the mildest of mild as far as tacos go. But they don't need to know that right now, I'm having too much fun.

Every other minute or so, my mind drifts back to an earlier time in the day. And when I think about it, I can still remember the cold feeling of the display case against my back as I huddled behind it, or the way the floor crunched beneath my feet when I made my way out of Candle Love. I don't know if I'll ever truly forget that experience, but being here in the warm kitchen with some of the best creatures in the world is definitely helping me to think of better, brighter things.

"Gentlemen, the starting course," Frankie says. She whips out a pair of tongs from the plastic bag and uses them to distribute the first tacos onto each of Chalice and Trent's paper plates. "Let the games begin."

CHAPTER SIXTEEN

The taco place on First Street was found totally on accident. Frankie and I were looking for a different restaurant her parents had suggested, and since they were never good at giving directions and we were even worse at following them, we ended up going the wrong direction on a one-way street in our search. After several screams from both of us, as well as from passersby on the side of the road, we found ourselves haphazardly parking the car in the first available spot and walking the rest of the way.

We never found the place but were so hungry that we finally stopped at a place simply called "The Pitt." I'll never forget the tall Demonnie working the register because he was the hottest guy Frankie and I had ever seen, and being the confident teenagers we thought we were, we tried our best to impress him by ordering the spiciest tacos on their menu.

It worked out for Frankie and earned her the cashier's phone number. It certainly did NOT work for me and landed my little human body a trip to urgent care. I have since been very selective in my spice levels.

"This is how it's going to work," Frankie points at the first two tacos. "You eat the whole taco, you earn my respect. You can't finish your taco, then you tell me a secret."

"What kind of secret?" Trent's tails twitch in agitation behind him, and Frankie gives him a normal looking smile.

"Nothing nefarious, Foxy Boy. Just something fun, or something you think will earn you points with me. I am, after all, judging both of you to see if you would be acceptable matches for my best friend, Julie."

"Frankie," I groan and roll my eyes at her. "You don't need to do that."

"Hush, Julie. Eat your tacos." She picks up the same kind of taco she just served to Trent and Chalice and holds it up to her mouth.

"Ready, boys?"

They both pick up their tacos. Trent takes a tentative bite, but after chewing thoughtfully, stuffs the rest in his mouth. Chalice, on the other hand, eats the whole thing all at once. Frankie chews thoughtfully as she watches their reactions, and I take a nibble of mine. I watch too because I know what's coming.

But nothing happens.

Sure, there's a small twitch to Trent's blue eyes and Chalice's cheeks turn a shade darker, but neither balk at the first spice level. Frankie eyes them, then eats her own taco in one swift bite.

"Good job," she purrs, then proceeds to serve the second round. These tacos are covered in small flecks of white onion and glistening cubes of pineapple. I recognize them as being further down on The Pitt's spice ratings but definitely not something I'd ever eat or even touch.

These two tacos are eaten without complaint from either of my roommates, though Trent does have to drink water afterward and Chalice lets out a small cough tinged with smoke.

"I'm impressed, Julie, it seems your two mates here can hold their own." Frankie eats her second taco and daintily wipes her mouth.

I try to hide my face so no one sees how my cheeks turn red, not from the tacos but from her choice of words.

Mates.

Fuck.

Did she really have to say that?

"Well, I am a Dragoon," Chalice says proudly, resting his elbows on the countertop. The kitchen lights reflect off the fine sheen of gold along his collarbone. "Fire and heat are in our nature."

"And I have a buddy who serves stuff way hotter than this at his restaurant," Trent adds.

Frankie nods absentmindedly as she serves up round three. There's a mischievous gleam in her eyes, probably because we've made our way to, according to Frankie, the actually spicy tacos.

Before Chalice and Trent take a single bite, she pops one of them in her mouth and chews loudly before swallowing and smacking her lips loudly. Her face is unreadable as she stares at them.

"So, Julie, what kind of secrets should we ask for?" She turns to me. "Just want to be prepared before we get to that point. I'm not sure about the Golden God here, but the other one looks like he'll last another round or two."

"Secrets, hmm." I take a second to think. "How about, the most interesting place you've had sex. That's a good one."

A harmless and entertaining question.

"I like it! Okay, so as soon as you get to a taco you can't finish, you have to answer the question. Best way to get to know some-one!"

Frankie chortles with laugher, and I giggle along with her but catch Chalice's face over her shoulder. He's looking at Trent with a grimace, and Trent's face is pale as I see him visibly swallow.

"Bottoms up, boys," demands Frankie.

Chalice sighs loudly and shoves the small taco in his mouth, his eyes water as he chews and eventually swallows. The golden shine to his skin quickly replaces with a coppery red, but he holds his hands out in triumph and grins. He finished the whole thing with tears rolling down his cheeks.

Trent follows his lead, eating the whole thing in two large bites. He handles the spice much better, but I can see the agitated way his tails swirl behind him and his ears flattening to the sides of his head. After he swallows the last of it, he flashes Frankie a toothy, if not pained, grin.

"You got a hot pair here, Julie. In more ways than one." Frankie makes a show of dishing out the last part of her challenge. She places the tacos carefully on each of their plates and all four of us stare at the unassuming food.

There's no way you could guess these are the spiciest tacos served at The Pitt. The tortillas are plain, but lightly toasted, and each boast very minimal toppings of cilantro flecks, tiny slices of red chili peppers, and a single swirl of creamy sauce. I don't know what's in that sauce, but it is spicer than the sun. There is even more of it hidden under the toppings.

"What do you think, Julie? Will they be able to eat their taco, or do I win?"

"Wait," says Trent. "I didn't realize there's a winner to this game."

"Of course there is; it's just usually me." Frankie smiles at him and takes a large bite of her spicy taco. It's hard to see, but there is the tiniest twitch to her left eye when she gets some of the sauce on her lip. She wipes it quickly away with a paper napkin and smiles. "Tasty."

Chalice, taking the bait, bites into the taco, chomping down on in as if it were a burger. He chews for a moment, his gaze drifting while he considers the taste. Not to be outdone, Trent does the same, only his bite is much smaller. His face is neutral in the seconds afterward.

"Wait for it . . ." murmurs Frankie

It hits them all at once, like bricks hitting a glass window, shattering their composure in a single throw. Chalice begins coughing and sputtering, doubling over and crying tears of equal parts pain and . . . laughter?

"What was that?" The words barely come out as he wheezes and pounds his fist on the counter top. I watch as he attempts to scrape the taste off his tongue.

A second later brings Trent to his knees.

"Goddess, fuck, who would serve something like that. It tastes like nothing but . . . fucking flames of fire licking the devil's ass!"

"Oh, points for the originality of swearing." Frankie laughs and eats the rest of her taco in a single bite. "I didn't think you'd be able to handle the final taco. Not many do."

"Frankie insists on marrying the first creature to finish one without shedding a tear.

"I have a feeling I'll be single forever." She throws the back of her palm up to her forehead and pretends to swoon. "Woe is me."

Trent composes himself and tries to finish the rest of his taco, but he stops at the last moment and places it back on his plate. Chalice has scrambled to the refrigerator and drinking straight from a plastic gallon milk jug. He offers some to Trent, but he waves him off and takes a drink of water.

"Whelp, I can't finish that." Chalice burps loudly. "Excuse me."

"Yeah," agrees Trent. "Me neither."

"Alrighty then." Frankie claps once and points to Chalice with intertwined fingers. "You first, where's the more unique place you've done it?"

"Waterpark bathroom, which I do not recommend. We both got ringworm from the moistness in there."

Frankie looks amused, but I'm mildly horrified. Chalice doesn't seem to mind, though, as he continues to drink milk.

"And you, my five-tailed friend?" All three of us turn to Trent.

He's staring down at the unfinished taco but closes his eyes and lets out a sigh.

"Nowhere," he mutters and in the silence that follows, Chalice sets his milk on the counter and looks at his friend.

"He's joking, I think it was in a park or something. Um, on the swings." He beams at Trent, who answers his look with a pained, but determined, expression.

"You don't have to cover for me, the truth would come out sooner or later." He straightens up, but while he holds his head and shoulders high, his five tails droop low to the ground. "I haven't done it anywhere unusual because I've never done it before. I'm a virgin."

Frankie is at a loss for words and drums her fingers on the countertop with stiff, straight arms. She turns her head to look at me.

"Did you know that?" she whispers.

"Nope," I say. After learning of Trent's, well, so-called "flaw," I
had wondered how exactly sex had worked for him in the past. I
guess this answers my question.

"Goddess, Trent, I'm so sorry. I didn't mean to put you on the
spot." Frankie turns toward him looking truly remorseful.

He shrugs.

"It was bound to come out sooner or later. I was going to tell
Julie, and as her best friend, I assume she would tell you at some
point."

"Not if you told me not to tell anyone." I chew on my lower lip.
"I will always keep your secrets."

Trent's tails lift a little higher, but my heart sinks for him. I didn't
want Frankie's "game" to turn into something like this. I reach out
and give his hand a squeeze.

"Thanks, Julie, I appreciate it. Besides, it's not a big deal. I mean,
do I look like a virgin?"

"Not at all," answers Chalice. "It looks like you fuck all day and
all night."

"Thanks, man." Trent flicks his tails at Chalice's back. "It's good to know I'm so fuckable."

Frankie clears her throat and nudges my arm. She leans in closely.

"Might be fun," she whispers. "You could be his first."

My face flushes again, and I swat at her shoulder, but her words land where she threw them and that's all I can think about now. Sex with Trent.

Sex.

With.

Fucking.

Trent.

Yes, please.

But wait, everything is moving so quickly and I'm seriously running out of steam to handle all these emotions flying at me today. This has been fun, well, until it got awkward. But while I'm in a better mood, I'm still exhausted and numb from everything that happened before I sat down at this kitchen counter.

As if the day finally catches up psychically, I let out a big enough yawn to attract everyone's attention. Frankie begins cleaning up our plates and napkins, and Chalice urges me to drink a huge glass of water.

"Do you want me to stay the night?" Frankie asks once every trace of spicy taco has been wiped clean from the countertop.

"No, that's okay. I'll be fine," I tell her. She looks to Chalice and Trent, then nods.

"Alright, but call me when you wake up tomorrow, okay?

"I promise."

She gives me the tightest hug I've ever received from her and then Chalice walks her outside. I hear them quietly talking but can't make out what they're saying.

"Come with me," Trent says quietly, taking my hand in his. Despite the slight calluses on his finger tips, his palm is warm and comforting against mine and it feels natural to be connected to him like this.

Trent takes us to the couch in our living room. He sits and pulls me down with him, encouraging me to kick my feet up so I can lay down against his propped up body. After picking up the TV remote, he wraps his arms around me. Just after the TV is turned on and tuned to a late night channel showing nothing but cartoons, Chalice comes in and takes a seat on the other end of the couch. He lifts my feet up and rubs them tenderly.

"What a day," I mutter and Chalice gives my heel a squeeze.

"Yeah, it was kinda fucked for you. I'm sorry you had to go through it," he says.

"I guess you'll at least get some time off work," Trent adds. His breath is warm and ticklish in my ear. It makes my spine tingle with giddiness, even though I know I'm too drained for any excitement of that nature.

"My manager, Marilyn, said to expect a call tomorrow with an update, but it's a good thing I have some savings, so I can still pay rent."

"The lawn and water bill will thank you for it, but I wouldn't worry about that right now. Trent and I will make sure everything works out."

"What about Misty?" I ask.

"Heh, I almost forgot about her."

"Does she still even live here?" Trent lets out a snorting laugh, and Chalice's body rumbles with quiet laughter.

"She's gone most of the time, so I guess not."

His hand has moved from my heel to my ankle, and now he caresses my calves, his long fingers press lightly against my bare skin, skirting their way up through my sweat pants.

"I'm sure his sister will be fine and if she's not, just leave her to us." Trent chuckles and his toned chest presses into my back. I suck in a breath and close my eyes when he shifts positions, and I feel him growing hard behind me. With my back arching, I lean my head backward to look at him.

"You promise?"

"I do," he murmurs, running a finger through my hair and tucking it behind my ear. His other hand tightens around my rib cage with one finger sliding under the band of my bra. I let out a sigh and let my gaze drift over our intwined bodies until it meets with Chalice at the other end of the couch.

We lock eyes and both swallow hard as the grip on my legs tightens.

I want nothing more right now than for him to push my legs apart and crawl on top of me while Trent holds me from behind, but I know—oh, Goddess do I know—that it shouldn't happen right now. Not until I'm sure what they both want.

Not until I'm sure what I want.

From the looks of things and the tension in the air, I have a feeling we're all on the same wave length, at least for tonight, but I need to know for certain. This also isn't the time. Its late, we're all tired, and today has already been memorable for mostly the wrong reasons.

So I, ugh, sit up.

The cold air hits like a ton of bricks as Trent's hands fall from my body and I swing my legs out from Chalice's warm lap.

"I'm tired," I murmur in way of an apology. "I think I'm going to bed."

I look to Trent first, who gives me an understanding nod.

"That's probably a good idea, Julie. But if you need anything at all tonight, feel free to knock on my door."

"I will, thanks." I bend over and kiss his forehead. "Thanks for being an awesome roomie."

"It has been a long day," says Chalice from behind, and before I can even move, his big arms scoop me up like I weigh nothing at all. He cradles me like a child against his chest and I burst into giggles.

"I'm not a kid, I can walk to bed on my own," I say.

"Nonsense, I got this. Let me take care of you," his words rumble from his chest.

I yawn in reply.

Chalice effortlessly carries me down the hallway and then nudges my door open with his shoulder. He even lays me down on the bed. He bends over me, his lips hovering above my mouth for a moment before he leaves me with a whisper of a kiss.

I watch him as he walks out and notice his eyes drift quickly to my nightstand, spying my CPAP machine in all its glory. Grimacing, I shrug my shoulders.

"That's, uh, my . . ." I start, but he holds up a hand to stop me, crosses back across the room, and cups his hands around my face.

"I know what that is, don't worry about it." He presses his forehead against mine. "I read about them in a book once."

"I didn't know you were a reader."

"There's lots of stuff I want you to learn about me," he whispers before pushing me gently back on the bed and pressing my mask into my hands. "I'll start telling you soon."

"Looking forward to it." I yawn. "Night."

"Night, Julie."

Chalice closes the door quietly behind him and my room is covered in darkness. I wait a few minutes for my eyes to adjust to the dim light coming through my window, then slip my mask over my face.

I'm in awe of how much happened to me today. From waking up for an early shift at work, to a car flying through Candle Love's front doors, to spicy tacos and almost asking my room mates for a threesome.

A threesome. Whoa. It makes me wonder and maybe . . . hope? It's something to think about as I finally drift off to sleep.

CHAPTER SEVENTEEN

The morning comes after a restless night of sexy dreams. Waking up hot and bothered is annoying. My whole body is wired and pumped for a release that I just can't see happening before breakfast. Unless . . . I sneak my vibrator into the shower with me. I'm pretty sure the thing is waterproof and if I make sure the door is locked and water running, I should have all the time and privacy I need to help ease this tension.

Yes, the perfect plan.

I wrap my trusty purple tool inside a spare towel and tuck her securely under my arm before creeping toward the bathroom I share with Chalice. But when I get closer, I realize the light is on and the door locked tight.

"Did you need to shower?" Trent's voice breaks the silence around me and I nearly drop my towel bundle.

"Oh, um, yeah, but it looks like Chalice is in there."

Trent makes a face looking at the door.

"He, um, might be a while. Chalice doesn't do so well with spicy foods. I think last night might have done him in. Come with me, you can use mine." He gestures for me to follow him and thinking that it might look suspicious if I were to chuck my towel into my bedroom on the way, I hold it close and walk with him toward his bedroom at the end of the hall.

Curiosity surges through me when he opens the door, and I realize I finally get to see the inside of his room.

Trent has the master bedroom of the house because he pays the most in rent, which means his room is much, much bigger than mine. However, I'm stunned to realize he has practically nothing inside it. There's a giant, king sized mattress laying directly on the floor, not even on a bed frame, a rack with clothes and a few aprons hung on it, and a small dresser. Everything is black and grey, and there isn't even anything on the walls.

He stands sheepishly behind me as I look around.

"I guess I'm kind of a minimalist," he mutters.

"It's not . . . bad. Maybe I could paint you something for your walls, though. That might brighten up the place. I think."

"I'd like that." He smiles and gestures toward a closed door. "Bathrooms in there. Take all the time you need, Diamond."

"Thanks." I pause. "Do you mind if I use your soap? Mines in the other bathroom with Chalice."

"Consider everything I have to be yours," he says. He lays down on his bed and takes out a book, which he begins to read. Goddess, he's going to stay in here while I shower?

Interesting.

"Careful what you wish for," I joke, and his eyes widen.

I take a deep breath, give him a smile, and retreat into the bathroom. Just like his bedroom, this bathroom is much bigger than the one in the hallway. It also has a normal sized shower. Well, normal by my standards. It's probably still bigger than something you'd find in a totally human bathroom. I'm guessing it's for all his tails.

There isn't much to the place and what there is has been sorted neatly into shiny black holding trays. All the products are unfamiliar to me so I spend time reading the labels while I wait for the shower water to come to an agreeable temperature. There are at least several different types of shampoos, conditioners, and body soaps, and it takes a few minutes to decide on which ones to use, but I finally choose a vanilla-scented set that smells like cookies.

After stripping my clothes and arranging them in a neat pile on the counter, I slip under the glorious water and let it run over me. Warmth and the smell of baked goods becomes my whole world as I wash away my extra thoughts and become nothing more than a cookie myself, fresh from the oven and steaming with shower sweetness.

But now I have a choice to make: do I or do I not masturbate? That was my plan for this morning, but having Trent just outside the door is giving me second thoughts.

What if he can hear me and he's not into that?

What if he's not into me?

No, I'm pretty sure he is. And if I'm reading between the lines correctly, there's a real chance he's okay with what happened with Chalice. But there's also a chance this whole threesome fantasy of mine is a recipe for disaster.

He hasn't come in here yet, but that doesn't surprise me. Chalice is bold like that, and Trent seems more calculating, like he wouldn't do something unless he was sure of the outcome. I guess we're both that way.

Back to the problem at hand

I reach out of the shower and grab my trusty vibrator from the counter and bring her inside with me. Once I feel the weight in my hands and the gentle hum under my fingers, I know I've made the right choice. The force of the shower water also feels loud enough to mask the buzzing.

Bringing a hand up to my chest, I pinch my nipples and watch as water and soap rinses down the smooth skin of my chest. It flows down in white streams across my belly and between my legs, and brings with it flashes of steamy shower sex with Chalice. It also makes me wonder what it would be like with Trent.

Slowly, I drag the vibrator across my skin, down my chest, over my belly button to nuzzle against my . . .

"Hey Julie?"

The sound of someone knocking on the bathroom door makes me drop my vibrator and it clatters nosily to the ground. I scramble to pick her back up and turn down the water.

"Um, yeah?"

"Chalice is making pancakes. Well, he's heating premade frozen ones but is assembling the toppings. Do you want some?"

"Sure!" I call back, biting my lip to keep from laughing.

"I'll let him know!" Trent calls back through the door.

"Thank you!"

"Are you enjoying yourself in there?" he asks.

"Um . . . yes?"

Wait . . . could he hear my vibrator? There's no way . . .

"Do you like my soaps? You've been in there for some time so I figured you must really like them. I got them from the Night Market on a friend's recommendation."

"Oh! Yes, they're lovely."

"Good! Okay, I'll leave you alone to finish up . . ." his voice trails away, but I still give it a minute before turning the water back on to hide my giggling. I'm still hot and bothered, but something feels like it's been turned down inside me. It's probably because Trent's right, and I have been in here a little too long.

A look down at my wrinkly fingers proves him right, and I hastily finish up and get out of the shower. Even though his soaps do smell really good and I think I might want to stay inside here all day.

As I dry myself off, I debate how to hide my vibrator on the way back. It's either putting my old clothes back on and hiding it in my wet towel, or walking out wearing only a towel and tucking the vibrator inside my dirty clothes.

Hmm, well, the guy has already came in his pants on top of me, he might as well get to see me in just a towel. Besides, it's not like it's any different than me wearing a bikini in the hot tub with him.

I pile up my wet hair on top my head, do a really good job at packing my vibrator inside my sweat pants, and secure my towel tightly under my arm pits. Then I open the door to a rush of steam and step back into Trent's room.

I walk into him laying in the same position on his bed, only this time he's holding his phone up and intently watching something on the screen. But his attention quickly shifts when he looks up and sees me.

His jaw drops open and the phone, once clutched in his hand falls to the bed screen side up. And . . . he's watching porn. I lift an eyebrow and lean over to glance at the screen. It's a petty human looking girl being railed by a trio of Fox Folk men.

"I hear the sequel is much better," I tease, but instead of a verbal reaction I look back up to see him staring at the way my cleavage practically hangs out of my towel.

Blushing, I tuck my bundle of clothes against me so at the very least, my towel doesn't fall off on him and stand up straight.

"Sorry about that," he mumbles, swiping his phone off the bed. It falls with a soft thud onto the carpet, and he looks up at me with a cocky grin. "I didn't think you'd be out so quickly."

"Hmm, sure."

"Go-ahead and don't believe me." He laughs lightly. "Or maybe, just maybe, I was too busy fantasizing about what you were doing in there and then got carried away looking at my phone."

"I believe you," I say with a wink. "Thanks for letting me use your shower."

"Anytime and anything for you, Diamond." He pauses, then flicks his tails a little before asking, "Hey, a friend invited me to his restaurant tonight to fill some vacant seats. Do you . . . do you want to go with me?"

"Go out to dinner with you tonight?"

"Yeah." His gaze lowers briefly to the exposed skin of my chest, but he looks swiftly back up at my face.

"Sure, I mean, yeah, that sounds great." I blush, clutching my towel just a little closer.

Trent, now with an obvious erection from the last few minutes of events, smiles broadly and not-so-discreetly adjusts himself.

"I'll meet you in the kitchen in a, uh, few minutes and we'll talk details."

"Sounds good, see you in a few."

We smile awkwardly at each other and I make a quick exit, because I know—I definitely know—that we're both going to go masturbate before breakfast!

Dinner with Trent's chef buddy, Angel, is scheduled for seven in the evening, which is about an hour later than I normally eat. So by the time we've driven to his downtown restaurant, Butter, and park in a structure across the street, my stomach is growling so loudly I wonder if Trent can hear it from the driver's seat.

It's not like I haven't missed a meal before, but I purposely ate a very light lunch so I could save room for tonight's feast. I'm now feeling this was not the best idea in the world because that bowl of cereal has long passed through my system.

Please learn from my mistakes, everyone!

Despite the gnawing hunger in my stomach, I'm having a really good time so far. Trent's taste in music is similar to my own, and we rocked out to some poppy jams on our way over here. Even now as we exit the car and make our way to the street corner near Butter, we're still exchanging lyrics back and forth.

We're in roughly the same area as Frankie's loft, but far enough away that I don't have to worry about her looking down at me from any of the apartment windows above the many different, small shops here. Still, there are enough creatures walking the streets that I wonder if I might recognize her or one of her neighbors.

What I do not except to see is the flash of six recognizable tawny brown tails swishing down the street ahead of us.

"Oh great," I mutter, and Trent looks down at me just before Portia stops a few strides ahead of us. I clear my throat. "Hi Portia!"

"Oh, hello, Julie," she says, also looking down at me. She is flanked by two very tall, though not as tall as Trent, Fox Folk guys each with their full set of nine tails. "Where are you headed?"

"We have reservations at Butter," Trent responds, and Portia's eyes grow wide. He follows by putting his arm around my shoulders.

"Butter? How did you manage that? I've been trying to get in there for ages, but they're always booked. How could *you*, of all creatures, get in there?"

I stare blankly at her. We've always been cordial to each other but always at work. Apparently, a work environment is different than a downtown street corner.

But I won't stoop to that level.

"Trent knows the owner," I respond, turning to look up at him. He smiles back and winks.

"Yup, reservations or not, he always makes the time for me." He slings an arm around my shoulders. "But we need to get going, I don't want Julie to miss the first course."

Portia looks disgruntled but steps aside with her two dates so that Trent and I can cross the street toward the restaurant. He tugs me a little closer as we walk.

"That one is trouble."

"Yeah, I've never really had too much of a problem with her at work before, but we've never interacted outside of world. It's kinda, I don't know, sad." I cast a quick glance over my shoulder to watch Portia continue down the street, possibly to another restaurant further away.

"Sad?"

"Well, yeah, that she feels like she has to be so nasty. There's something sad about that. Maybe even mysterious because I would bet there's a reason why she's like that"

Trent gives my shoulder a squeeze before letting go and opening the door to Butter for me.

"I get that," he says. "Sometimes we hide ourselves behind masks, and sometimes those masks can be a real bitch to take off."

Masks. I wonder if I'm wearing one as well and that I'm hiding everything I'm feeling behind a veil of normalcy. I certainly haven't been truthful with Trent and Chalice yet about how I want them both, and I cannot fathom picking just one of them. That would be heartbreaking.

It's well past time that I talk to them, and it needs to happen soon. As we walk into Butter, my mouth opens to say something, but instead of any words, my stomach just growls loudly and Trent cracks a wide grin.

"Come on, Diamond, let's take our seats and get you fed. You're going to love this place."

Future Julie here! My date with Trent is a night of communication failures and good food. I would attempt bringing up relationship topics, but then some sort of outstanding food would come by and, of course, I couldn't resist their temptations.

One thing I didn't have to handle, though, was a packed and crowded restaurant. Trent chose seats at the end of a very long bar, and while I may have been directly across from one of the assistant chefs in residence, I didn't have to be sandwiched between Trent and some stranger. Not like Butter was crowded at all, the place only seats twelve creatures along a long table bar facing the chef. That number would be even less if the guests are Minotaur because they're just a little bigger and this place is super small. But I guess it helps keep the experience more intimate.

Everything on the menu was pumpkin-themed in celebration of the changing seasons, which worked to make the experience even more memorable. Portions were also on the small side since there were so many, but I did manage to bring home a small take-out box of goodies at the end.

So, here for your reading pleasure, is a course-by-course summa-rized version of our memorable and frustrating evening:

First Course - Bread. But not just any bread. This bread came straight from the oven to a plate placed directly in front of me. It was round with a perfectly golden crust, was baked to perfection, and had the lightest glaze of sea salted butter on top. It was so good that I was too busy obsessing over it to even think of bringing up any hard topics with Trent.

Second Course - A spoonful of whipped feta cheese with pump-kin and honey. Since this literally disappeared in a single bite, I let Trent know there was something I hoped to speak with him about. The grin he answered with was as sharp and sweet as the contents of my spoon.

Third Course - Pumpkin and sweet potato soup with basil cream. Another dish that was too good and I couldn't concentrate on much else. Trent, waiting with perked ears for me to "speak with him about something" only received a couple of well-placed moans of enjoyment instead of words whenever I slurped the soup.

Fourth Course - A much-too-small slice of pumpkin crust pizza with garlic, thyme, mozzarella, and more feta. It was not enough; I could have eaten an entire pizza made like it. I discreetly took a photo of it and made a mental note to recreate it at home. Still rid-ing on my good-food-high, I totally forgot to talk about anything other than cheese with Trent.

Fifth Course - Pumpkin and quinoa salad with roasted cranberries. This was okay, probably because I'm not a big salad fan and was still mourning the fact that I ate all of my small pizza slice. As I poked at it, mainly eating just the cranberries, I attempted to bring up relationships in general, but Trent distracted me when he started flicking his cranberries onto my plate, which I then ate.

Sixth Course - Pumpkin and spinach lasagna. Savory, warm, and comforting, this dish made me stop talking completely as I devoured it. Though once my plate was clean, Trent and I got into a conversation on guilty pleasures, and all the things required for a soothing night of self-care rituals.

Seventh Course - Turkey meatballs in creamy pumpkin sauce with sage. Why does sage make everything taste and smell so fancy? This was Trent's favorite dish, and he spent some time asking the chef, Angel, questions about how it was prepared. I listened carefully, but couldn't follow all the culinary jargon, but do have plans to ask Trent to attempt making them for me sometime.

Eighth Course - Basil and sage-infused sorbet. Every bit as weird as you'd think but definitely a palette cleanser. There was also some sort of mystery ingredient that Trent and I spent time trying to figure out. I thought it was popcorn puree, and Trent was sure it was browned butter. The friendly debate took up the entire course.

Ninth Course - Pumpkin butter cake with cinnamon glaze. When you get this far in a ten-course meal, you're bound to slow down sooner or later, and this is where my body decided it couldn't handle anymore food. Well, I forced myself to have several bites because how could someone say no to cake?

Tenth Course - Coffee and flaky pumpkin pie twists. By now, I was truly disappointed in myself for having not brought up anything of substance. Sure, we had a good time and had real conversations, but I was still nowhere close to discussing our future together. So as the amazing meal closed out, I drank my coffee and tried to summon the courage, as well as the energy, to stay awake and talk to Trent after leaving Butter.

CHAPTER EIGHTEEN

The night is crisp and mostly quiet when we leave the restaurant. Thick, warm air surrounds us and feels like the bread rolls from earlier tonight: pillowy, soft and comfortable. The soft murmuring voices of various creatures out at this hour float by us upon the wind, but the gentle swelling sound of the nearby ocean sings loudest of all.

"We're next to the coast, right?" I ask Trent.

He points down the street and it causes his sleeve to ride up his arm enough to see his tattoos poking out from beneath. Fuck, he looks hot tonight. He's put together, but somehow still a rugged bad boy. No, he's not a bad boy, but maybe not your average golden retriever-type-of-guy, though he acts a little like that sometimes.

A tattooed golden retriever.

I really love it, though. The way he looks like a rock star but with a heart of gold. He makes my thoughts fracture, but mostly I just want him to be mine.

But Chalice . . .

"Just down the way, did you want to go?"

"I think I do," I answer, unable to keep the dreamy, love sick sound from my voice. Though all bets are off when I have to hold back a burp. "Besides, I probably should walk off a little of this food."

The portion sizes were small tonight, but I guess when you eat enough courses of them, they add up. I even have a small takeout container tucked into an artsy little brown bag.

"Anything you want, Diamond," he wraps his arm around my shoulders and pulls me close. "Anything you can ever, ever want. I promise."

"Anything, huh? I'll keep that in mind."

Careful what you promise, Trent. A girl can get used to dates like this.

We continue on in silence for just a few minutes until we come to the last building before the main street ends. Here the sand begins to take over, covering the asphalt road in an ombre of yellow and grey in the moonlight.

Before us, I can hear the steady rumbling of waves, and while the sea is black before me, lights from the shoreline illuminate the crashing, bubbly water. Far out in the distance, a cruise ship sails by in a cluster of starry lights.

I can see why some say the ocean is endless. It's like a black table covered in a sparkling tablecloth stretching so far out that you can't tell where it stops against the horizon.

We pause to take our shoes off and tuck them under our arms so we can make our way toward the breaking waves. I don't see anyone else out here, and I wonder if the beach is actually closed for the night, but that only makes our adventure more thrilling.

A lone lifeguard tower stands sentry over the vacant, dark sand, and since neither of us want to dip our toes in the cold water, we head there.

Someone forgot to lock the small wooden box at the top of the short ladder, and after we both make sure there isn't any alarms to give us away, we sneak inside. It's private in the little area since the sides are closed off, but we still get a very good view of the ocean spread before us.

"Feeling a little less full?" Trent asks as he pulls me toward him so I'm snuggled against his chest.

"I think so," I mutter softly, leaning into him.

"Good," he murmurs back and dips his face into my neck.

I can feel his lips against me, followed by his soft tongue probing at the ticklish skin. When he grazes his teeth again me, I let out a small gasp.

"You smell good." He drags his nose up my neck toward my ear and gives my ear lobe a playful bite. "A little like cupcakes."

"Delightful Praline Pumpkin by Candle Love," I tell him, squirming in his grasp when I feel his hot breath in my ear. "I have it in the lotion and body spray."

It's like he's breathing life into every nerve ending in my soul and no matter how far back I lean into him, I can't get close enough.

"You'll have to loan me a bottle of that lotion." His hands roam under my shirt from behind and he squeezes both of my breasts. "I want to be able to smell you whenever I want."

"Sure, I can do that," I squeak. His fingers dip beneath my bra and pinch my nipples gently. He chuckles behind me.

"Even when I use it to jerk myself off?"

I mewl in response, at a loss for words because one of his hands has moved further down, grazing over my belly and tugging at the hem of my pants.

"Can I play with you, Julie?" he whispers in my ear.

It's not lost to me that he uses my real name, but that's about it. Every other sense in me has long since left the building. It is only Trent and how his hands are making me feel, which is amazing.

"Uh huh."

"Sexy answer, Julie. Real sexy."

Trent laughs softly in my ear again, and I shiver with anticipation when I feel his hand dip below my panty line. His other hand curves over and, with my help, undoes the button to my slacks.

He starts slowly with one finger dipping between my legs.

"We've barely started and you're already soaked," he says. "Fuck, I love that."

I respond by wiggling against him, but he pulls his hips back.

"Sorry, I want to make sure I take care of you before . . . before .
. ."

I reach back and am able to place my palm against his cheek. It's
rough and unshaved, but his lips are smooth and supple when I
run my fingers across them.

"Okay," I breathe, and he kisses my thumb.

Trent resumes his gentle caresses until I can't help but squirm
again and push my hips toward his hand.

"Is this what you want?" he inserts a long finger inside me, and
I wiggle in pleasure and let out a shuddered breath.

"Yup."

I really need to work on my sexy talk.

With one hand slowly pumping one and then two fingers inside
me, he uses his other hand to apply a steady pressure to my clit. It
makes my hips buck madly against him when he picks up the speed
and makes me gasp for breath.

"Fuck, Julie, you sound so hot when you're panting for me. You
sound like you really love this."

I reach behind me to grab him in any way I can and successfully
get his hair with one of his ears trapped under my grasp. When I
hear him hiss in pleasure, I lift my other arm up to gently tug on
the furry points.

"Good to know you like that." My voice comes out in strangled
gasps, but I'm proud that I was at least able to form a sentence.

"Fuck," he groans and buries his face between my neck and shoulder, biting down hard. I can feel his body tense behind me, but only for a moment because my own body begins to buck uncontrollably against his hands as my orgasm crashes into me.

Waves, like the ones crashing against the shore outside the life-guard tower, pummel me with pleasure as I let out a sharp cry when they peak.

Trent, breathing heavily, pulls his shaking hands from my pants and grips tightly to my waist. I can tell right away that his cock is still rock hard behind me, which is good because that means he hasn't come yet.

I twist my body around to crawl over him, but he stops me.

"We should get out of here," he says with a wry grin before taking my hands and kissing my knuckles.

"I want to . . ." I start, but he puts a finger to my lips.

"Trust me, I want you to do a lot of things to me, but right now I want us to go home and fuck. Please."

My eyes open wide as Trent's admission from the hot sauce night plays through my mind.

"You want me to take your virginity?"

"No, I want to give you my virginity. But not in here. Theres too much sand, and I don't think it'd be very comfortable for either of us."

We both look down and see the stray bits of sand and even some shells that have made their way to the lifeguard tower floor, and I grimace when Trent stands up and shakes sand out of his pant legs.

He helps me down the short ladder back to the beach, and we make a hasty retreat through to the rows of shops and restaurants, all closed at this late hour except one, a rowdy bar down the street near the parking structure.

They're playing music, and it drifts down magically across the sidewalks as Trent and I walk hand-in-hand toward his car, ready for what will probably be a very long, sexually tense, drive home.

When we arrive at 1414 Cumberbatch Way, the first thing we both notice is that Chalice's truck is gone from the driveway. I glance at the empty space quickly, thoughts and guilt rummaging through my mind, and it slows my steps as we make our way to Trent's room.

Then, as soon as he closes the door behind us and threads his fingers through my hair, I open my big mouth to say something.

"Trent, there's something you should know." My words sound weak as he backs me against a wall, giving me slow and lingering kisses along my collar bone. "It's about Chalice."

He slips his shirt over his head and looks down at me. When I look back up at him, his five tails fan out behind him like a five-pointed star and his tattoos form beautiful patterns and rainbows on his whole body.

I don't think I've ever really studied them in detail before. It's like I just knew he had them and that was enough, but now I can see the interlocking patterns of various foods, kitchen knives, a good number of ravens or crows, and a few stars. They curve around his arms, shoulders and chest, and a few dip below the waist line of his pants, all beautiful, colorful and entrancing. I can't help but stare at them in the dim light as he waits for me to continue.

But when I don't, he starts talking instead as he leans toward me.

"I know you already fucked Chalice and will probably do it again and again and again," he says softly into my ear. I shiver against him. "But who wouldn't? He's a Golden God. I probably would if I was into that, which I'm not really. But it's okay for you to be into him too, Julie. I don't mind sharing your body and soul with my best friend, as long as its only him, and no one else."

"Wait, what? Really?"

"I don't mind. It's kind of hot, but really I just know he would take good care of you." He kisses my neck. "But we still have to even things out because I haven't had my taste of you yet. Can I fuck you, Julie?"

"Are you, uh, sure that you're ready? Because isn't this your first . . ."

Trent growls and hoists me up by my thighs, pressing my back uncomfortably against the wall. I'm not the smallest, most petite lady in New California, so it's a testament to his lean, muscular arms that he can lift me so effortlessly.

"Yes, I'm sure, and I'm not gonna lie to you, this is going to be fast and rough."

I whimper in his arms, already feeling moistness between us, either from him or my soaked panties.

"Okay," I breathe into his mouth as he closes in to kiss me.

Trent is a really good kisser because he uses his hands. A LOT. After setting me back down on the ground, he moves his fingers through my hair, moving my head so he can have the perfect angle to claim my mouth. He doesn't ram his tongue down my throat like this one guy I dated years ago did, but he's soft and exploratory, making sure to leave no corner of my lips untouched.

It makes me wonder what it would be like to have his mouth between my legs, but that's going to have to wait for another day. With the way things are going right now, this is going to, indeed, be fast and rough.

Trent's hands move to my shirt, yanking it over my head with one swift tug, I help things along by kicking off my pants and helping unhook my bra. He bends his head, leaving slobbering kisses along my shoulders as he watches me unbutton his own pants and slide them down his thighs. He kicks them off as well, then when we're both only in underwear, he tackles me on the bed, hovering protectively over my body.

"I'm not going to last long." His eyes are closed tight in concentration now, but he's pressing himself between my legs. I can feel the moist head of his cock pressing against the fabric of my panties, and I wiggle against it.

"It's okay." I cup his face between my hands and catch his eyes when they open. "You've already given me one amazing orgasm tonight, let me help you with yours."

"Fuck, Julie," he bends his head down and breathes into my neck. At the same time, one hand roves down my sides to grasp the hemline of my underwear. He manages to tug them halfway down my leg, and I reach down to help, then grab his boxer briefs and start pulling them down as well.

We're not at the greatest angle for this, and we both have to separate and lay on our back for a moment to fully get our underwear off and to the side, but we're quick to roll back together, each laying on our sides and entangled in each other's arms.

His cock is rock hard between us and slick with pre-come as it slides against my stomach. The feeling makes my body quiver in anticipation of wanting to see how he feels inside me.

Trent takes one of my legs in his hands and his fingers grip onto the flesh of my thigh as he hoists it around his hip. That's when I feel his cock beginning to press into me.

"I want you to take my virginity." Trent's voice is strained and hoarse as he nuzzles against my ear. "Julie, it's yours."

"Trent," I breathe his name, pushing my hips toward him. I don't have to do much movement, because the grip on my leg tightens as he flips over on top of me. We're very near the edge of the bed, almost about to fall off, but he holds us secure as his hips push between my legs and his long cock glides into me.

My back arches from the pressure, while Chalice may have more girth, Trent's cock is equally as amazing and longer. The pleasure that shoots through my body when he finally becomes flush inside me is consuming.

His body suddenly tenses and soon after, his hips begin moving, pumping into me in a frenzied dance as he pants and gasps above me. Protective arms encircle my shoulders as he rolls to his back, taking me with him.

I suddenly find myself sitting astrid his hips while I continue to grind on top of him. The change of position allows me to access my clit with one hand, the other having to keep my balance. Trent cracks an eye open to watch while I join in the manic moment and bring myself to the verge of erupting pleasure.

"I can't . . . I'm going to . . ." Trent gasps, but I can tell what he's trying to say.

"Me too," I whimper just as my muscles clench together in glorious release. This one is different than in the lifeguard tower and feels much more intimate and powerful.

Trent lets out a strangled moan and follows after, coming full force inside me as he finishes up his last few frantic pumps. His shoulder muscles ripple and his hips shake against me during his own release before finally relaxing and going slack.

I collapse on top of him as a sweaty mess and kiss his forehead before gently pulling myself off him. Come spills from me to the sheets and drips down my legs, but I'm too exhausted to care and instead focus on catching my breath as I lay next to him.

Trent, breathing and sweating just as hard, feels around for my hand and grasps it, entwining his fingers with mine.

"Thank you, Julie. That was amazing."

"Anytime."

He chuckles and gives my hand a squeeze.

"I think you only lose your virginity once, but we can always pretend." He brings my hand up to his mouth and kisses my knuckles.

"Didn't realize we were already in the role-playing stage of the relationship."

"Is that what this is?" he asks. "Are we in a relationship?"

"I . . . hmm. Are we?"

"You and me are, at least in my opinion, but I get how you have some unresolved feelings with my better half. We can talk about him some other time, though."

Part of me wants Chalice to barge in here right now and proclaim his love for me, then fuck me raw while Trent holds my hand and watches. But that wouldn't be fair to Chalice. He deserves a chance to tell me himself how he feels about this, um, situation.

But Trent's right; we can talk about it later.

"But for now," he leans over and kisses my cheek lightly, "Just know that I think you're the most amazing thing to every come into my life, you are every love song I've ever written, and I'm falling more in love with you every day."

Words fail because I'm too choked up to say anything, so I simply turn my head and whisper, "I'm falling for you too," before pressing my lips to his.

CHAPTER NINETEEN

I t isn't long after we stop talking that Trent drifts off to sleep with his arms still wrapped around me. I can't blame the guy; we stuffed ourselves silly then had some intense sex. That's enough to put anyone to sleep, especially me.

I'm fighting my own fatigue as well, but I don't want to risk falling asleep in his room. The headache I will get from sleeping without my CPAP machine isn't worth it. The headaches occur when your brain, starved for oxygen, wakes you up from sleep because it thinks you're suffocating. They are not fun.

So I use my fading strength to stay awake and then, when Trent's breathing becomes slow and steady, I extract myself from his arms and leave his bedroom as quietly as possible. A quick check of the time, and I realize it's just past two fifteen in the morning. This night went by much too fast.

My skin feels sticky from the salty air around the beach, as well as from my steamy session with Trent, so I make the decision to take a late night shower. Even though it means I'll be going to bed with wet hair, at least everything will be clean. It's the best way to fall asleep.

The house is quiet when I get to the hallway. I can't tell if Chalice is home yet, but I don't think hearing the shower going this late will bother him even if he is. Besides, Trent said he's a heavy sleeper. Also, I live here too; so I'm within my right to shower whenever I want. Even if it's almost three in the morning.

Every day that's passed has made me miss my old home with my parents and brother a less. Sure there are times when I wake up and the first few minutes of the morning, before my eyes open, it feels like I'm back in my childhood bedroom. It's a strange feeling but hasn't happened in a while now.

When I close my eyes and think about it, I can still remember every detail about the house I grew up in, but the memories hurt much less. I miss my parents and to a lesser extent, my brother, but I know they're all just a phone call away. I think, too, that I once missed the familiar way that home and the creatures inside made me feel. Now, that feeling of home comes from 1414 Cumberbatch Way and the two creatures within, Chalice and Trent.

I've finally gotten used to living here. I guess home is where you make it, after all.

Just in case it does disturb anyone sleeping, I make my shower a quick one. But even short, it's still extremely refreshing and I'm glad I did it. It feels like a reset for my thoughts and now I can think a little clearer.

After I'm mostly dry, I wrap myself in a clean towel and scurry into my own bedroom. Because it's so late and I need some time to myself, I lock my door and rummage around for my little white-noise machine. I set it to some gentle ocean waves, but they only serve to amp me up, so I change it to the thunderstorm setting.

It's past three by the time I finally lay in my bed, but no matter how much I try to clear my mind, I just can't sleep. It's exhausting to be this exhausted and not be able to calm your mind.

So I do what I usually do when that happens.

I text Frankie.

It takes a minute for her to respond, though I don't know if it's because she was asleep or up with some art project or another. Frankie tends to keep different hours than most normal creatures. I have no idea when she actually sleeps and think she just runs on coffee like some sort of machine.

When she does text back, it takes me off guard because she says to just call her. I guess that would be easier, even though it feels weird to call her at this hour.

She answers on speaker and sounds like she's had an energy drink or two. She was definitely not sleeping.

"Julie! Sorry, I can't text right now. I have too much glitter glue on my hands and don't want to ruin my phone."

"Glitter glue? I didn't get the memo that first grade started already, or that they make that stuff anymore."

"You'd be surprised at what craft supplies from our youth are still going strong. They're just more expensive and not as high quality." She pauses and laughs loudly. "I'm using it for this amazing piece for a festival next year. Those judges aren't going to know what hit them. But, anyway, I know you didn't text me at three in the morning to talk about art. How are things? You doing okay? Do you still hurt from that car crash or did someone fuck you too hard?"

"I don't know if I'm okay," I answer quietly and stare at the ceiling. "I went out with Trent tonight."

"Did the date end with you doing him?"

"Goddess, Frankie."

"So you did?" she asks hopefully.

"Yes."

"Nice."

"It really was, actually. It's just, I don't know how I'm feeling about the whole situation. I think I want to be with Chalice and with Trent. Is that weird?"

"Not at all." Frankie pauses, and it sounds like she's shuffling around her glitter glues. "As long as everyone's cool with it."

"Trent said he was."

"That's good!"

"But I don't know about Chalice."

"That's bad."

"But I haven't talked to him about it yet."

"That's good! If his buddy is fine with it, chances are that he will be too. It sounds like you just need to get a one-on-one with the Golden God and see what he says."

"Ugh, you're right. I guess I'm at least fifty percent there."

"See, all you gotta do is talk to him and be open about how you're feeling. Honestly, it's the best way to avoid miscommunication tropes and such. Oh hey, I forgot to ask, did you end up entering that contest at work? The candle design one?"

"Oh, um, yeah . . . I did. I wasn't going to say anything." I let out a long sigh. "Because I doubt they'll even consider me. I also turned it in the same day a car parked itself inside Candle Love."

"I'm still proud of you for doing that, but if you want me to be even more proud of you, you'll talk to Chalice and validate this throuple thing between all three of you."

"Is it even still a throuple if not everyone is sleeping with each other?" I ask.

Frankie hums to herself as she thinks, or maybe she's painting again. It wouldn't be the first time she became distracted while talking with me on the phone. Finally, after what sounds like something wet being slapped down against something hard, she speaks again.

"Eh, those two are best guy friends. That's close enough for now and who knows for the future!" She lets out a peal of laughter that is much too loud for this late at night or early in the morning.

Her poor neighbors. Sometimes I wonder what they think of her odd habits. Can they tell she's up at three in the morning creating art and scream laughing on the phone? What am I talking about, of course they do! It's Frankie and she probably warned them about it herself.

I let out a big yawn and snuggle back down in my sheets, hugging a pillow against my chest. Even though she's a little loud sometimes, talking with Frankie always makes me feel better.

"Thanks for talking with me, Frankie, but I think I'm finally tired enough to sleep."

"Anytime bestie, call me when you have an update on things!"

"You know I will!"

I take a quick moment to slip my CPAP mask over my head and lay back down on my bed. While I find myself staring at the ceiling again, it's not for long because sleep rapidly descends on me.

But the sleep that comes is pummeled by dreams both sweet and angry. Maybe its coming from all the rich food earlier tonight, or perhaps from the mix of emotions swirling inside my head, but I spend the short remainder of the night tossing and turning within the turbulent dreamscapes.

The dreams keep forcing me awake, and when I crack open my eyes between them, I can see the dim light becoming brighter and brighter as the sun steadily rises. It's only just after the sun begins to peak through my blinds, that I finally get out of bed. Even then, it's much later in the morning than I normally wake up, so I find myself forcing my body to get up and get moving.

It's time to, as Frankie said, stop this whole miscommunication thing. I guess it's my least favorite romance trope anyway; so theoretically, this should be easy. I just need to somehow get some courage and bring up the subject without the fear of rejection. Maybe I'll get lucky and Chalice will beat me to it, like Trent. But I just have this feeling that I'll need to take charge on this one.

Oh Goddess, give me the courage because I have to talk to Chalice!

I need to feed my anxiety, so after rolling out from bed, I wrap a bathrobe around my night shirt and kick on a pair of fuzzy slippers. My box of leftovers was stashed in the refrigerator last night, and I plan on having them as a quick, amazing breakfast.

Last night was amazing on so many levels. Not only was it filled with great food, but Trent and I took our relationship to the next level and he even said he's okay with my feelings for Chalice. Now, I just have to find the right moment to bring it up with Chalice himself.

Distracted from thinking about my pumpkin-flavored treats and feelings, I don't notice the Golden God standing behind the open fridge doors and nearly walk into them. Throwing my arms up at the last minute, I make an undignified *thump* when I hit the doors, but at least they force me out of my tired stupor.

"Good Morning!" A beaming Chalice closes the refrigerator doors and looks down at me. His golden skin shines in the early morning sunshine, which is magnificent and all, but I swiftly realize he's holding my box of leftovers.

"Oh no," I say quickly, snatching the box from a stunned set of gold-colored hands. "These are mine."

He laughs loudly, thumping his tail on the ground.

"I know, I was just moving them out of the way so I could grab Trent's box. The big letters spelling out your name on the container kind of gave it away."

I look down and realize I did very clearly, and very largely, write my full name and an expiration date.

"I guess I took Misty's words to heart. The only fridge 'monitor' I ever lived with was my dad and he wasn't that strict."

Chalice beams.

"You did good; she will throw your food out if she can. It's nothing against you. She's been doing it to me ever since we were kids. To be fair, though, I ate most of her leftovers whenever I had the chance. Maybe that's why she's so annoying about the fridge now."

Chalice's face goes distant in thought for a second, but he comes back quickly enough. It makes me wonder what his own family life was like growing up. Did moving out on his own affect him, or was he okay because his twin went with him?

"If you're hungry now, you can have some of my leftovers. I doubt I'll be able to eat this whole thing."

"I would never deprive a lady of her food, but I will take my best friend's." Chalice opens the fridge again and sticks his large hands inside, coming back out with Trent's box from Butter.

"Does he know you do that?"

"He sure does! You don't become best friends with someone and not learn both their good and bad habits." He beams with pride.

"Well, if we ever become that close, you'll need to ask me before eating my leftovers. I have to set some boundaries."

Chalice's laugh fills the room and he casually hands me my own fork.

"I'll keep that in mind. Come on and eat breakfast with me, we can eat our leftovers on the couch."

I follow him to the living room, and we take up opposite sides of the couch with our feet meeting together in the middle. There's a slight chill to the air this morning, which is considered cold by New California standards, and Chalice drapes a blanket between us.

The leftovers are almost just as good as last night, though I find myself missing the fresh from the oven bread. Cold lasagna, though, hits just right. Chalice seems to be enjoying Trent's food as well and I wonder briefly what Trent thinks of this habit of his. I guess he's probably used to it by now.

"Did you two have fun last night?" Chalice asks, and I pause with my fork still in my mouth.

"Yeah, a lot of fun," I mutter in response, and he raises a perfectly chiseled eyebrow.

"Sure sounded like it," he chuckles.

I feel redness creek up my neck and heat my cheeks while my pumpkin-themed food suddenly feels cold in my stomach.

"Um, well, I . . ."

Chalice nudges our feet together under the blanket. They're warm and surprisingly soft given that the rest of his appearance is more cut and rugged. It's incredibly comfortable under the blanket with him and when I look up to catch his eye, he smiles.

"You look like you want to talk to me about something," he says.

Deep breaths, Julie. You just gotta get this over with.

"Actually, yeah, I do."

Chalice leans forward and the blanket begins to fall off us, but he grabs it and holds it close. The golden sheen goes ashen for a moment, and my heart catches in my throat at the pain on his face.

"What," he clears his throat, "did you want to talk about?"

"Well," I start, but then take a moment to smooth the blanket out against my legs, focusing on the little swirls and heart design on the fabric. "About us."

He sucks in a breath.

"About all three of us," I continue quickly. "Trent and I talked about it last night and he, uh, well he said . . . hmm."

"All three of us?" Chalice asks hopefully. He takes hold of the blanket and throws it aside as he crawls across the couch toward me. His large body hovers over mine as I stare up into his hazel eyes. "So, you do still like me?"

"What? Yes, of course I do." I place a hand over his cheek, and he closes his eyes. "I just wasn't sure if you still wanted to be with me considering I, um, also want to be with Trent."

He opens his eyes again and looks into mine.

"Is that all?" His chest rumbles with soft laughter. "Trent's my best friend in the whole world, well, besides my sister, but Misty doesn't count in this situation. What's his is mine and what's mine is his."

I snort.

"You make me sound like leftover food."

He smiles and kisses my forehead.

"Nah, you're better than leftovers. I don't really love leftovers, but I love you and everything about you. Even if you don't share your food with me."

I start laughing, but he closes in and swallows my laughter with his mouth. At the same time, he lowers some of his weight, trapping me under his warm body on the couch. He kisses me deeply as I wrap my arms around his broad shoulders and listen to the old couch creak in protest.

"I better tell you that I feel the same way before the couch breaks and we fall to the ground," I say when we finally break apart for air. He lets out a strangled gasp and claims my mouth again.

"Hey now, what's this?" I hear Trent's voice behind us and look at him upside down from my position under Chalice.

"Just a little breakfast," Chalice murmurs into my neck.

Trent kneels beside the couch and runs his fingers through my hair, moving it out of the way for Chalice to continue nuzzling and nipping at the skin of my neck.

"Mind if I join you?" His voice is warm and husky as he bends over me from above. He hovers his lips just above my mouth, waiting for my reply as Chalice moves back.

"Sure," I breathe, but he's already on me, exploring my mouth with his tongue as Chalice's hands roam down my shoulders to my chest, massaging and squeezing my nipples.

A moan escapes my mouth, but just as my back arches in pleasure and an arm wraps around my waist, the front door opens.

"I'm back!" someone yells out over the sound of luggage being kicked inside. "Chalice, get your ass over here and help me bring my luggage up the stairs!"

I'm a cluster of chaos as I scramble from the couch and stand awkwardly beside Trent just as Chalice's sister, Misty, saunters into the room. Her nostrils flare as she takes us in, and I give her a sheepish grin.

"Hi!" I squeal just a little too loudly.

"I thought you were coming home later tonight?" asks Chalice as he swings his legs from the couch and stands up next to us. Trent and I exchange a glance when we both look down and see that Chalice clearly has a large erection. Like, it's literary straining out of his shorts.

I catch Misty's eyes flicker downward and notice it as well, but she looks away quickly and clears her throat.

"I caught an earlier flight because I felt like treating myself and upgrading to first class," she says, her tail swinging delightfully behind her. "But I had to be awake and at the airport before five in the morning, so I'm beat."

"Welcome home, Misty." Trent, who was smart enough to stand behind the couch to hide his massive boner, smiles at Misty. "Leave your luggage by the door, we'll get it in a moment."

Her face twitches like she's trying to hide a smile.

"Looks like you've settled in nicely, Julie." She looks at me and I do my best to look as natural as possible, which is nearly impossible considering what we were just doing.

"Yup, it's great! I love it here!"

Smooth, Julie.

"That's awesome," she says, her eyes darting between the three of us. "Well, I'm going to go take a shower, so I'll see you three later."

"That sounds like fun. I mean, not you showering, a shower sounds . . . good as well . . . for me. I'm going to go take one too. Um, bye!"

I scamper ungracefully out of the room and hope Misty doesn't see how red my face is. I think I hear Trent snickering behind me as I flutter out of the room like a hummingbird hyped up on energy drinks.

As I go, it feels like I'm walking on clouds as I hurry to bathroom, slam the door shut, and begin brushing my teeth just for something to keep my hands busy.

Is this my life now? Do I really have two boyfriends? Also, do I really need another shower? No, but I feel like I should take one because I don't want to go back out there right now. I'm not ashamed of anything, just embarrassed and really, really don't want to look Misty in the eyes right now.

CHAPTER TWENTY

I spend much too long in the shower, and when I get out, my skin is wrinkled and I'm lightheaded. But it was time well spent because I, apparently, really needed a moment to myself because I feel calmer and more composed now.

Even though I do plan to avoid Misty for the rest of the day, I'm not nearly as embarrassed as I was when I first heard the front door open. I'm an adult, I think. Yes, I am. No . . . well, fuck, I'm at least old enough to engage in sexual encounters. Goddess that makes me sound ancient, so I must be old.

Maybe it has more to do with the fact that I was grinding against Misty's brother. I mean, how would I feel if I walked in on my adopted brother and someone.

Hmm.

No . . . gross, which is probably how she felt.

Still, I think I may need to tread lightly on this. At least until I know where she stands on this whole thing I have going on right now.

Multiple partners is not unheard of in the Dragoon world, but I'm not sure about my human side. And I'm fairly certain it's extremely uncommon for Fox Folk, at least for the traditionalists that is. Which means that Misty, and probably my parents, would be fine with me having two boyfriends. But I've never talked about that kind of stuff with them and don't plan on doing so now, so that's a moot point.

After my shower, I stand at the door and listen for voices, and when I'm certain no one is around, I bolt for my room and lock the door. As much as I really want to round up Trent and Chalice and finish what we started, something tells me it isn't the best time in the world.

I want to at least wait till after lunch to be railed by two guys at once.

My phone buzzes with unread text messages, so I slip into a pair of sweats and sit on my bed to go through them.

Several are from Frankie and involve everything from asking about my evening with Trent to random pictures of phallic shaped art she saw at a nearby store. Another mentions her neighbors are giving her trouble again because they think she's too loud. She really needs to be careful, or she's going to be kicked out of her loft.

I have one text from Eddie showing signage from a local club and telling me I have to go there and try their drinks with him. Hard pass. The thought of so many people packed into a dimly-lit room with blasting music makes my skin crawl.

Another text is from Rose, and it's a picture of a flower growing from a crack in the sidewalk outside the wrecked Candle Love store. She asks if that would be a good picture for the art contest, but with all the crying emojis she adds on, I know she's not serious. Somewhat traumatic but funny I guess.

The last text is super long and from Marilyn. She says that a cleanup crew was dispatched to Candle Love and that all salvageable merchandise from both the floor and backroom has been brought to a temporary location on the other side of our parking lot. She stresses that while care was taken to not break anything, the crew didn't really keep track of what goes where and that absolutely nothing was labeled in the process.

I put my phone down and swallow a growl of frustration. While I'm happy that I didn't have to sort through broken glass, bent steel, and smashed car parts, I would have REALLY appreciated them labeling the stuff they moved. Over half my job is stocking, sorting, cataloging, and keeping everything in beautiful order.

Deep breaths, Julie. Deep, deep, deep breaths.

The second part of her long message lets everyone know we'll be meeting this afternoon at the new location to start setting up our temporary store. That makes sense, with Samhain and Yule around the corner and all the Mabon sales. It's the busiest time of the year.

I text her back and let her know I can't come tonight but promise to be there all day on Saturday. It's my normal night off anyway because I'm expected at New Harvest today for volunteer work. I wonder if Chalice and Trent would want to tag along.

She responds immediately and claims to have known already and that nothing is getting done tonight anyway and that they're just looking at things. Great. All the work will be saved for me on Saturday. Ugh.

Then, instead of sending Frankie a long string of texts, I decide to call her instead.

The line rings for a few beats before she answers with what sounds like someone pounding on a wall.

"Frankie?"

More pounding.

"Frankie!"

"Ugh, sorry, I had to get out of the hallway. I couldn't hear shit in there." She sounds out of breath, and I can tell from the clanking of metal steps, she must be leaving her apartment.

"Everything okay?"

"No!" She sighs loudly. "I think my neighbors have decided to fight fire with fire. You know how they're always complaining that I'm up late and making noise? Well, they've decided to pay it forward ten million times. It's torture and not the good sexual kind. It's the kind they would show on a historical miniseries or something."

"Have you tried talking to them?"

"I think we're beyond that now." She laughs manically. "But enough about my problems, how are things with you? Last I remember, you had just fucked roommate number two. You didn't also tap the sister, did you?"

"Frankie!"

"Sorry." She laughs again. "So what happened?"

"They both are okay with it, Chalice and Trent both want me, and I don't have to choose. They're okay with sharing!"

"You lucky bitch!" Frankie cheers. "I'm so happy for you! So are you guys like a throuple now?"

"Um, I don't think so? Maybe? Well, Chalice and Trent aren't sleeping together, and I don't think they plan to from what I can tell."

"It's not uncommon among Dragoons to have multiple mates, so it makes sense for Chalice to be fine with sharing. Not so much for Trent, though, and even though I know you barely consider yourself a human, they are also not huge on sharing. I'm happy for you, but you may get some stares when you're out and about."

"Aren't you a spoilsport?"

Frankie snorts in laughter.

"Just being protective of my best friend, who I hope will still have time for me in between spreading her thighs for her two hunky boyfriends."

"Goddess, Frankie . . ."

"In all seriousness, you sound really good. I was worried for you, well not a lot because you're a badass lady, but I know it was hard for you to move out on your own. I guess I was right in that all it took was for some good sex with a couple of off-limit guys to break you out of your funk."

"I still miss my old house sometimes and the way things were when we were young. But it's strange, I don't feel as sad about it anymore. Moving out was just another milestone in life, I guess, just something I needed to do in order to really grow up and mature."

"Ah, so you weren't grown up before? That explains your taste in bedsheets. Are you still sleeping on rainbows and unicorns? Goddess, did you fuck on those sheets? Did they say anything?"

Now it's my turn to laugh, though she brings up a good point.

"Well, we haven't all three fucked at the same time. I've just had some good one-on-one things with them, nothing, uh, all together."

"Something to look forward to then." I hear a car door open and an engine start up. "It'll probably happen soon, though, I would put money on it."

"Please don't make bets on my sex life."

"It's how I live life on the edge. Anyway, I gotta run, I'm going to go check out a new apartment downtown. I don't think I can take my terrible neighbors anymore. But you had better call or text me later with all the details of your sex life."

"Um, no."

I can hear her smile through her laughter.

"Don't stress, I don't expect you to kiss and tell me every detail or every single touch or lick. I'm more interested in that they're taking good care of you. You're my best friend, Julie, and if they ever hurt you . . . they'll have me to deal with."

"Thanks, Frankie, I know you always have my back."

"Anytime, Julie. Okay, have fun with your roomies! I'm winking right now, but you're not here to see it so just take it on my word. Talk to you later!"

"Later, Frankie!"

My room feels quiet after I'm off the phone, and I fall backward on my bed, staring at the ceiling and thinking about the home I grew up in.

It feels different now. Sure, there's that nostalgic feeling that feels like a cloudy mist, but now its tinted with sunlight streaming from the window of my new room. While I'll always have fond memories of that house and growing up with my adopted family,

I find that I'm really looking forward to this new path in life and am excited for what the future holds.

It's a lazy afternoon for me. At some point, Chalice leaves to go to work for a few hours and Trent is left with the task of helping Misty move her gigantic luggage up the stairs to her room above the garage. He's a sweaty mess by the time he's through and excuses himself for a shower and nap. With Misty resting in her room, I'm left alone most of day.

As I'm sorting through some laundry, there's a light tapping on my door, and I open it to see Chalice standing there. He's freshly showered because he does not smell like burgers and fries. Instead, he's absolutely glowing with that dark, smoky amber scent.

"Hey there," he says casually, pushing into my room and taking my head in his hands.

"Hi," I breathe just as his lips seal against mine in a sultry kiss that makes my toes curl.

I wrap my hands around his, intending at first to move them to my waist and fall into him, but then I notice his short nails and instead I thread my fingers in one of his hands and hold it in front of his face.

"So, why do you keep your nails so short? I know that's not typical for a Dragoon."

He smiles, but I detect a slight flush in his cheeks.

"It's silly," he says, avoiding catching my eye and staring instead at our hands. "You sure you want to know?"

"I do."

"Well, alrighty then. Come with me."

Chalice grabs my hand and takes me toward his room.

It was dark the last time I was inside here, so I don't remember much. But today, the first thing I notice is that it's similar to Trent's room with just a giant mattress on the floor, though it's also covered with a pile of laundry he has yet to put away. I must have been too tired to notice after our shower sex when he brought me in here.

What is with these guys and no bed frames?

Chalice must see me looking at it because he cocks his head and grins.

"I'm a big guy, and it's just easier this way. I don't have to worry about breaking anything."

"Have you been, uh, known to break beds?" I ask.

"Yes, but it's not what you're thinking. Trent and I were rowdy little kids. Together, we've broken at least five different beds, both at home and friends houses, just from wrestling and jumping around. You know, totally normal behavior."

"Hmm, my brother never broke any beds before."

"Well, he probably didn't play Caves and Cryptids. It can get intense when your level forty-four warrior casts slamming shield on a pile of possessed garden gnomes."

My limited knowledge of Caves and Crytids flashes through my brain. It's a pen and paper role-playing game where you make up characters with various traits and invade dungeons and battle magical creatures. All your moves are based on the roll of a multi-sided dice.

"Oh, I have heard of that game. I haven't played though but sounds like I shouldn't if I wants to keep my bed intact."

Chalice waggles his golden eyebrows at me and grins.

"We'll get you to play someday, trust me. If you're going to be a part of our lives for the long haul, you'll be around it so much that you'll be begging for us to allow you in our campaign."

"I'll take your word for it," I respond and try to fight the redness in my face. *Part of their lives for the long haul? Yes, please.*

"Okay, take a seat," Chalice says and gestures toward the ground mattress. I sit down heavily, unaccustomed to sitting on a bed that low to the floor. He grabs something from a nearby desk and plops down next to me.

It's a laptop with a stack of books, and from the looks of it, the books have been read about a million times each. The spines are white from repeated bending, and while the covers are worn and faded, I can make out a few spaceships on them.

"So, what you might not know about me is that I like, um, fantasy and sci-fi stuff." He scratches one of his gold cheeks with a short nailed finger. "Like wizards and magic and spaceships and, um, aliens. I really like old science fiction, the stuff from fifty years ago when it was mostly just speculation and themes of feminism and social upheaval."

He's right, I did not figure that from him. But maybe that's my fault for assuming he wasn't into that stuff just because he's tall and muscular. I think I labeled him as someone I thought he should be based on looks, so I'm really glad we're taking the time to get to know each other better. It makes my fondness and love for him grow even more.

"Interesting," I say with a smile. "But what does that have to do with your nails?"

"Well, I . . . um, I really like to read so I thought I'd give a try in writing my own, um, a science fiction novel."

My eyes go wide.

"You actually wrote a book? An entire book?"

"Well, yeah. I did."

Chalice goes quiet as he bends his head to look down at his laptop. When his eyes dip, I notice that his eyelashes are a perfect shade of golden brown that compliments the shine of his blonde hair. He's gorgeous and extremely talented. How did I get this lucky?

"That is . . . incredible!" I throw my arms around his shoulders. He's way bigger than me so I can't really get all of him in a hug, but I do my best. "I can't imagine writing an entire book; that must have taken you forever."

Chalice laughs loudly. He then kisses my cheek and hugs me back before pulling away so he can open his laptop.

"I'm still doing a final read through before I send it to an editor friend, but you're welcome to read it after it's been polished."

The screen of his laptop flashes to life and after a few clicks, he opens a file called "Homecoming."

"Oh, I have so many questions," I breathe, scanning what I can of the first paragraph on screen.

"Such as?"

"How did you get started in writing? What inspires you to write the most? Can I read it? Are you self-publishing it?"

"Let's see . . . a long time ago, everything, and 'yes' times two." He reaches around and strokes my hair. "Can I ask you a question?"

"Anything." I lean into him.

"You don't find this kind of thing, weird?"

"Why should I? I think it's awesome and it makes me feel, I don't know, closer to you. I appreciate you telling me. Still doesn't really explain the nails though."

"It's dumb, but I can type better with short nails. Long finger-nails get in the way of the laptop keyboard."

A valid reason if I ever heard one.

"I'm assuming Trent knows?" I ask. "And Misty?"

"They both do, but Trent is the only one who really cares. Misty isn't really into reading and writing. She's super smart, but I think I sucked up all the creative genes in our family."

"Well, I'm envious of your talent. I can draw and paint, but I don't think I could write an entire story with a beginning, a middle, and an end. It would be a bunch of gibberish, or I would just give up."

"Maybe we can work together one day. I'll write, and you can illustrate." Chalice closes his laptop fondly and gently places it back on his desk. "Uh, if you'd be okay with that, I mean."

More future talk. Yes, yes, yes, a thousand times yes.

I nod and smile, hoping my eyes say what I know my words will fail at. Maybe that's just how it is with me, I can't put into words what I feel, but I can illustrate it. Perhaps Chalice completes that part of me.

"What are you up to tonight?" Chalice asks and slips his arm around my shoulders, tugging me into him. We fall to the bed, our limbs tangled together and his tail curled around us. I reach out and stroke it while scaled; it's velvety smooth when I slide my hand along the right way.

"Volunteer night at New Harvest. I already signed up, so I should go down there."

"Hmm, mind if we tag along with you?" he asks.

"Of course not, I'm sure Tom would love the help. They've been short-staffed lately."

"Good," Chalice murmurs, running his fingers through my hair. "Whatcha up to right now?"

"Nothing," I say with a sly smile and scoot closer to him.

"Well, we have about an hour or so till we'll need to leave for New Harvest. Wanna hang out with me?"

"What do you think?" I reach down and grab the waist band of his pants so I can flick open the button of his jeans.

Chalice let's out a hiss of pleasure containing a very small amount of smoke before he curves over my body and buries his face in my neck. The kisses he gives me there are hot and steamy as his hands dart down and help pull off all our clothing.

Then, just before he lines himself up with me and I feel the sweet, hot pleasure of his cock beginning to slide inside me, some-one knocks on his bedroom door.

CHAPTER TWENTY-ONE

"Who is that?" I whisper, squirming restlessly under Chalice. I'm worked up now, waiting for him to press his hips forward a little bit more . . .

"Ugh, probably Misty. Trent would have come straight in." He looks over his shoulder and narrows his eyes at the door.

I pat his arm and give him an encouraging smile even though my body screams in protest. Chalice returns an apologetic look and shifts his weight from me to the bed.

"Yes, sister?" He calls out in a more than irritated tone.

"Hey, do you have a moment. I need to talk something over with you." Her words sound tentative, like she's debating if talking to him is a good idea or not.

"Well . . ." Chalice makes eye contact with me and grimaces, but I mouth the words, "It's fine."

He sighs and sits up on the bed as we fall apart from each other.

"Give me a few minutes, and I'll meet you upstairs," he groans in reply.

"Kay!" She yells out from the hallway, and Chalice lets out a deep-throated and low growl as he reaches around for his shorts.

"Does she know I'm in here?" I ask, slipping my clothes back on.

"I don't think so. My sister can be bossy sometimes, but she's respectful. She wouldn't have interrupted if she heard us. I wasn't sure if you wanted her to know you're in here or not, but we can always just be louder next time. That'll keep her away."

"I don't think I want to be loud for your sister."

"Yeah, that sounded better in my head, and I regretted it the moment I said it." He laughs lightly and leans over to kiss my forehead.

"Let me get this over with, and I'll come find you."

"Sounds good," I say, rising from the ground mattress and stretching. "You know where to find me."

"In my heart?" he asks, leaping up and cupping my face in his hands.

"So cheesy, I thought you're a writer. Shouldn't you be able to think of something better than that?"

"Sometimes the cheesy moments are the perfect way to end things. So you had better get used to it." He kisses me so deeply that we both break apart and gasp for air.

"I'll make sure to do that," I pant into his mouth just before he kisses me once more and pushes his hips toward me. The bulge in his pants grinds against my body, and I whimper when his hands start groping my chest, pinching my nipples through my shirt.

It's such a tease because I know we don't have time to do anything now, but it doesn't stop me from thinking about it when I feel his hard cock straining through his shorts. He lets out a hiss of pleasure when I give it a squeeze over the fabric.

"Chalice?" I hear Misty's distant voice echoing through the hall, and we reluctantly pull away from each other.

"Later?" he asks.

"Later," I promise.

But later doesn't come, and I don't make good on that promise because I fall asleep on the couch. In my defense, I put on a cozy cooking show and the gentle tone always puts me to sleep in seconds. When I wake up, it's almost time to leave for New Harvest, and I reluctantly drag myself to my room to get ready to leave.

Chalice hasn't come down from his sister's room yet, but I finally hear him stomping down the stairs just as I'm grabbing my purse and car keys.

"I'll drive," he grumbles, casting a disapproving look behind him as he opens the door to Trent's room and sticks his head inside.

I look around his body and watch as Trent lazily rolls off the bed and runs a hand through his messy hair. How can it be possible for someone to look that attractive after waking up from a power nap is beyond me.

"Was that Misty I heard yelling in the hallway?" he asks with a big yawn.

"Yup, she's back for now." Chalice frowns and looks pointedly at Trent.

"For now?"

"For now," he repeats and Trent returns the frown.

"What are you guys talking about?" I ask as we walk to Chalice's truck. He opens the door for me and scrunches his eyebrows.

"Apparently, Misty is moving out." He rubs the bridge of his nose. "Got a job up north or something."

Trent sucks in a breath and twirls his tails in thought.

"Shit, that's a big chunk of our rent."

"I know," Chalice mutters and shakes his head, but then catches my eye and gives me a forced smile. "We have some time, it's nothing we have to worry about tonight at least."

"Kinda hard not to worry." One of Trent's tails whacks my arm as I climb into my seat. "Sorry, Julie."

"It's fine." I reach out and stroke his arm before looking at Chalice in the driver's seat. "We'll figure it out . . . somehow."

"I'll remain optimistic for you," Chalice says with the click of his seatbelt.

Trent sits in the small backseat with me, even though his tails are smushed behind him. He slides an arm around my shoulders and lets me lean into him. Chalice angles the rearview mirror to watch us.

"Not fair," he murmurs as we back out of the driveway.

"You're the one who offered to drive," laughs Trent.

I want to laugh along with him, but the nagging worry of being able to pay our rent sits heavily on my mind. *What if we have to move? Would we all be able to stay together, or is this wonderful life I've finally found myself a part of just too good to last?*

"Julie, I can see you thinking back there," Chalice warns. "We'll figure everything out somehow. It will be okay, we're going to take care of you."

"I know, but it's hard not to think about it," I respond.

I don't want any of this to go away.

"Hey, Trent, why don't you help her think about something else."

Trent chuckles and shifts around in his seat, pulling me as close to his body as my seatbelt will allow.

"Hear that, Julie? Let's get you thinking about happier things."

I let out a small gasp when one of Trent's hands slips under my shirt and he pinches my nipple until I squirm against him.

"What if someone driving next to us sees," I mumble and tilt my head back to look at him. "Besides I can't just not think."

He laughs in response and starts to kiss my neck.

"The windows are mostly tinted," says Chalice. "Mostly. And yes, you can 'not think' if we do a good enough job at distracting you."

"And I don't care if they see me worshiping your body," adds Trent. "You're fucking mine, and I want the world to know it."

"Ours," corrects Chalice.

"Ours," Trent repeats into my neck.

He draws slow circles with his tongue and his breath tickles my skin. The hand not under my shirt skirts over my stomach, dipping down between my legs. Then just as I feel the car shift to a stop, probably at a red light, his fingers begin to circle my clit beneath my underwear.

A mewl of pleasure escapes my lips as I shift around in my seat, desperate for more but restrained by, well, my seatbelt restraint.

"Sounds like she likes whatever it is you're doing back there," I hear Chalice say. "Keep going, I want to hear her come."

"I think I can manage that." Trent's voice is low and hoarse in my ear, and his breathing picks up as he works his fingers fast against me.

"Better come for us soon, Julie. We're almost at New Harvest." Chalice's voice is tense and needy, but I get the feeling his attention isn't fully on us. Which is good. He is driving, after all.

"You heard him, Diamond, we want you to come all over my fingers."

A second later, I feel my body pull in on itself as the muscles inside burst into exploding pleasure. My back arches against Trent who keeps his fingers working swiftly and deftly against me until every lingering spasm finishes and I'm left a floppy mess leaning against him.

For a moment, the truck cab is quiet except for my labored pants as I catch my breath. The streets are blurry when I look out the window, my eyes refusing to focus after such an intense orgasm.

"What a good girl," Chalice purrs from the driver's seat. "But I hope you saved some of that for later."

I giggle in response when Trent squeezes my sides and kisses my cheek as I attempt to straighten out and sit like a normal person.

"Of course," I say, catching his eye in the mirror. "I like to keep my promises."

Am I in a better mood? Yes. Do I still have a lingering pit of anxiety deep within my core? Also yes.

I think I could move somewhere else now.

If I had to.

But not without them.

It's only a matter of minutes before Chalice is pulling into a parking space just outside New Harvest. It's dark already, but the inside of the warehouse is exceptionally bright and, oddly, welcoming.

I've been coming here for a really long time, and it's only changed slightly over the years. Thinking about it, I've been here so often that it feels like an extension of home, a satellite location in a way. I can't ever go back to the house I grew up in, but I can still come here, and that's almost as good.

As we walk to the back door, I can't help but notice a line of creatures forming near the main entrance and loading dock, which is unusual for this time of day. Typically, they only distribute care packaging during the mornings when I'm not here.

"Thank Goddess you brought your friends," Tom practically screams as he rushes to greet us at the door. "We are desperately short-staffed tonight so we can use all the help we can get."

His eyes sparkle when he looks at Chalice and Trent, to which Chalice looks away with a blush and Trent gives a cocky smile.

"We're relaxed and ready to go with whatever you need." He gives me an exaggerated wink, and I hold in a snicker.

"Fantastic! We got a huge shipment of fresh foods and everything needs to be sorted before eight tonight."

"Why tonight? We usually have all weekend to get the packages done." I glance at Tom, who runs a hand down his face and sighs.

"It's my fault, I dropped the ball on this one. The warehouse needs to close for a deep clean tomorrow, which I totally forgot about until a reminder on my calendar popped up. Sent out an email last night to all the shelters and our regulars that we'll need to do a special evening pick up. So . . ."

"So?"

"It means I'll need help with not only packaging but distributing as well. But it's easy, you just have to hand stuff out. We don't ask questions around here, if you need help and ask us, we'll offer it to you."

My hands begin to sweat immediately. I've driven by and seen the lines of creatures who come by New Harvest, and while I'm glad we're here to help as many as we can, I don't think I can be around and help without seriously panicking from the sheer number of creatures surrounding me.

Chalice puts a hand on my shoulder, and Trent leans in close.

"We'll figure it out," Trent whispers into my hair.

"Everything will be okay," echoes Chalice.

Tom sets us up with safety vests and leads our trio to a table toward the back of the warehouse. Here, we're set to work sorting huge containers of bananas and tasked with pulling any that are just too brown and mushy to be of use. Eventually, another volunteer comes by to collect our sorted bananas and exchanged them for cans of creamed corn.

"Something keeps buzzing by my leg," says Trent, moving back to look down at the table.

"Oh, sorry, I think it's my phone. Someone's been texting me nonstop, but I'm too covered in banana goo to check.

"Oh, Diamond, there's nothing more I'd rather do than stick my hands down your pants again to check your phone, but I don't think you'd appreciate a coochie full of banana."

Chalice snorts.

"I dunno, Trent, sounds kinda tasty to me."

Even through the anxious pit in my stomach, I have to laugh at their comments.

"No, I'm with Trent on this. I'd rather not have bananas inserted in me."

I'm surprised by Tom's laughter from behind, and I turn to give him a sheepish grin.

"I won't ask." He throws his hands up in the air. "But we're about ready to open the doors. It'd be great if you three could man the right table with heavier boxes. That way you can help load them into cars if anyone needs the help."

Chalice and Trent exchange glances, and I open my mouth to say something to Tom, but he's already walking quickly toward another group sorting cans of pasta sauce.

"Come with us to the table, Julie, we'll deal with everyone. You can just sit there," says Chalice, and I glance up nervously when I hear the big warehouse door creaking open.

Trent's tails swish in thought as he looks from the distant table back to me.

"That line isn't so long, I think we'll be fine without you. Why don't you wait in the car? If anyone asks, we'll tell them off for you."

"You don't need to tell anyone off," I grunt, loading up a box onto a trolly to take our sorted cans and bananas to the last few volunteer sorters. "I promise to let you know if its too much."

"Okay, we'll let you decide." Trent bends over and kisses my cheek.

"Just let us know," Chalice comes in and kisses the other side.

Somewhere I hear someone giggle at us, but I don't pay any attention to them. How could I care about what they think when I have such a good thing going now?

But that high doesn't last long because as soon as we arrive at the table and I see the long line of creatures and waiting cars in the night, something clicks inside me and I feel like my body is turning off.

"Julie?" I hear Trent's voice distantly as I scan over the crowd before us.

For one thing, we need to do better as a society because there are way too many creatures here. But another thing is that we need a much better system for our distributing process and crowd control, because the literal sea of faces before me is causing beads of sweat to trickle down my spine.

"Julie!" Chalice's big voice picks at the walls that have gone up, but it isn't until Trent takes my hand and gently leads me away from the scene that I finally float back into myself.

"Wait in the car." He hands me Chalice's keys. "In case you haven't noticed, we're big strong guys with lots of muscle. We'll get this line handled in record time, and you're going to be blown away by how awesome we are. Tom will be singing our praises until at least next month."

I laugh lightly and turn to face him.

"Thanks," I say softly, and he brings his forehead to mine.

"Anything for you," he says before we break apart, and he hurries back to help a very overwhelmed Chalice.

I grip the keys until my knuckles turn white and practically run to Chalice's truck, but just before I get to the backdoor leading to the parking lot, my phone starts to buzz against my pocket again.

I decide to check it and see that Eddie has called me no less than ten times! There's also a very long text message I refuse to read, so I quickly tap his little icon on my phone to call him directly. It barely rings once before he picks up.

"Where have you been? I've been trying you all night!" Eddie ex-
claims breathlessly. Music pumps in the background, and I assume
he must be at some club. I've been told he's in his element when
he's dancing around in those, so I'm surprised he's had the focus
to keep calling me all night. Something must be up.

"I've been at New Harvest, it's kind of hard to talk here. What's
up? Is everything okay?"

"No!" he screams and the music becomes somewhat dulled,
though I do hear toilets flushing in the background. "Things are
not okay in Portia's head."

"What are you talking about?" I have to hold the phone away
from my head because he's so loud on the other end of the line.

"The day of the accident, you put your entry for the art contest
in the office, right?"

"Yeah, it was in there. I was a little distracted with having almost
been run over, so I didn't check it afterward, but I'm assuming it
was fine since it was in there."

"Yeah, back there with Portia! That bitch stole it."

"What are you talking about?"

"I heard her talking about it tonight, and since I was the one
setting up the temp office at the new place, I sort of . . . looked
through Marylyn's computer and saw it. She put her name on your
entry!"

"You're kidding!" I have to lean up against the side of Chalice's truck because my knees have gone weak. "Why would she do that?"

"Because she's just that kind of person, I think." It sounds like someone nearby is drying their hands on crinkly paper towels and another may or may not be peeing.

"Did you say anything to Marilyn about it?

"I can't do that, then she'll know I was snooping around her office logs. I could get fired for that." Now it sounds like Eddie may be peeing, and I don't know how I feel about that.

"I need a moment to process this. We'll talk tomorrow at work, okay?"

He's silent for a moment, and I only know he's still on the line because I can hear the occasional toilet flush.

"Hey, Julie, are you hanging out with your roommates right now," he finally asks.

"Um, yeah, I'm with them. Why?"

"Nothing, never mind." He pauses. "I'm just draaa-unk."

"Okay, well, I'll see you tomorrow then."

Eddie hiccups, then burps. He's a good guy but really needs to cut it out with the clubs and bars. I worry about him sometimes.

"Yeah, alrighty. I'll bring the coffee," he says.

"Yes, please. It sounds like you're going to need it!"

CHAPTER TWENTY-TWO

L ast night was tense in more ways than one. I was still worked up from my call with Eddie by the time Chalice and Trent, sweaty and tired, finished their volunteer shift at New Harvest. Then, to top everything off, my whole body was worked up in a very different way from seeing my two guys pumped and sweaty from lifting boxes all night.

For example, I did not complain when Chalice took his sweat-soaked shirt off and swapped it for another he had stored in his car. Nor did I say anything when Trent drank greedily from a bottle of water and it sloshed down over his chest until his shirt was practically translucent.

But I could tell from their body language that they were exhausted, so I didn't press them for sexy time, even though it was heavy on my mind.

I also decided not to tell them about Portia. I didn't like feeling that I was hiding something from them, but it didn't seem like the right time so I kept it to myself. However, now that it's the next morning I'm sitting at the kitchen table with Chalice pouring myself a giant bowl of sugary cereal, and I feel like I should bring it up.

"Hey, can I ask your opinion on something?" I ask him. He raises an eyebrow and sits across from me. Trent hasn't gotten up yet so it's just the two of us.

More often than not, I'm an early riser and Chalice seems to be up and about at all hours of the day—thanks to his job in the quick service food industry. Trent, on the other hand, likes to sleep in whenever possible.

"Of course you can," Chalice says and sips from a glass of orange juice. "Ask away."

"So, as a fellow creative, if you knew someone, uh, took credit for something you made, how would you handle it?"

Chalice blinks.

"I'd beat the shit out of them," he quickly replies.

"Okay, well, what if that's not an option?" I ask. "Also, you shouldn't beat creatures up. I really wouldn't like that."

I'm not one hundred percent sure, but I think Portia could beat me in a fist fight if it came down to it. I'd have to ask Frankie to be my champion and fight on my behalf. But violence is never the answer, and I need him to know that.

"I respect that, but please know that all bets are off if it ever comes to your, or possibly Trent's, safety."

"Thanks, Chalice." I give him a warm smile, and he winks.

"So, why do you ask? Did something happen?"

I take a deep breath.

"There's this Fox Folk at work, a very rich nine-tailed one, who I've been told has put her name on an art piece I submitted for the contest at work."

Chalice blinks again.

"Do you want me to kick her ass?"

"No!" I yelp, and he cracks a wide grin.

"I don't normally beat up other creatures, but exceptions can be made." He cracks another smile, but his face falters, and he drums his fingers on the table. "But in all seriousness, I wouldn't do that. What are the details?"

"Well, Candle Love Corporate is having a candle design contest, and I submitted something on the day that car drove through the store. I left it on my manager's desk, which was untouched by the damage and so it survived the accident. A coworker, Portia, then somehow got hold of it and put her name on my entry before it was sent in to Corporate."

"Whoa, how'd you find that out?"

"Another coworker called and told me." I dip my spoon in my cereal and pull it up just to dump it back in the bowl. "I can't call her out on it because Eddie will get in trouble. He didn't exactly use the, um, most legal way for his snooping."

Chalice takes a thoughtful sip of his juice and thinks for a moment. Just as he sets the glass down on the table, Trent walks into the kitchen wearing nothing but a shirt. He may or may not be wearing underwear, I can't tell.

"Trent, you forgot pants again," mutters Chalice.

"Again?" I choke on a bite of cereal.

"I didn't forget them, just didn't feel the need to put any on right now." He comes over and kisses my cheek. "Morning, Diamond. Slept well?"

"She did not," answers Chalice, getting up and going to the counter with him to pour a cup of coffee.

Trent looks at me with a frown as he waits for my response. He looks absolutely gorgeous with his rumpled hair, tattooed arms, and a sleepy sexy look to his eyes. I have to take another bite of cereal to reset my mind and answer his question.

"I was just telling Chalice that Portia took credit for my entry into the candle design contest at work."

"Portia? The one we met the other night outside of Butter, right?" He fills a cup with some coffee and sits next to me at the table. "Are you going to confront her?"

"I'm not sure, I was just asking Chalice what he thinks I should do."

"Hmm." Trent stares into his dark coffee. "She looked like trouble."

He's not wrong. Portia is trouble, and confronting her feels too intimidating to manage. I don't know how she'll take it.

"Maybe it will be fine. I'm not going to win anyway, so it's not like it'll go anywhere. I wasn't even sure about entering in the first place. No one there knows I entered, except Eddie, so it will be easy for her just to say she painted and submitted it. I didn't even show it to anyone."

"Julie," Trent says softly, reaching over and cupping his warm hands over my own. "No."

"Exactly, no." Chalice leaves his position by the counter and walks over to me. He puts his warm palms on my shoulders and stoops down to give me a hug from behind. "You entered that thing with something you made, don't let her take the credit for it. I know it can be hard to share your creativity with others, trust me, but you had the courage to do it."

"So now," continues Trent, "you just need the courage to own it and confront her. Don't give it up easily."

I think back to the artwork I submitted. It was inspired by both Chalice and Trent, as well as a touch of life before the move. It was a feeling suspended in time as my inner longing for my old home melted into my feelings for both of them. Deeply personal, at least to me it was. She has no right to what's in my heart.

Heh, look at me, maybe I should be writing novels like Chalice!

"Well, I'll see her at work later today. I'll think of something to say or do." My words trail off in thought as Chalice releases his hug and moves his chair so he's closer to me. His hand reaches out and rubs my back in a soothing way and Trent watches fondly from across the table, sipping his coffee and swishing his five tails.

There's a window in the kitchen that overlooks the backyard, and I can see the pool water glistening in the morning sun. Sparkle, shine, the smell of fresh coffee, and my two favorite guys. I'm happy in this moment, so do I really need to say something to Portia and ruin today's perfect feeling?

But deep inside, I think I know the answer to that.

I just don't know how I'll do it.

"What. The. Fuck." The first words utter from my mouth as Rose and I step into Candle Love's temporary location.

What was once a home goods store is now a vast cavern of white-tiled floor and vaulted ceilings decorated with webs of exposed air duct. Situated in the endless empty space are piles of brown boxes packed full of everything salvageable from the original Candle Love store. Another pile off to the side consists of a mish-mash of castoff display cases donated to us by a few other Candle Love locations in the area, as well as property management.

"This place has been vacant for years," Rose mutters, running a finger against a window and flicking the grime off to the floor. "I think this is where they normally put the Spirit Samhain location until it moved across the street."

"I am . . . overwhelmed." I say with a nervous laugh.

"Me too." Rose floats by me into the space and squints into the distance. "Goddess, is the bathroom way over there?"

I follow her gaze to the very end of the enormous space in time to see Eddie exiting from one of the doors.

"Good morning!" he shouts, and his echoing voice makes both Rose and me cringe.

"I guess I should be glad to still have a job." I look to Rose. "But how are we going to make this work?"

"We'll make the best of it, though we may have to take longer breaks because half that time will be spent walking to the bathroom."

We both look over and notice Eddie still walking toward us in the distance, so we meet him halfway at the mountain of boxes. I've been in the backroom during massive shipments from Candle Love Corporate, but this is like nothing I've ever seen before.

The boxes look pristine and crisp, like someone picked up brand new ones from a store. But, just as I was told, none of them are labeled. The colored tape indicting their contents is nonexistent except for the few that had been moved directly from our backroom and brought here. The majority of our floor stock seems to be packed tight into each mystery box.

Rose and I are peeking inside a few of them when Eddie finally makes it back to us.

"Marilyn wasn't kidding; everything is out of order," he says, surveying our cardboard landscape.

"I expected it would be bad, but I did not except this," I gesture around the cavernous space. "They couldn't find us a smaller location?"

"We can't be picky, at least they were able to put us somewhere." Rose glances up at the ceiling when something makes a noise up there. "Though I hope there aren't bats in here."

Eddie shuffles his bronze wings and yawns. Part of me wants to ask if he'd be able to fly up to the rafters and check for us, but he looks beat. I bet he was at that club all night and doubt he really slept at all.

"Hey, weren't you supposed to bring coffee?" I ask him, and he blushes.

"Sorry, I slept in. I'll grab you some on break." He cracks his knuckles and grabs a few box cutters that then hands out to us. "We'll just have to suffer through this until then."

"I brought some tea. Would you like some?" Rose offers, but I politely and quickly decline.

Rose and I decide to move any box with an original Candle Love Corporate logo to the very back of our temporary set up while Eddie spends time wheeling around makeshift display cases to form the basics of a Candle Love store, just with ceiling that spans nearly two stories and no walls. Then, we spend the next three hours before lunch sorting through a majority of the boxes, opening them, and taking turns in sorting them into different themed piles.

"I don't know about you, but I never want to see another brown cardboard box again," Eddie groans, sitting down on a pile of folded and discarded packing materials.

Rose flops down next to him.

"Agreed." She stretches her rose gold tail straight behind her and yawns largely. "I'm going to take a nap for my break."

"Do you want us to bring you back some coffee?" I ask her, but she's already dozing off and waves Eddie and me away.

"Come on." I grab Eddie's arm and haul him after me. Once we're outside the doors and walking across the parking lot toward the closest place that sells coffee, the cafe inside the bookstore, I turn toward him.

"So . . . Portia."

"Ugh, I know." He runs a hand through his shiny black hair. "I can't believe she would do something like that. I mean, who does she think she is?"

"She thinks she's Princess Portia," I grumble. "Is it even worth saying anything to her about it?"

"Whatever you do, just leave me out of it. I don't want to get in trouble."

"You kind of got yourself into the middle of it by snooping around and telling me. And then calling me a million times about it while drunk at the club! I think you're pretty much in the thick of it now."

Eddie shrugs as we walk into the cafe together.

"I guess you have a point," he mutters, barely looking at me because he's focused on a pair of pretty Mousequeek barista girls behind the counter. He gives them a charming smile and wander toward them, leaving me alone by the door. Goddess, he's pretty but there's a reason I never felt more for him than friendship.

"Are you going in or out?" a voice suddenly snaps from behind me, and I spin around to let whoever it is through, BUT it's Portia. I can't help but stare dumbly at her, the words I want to say to her lost in my lack of nerve, as she pushes by me.

"Here by yourself? I thought your boyfriends would be here with you." She flips her hair over a shoulder and waits for my response.

"My boyfriends are at home," I snap back at her, narrowing my eyes a fraction. "They don't have to escort me everywhere, I'm a big girl."

Ugh, why did I say that? Am I trying to prove to her that I'm wearing my big girl panties? Fuck.

"Huh, boyfriends," she repeats, stressing the plural. "Interesting, I wouldn't figure you for the type to land one, let alone two. Must be something wrong with them. I mean, they were hot and all, but they're obviously a couple of idiots to want to be with you."

The blood that rushes to my face is fiery and hot. Our exchange has attracted the baristas' and Eddie's attention now, as well as a few other cafe patrons.

"Look, I don't appreciate you being so mean to me all the time and I don't know what you think I did to deserve it, but maybe if you tell me, we can work on it. We have to work together after all; however, you do not insult Chalice and Trent, ever. Do you understand me?"

"You know, technically, we don't have to work together." She points out with a swish of her nine tails. "You could always quit. I don't think anyone would miss you."

The whole cafe turns quiet and the only sound penetrating the air is the internal churning of a nearby ice machine.

"Do you understand me?" I seethe. My body shakes from the rush of conflict and the edges to my vision have gone blurry. I'm not like this. I do not like confrontation. But it feels like I've backed myself up into a corner and, like a scared animal, have nothing more I can do other than lash out. She ignited something in my chest with her comments about my guys.

"Oh, I understand you," she starts, "but also know well enough that you're not the type of person to cause problems. Scared little Julie who runs and hides when it's too crowded. Little Julie who can't even stand up for herself." She lowers her voice and tilts toward me. "It's a good thing I stole your contest entry, you wouldn't last a day with the popularity if you won."

"Stop it, Portia." I take a deep breath. "I'm really trying to ignore you and your, ugh, attitude. But I would appreciate, like really fucking appreciate it, if you never spoke to me again. And that you never say a bad thing about Chalice, Trent, or me."

She scoffs loudly.

"We can't ignore each other forever, Julie. Remember, we work together!"

"We'll see about that," a familiar voice booms behind me.

I turn around to see my manager, Marilyn, standing beside the pick-up counter. There's a forgotten cup of coffee resting between her and the stunned barista who keeps looking between me, Marilyn, and Portia.

"Ma-Marilyn!" Portia stutters her name, backing away only to bump into Eddie. He stands there with his arms crossed and a wide smirk as she cowers in front of an approaching Marilyn.

"Why don't you take the rest of the day off and meet me at the new store bright and early at eight tomorrow morning. I'll have your final paycheck ready for you to collect."

"Wh-wait, you're firing me?" The nine tails spring up, shoving several customers' and their coffee cups out of the way. "You can't do that!"

"Yes, I can, because I'm the manager. Today you've proven you're not the caliber of character I'd like to see working in my store. With an attitude like that, we can't trust you to provide the kind of customer service we strive for. And . . ."

"I'm great at customer fucking service!"

Someone in the cafe gasps and someone else snickers loudly. It might have been Eddie.

"And," Marilyn continues, "not only did you steal your coworker's property, but your behavior toward her is inexcusable."

Just then, Marilyn seems to realize the entire cafe's attention is glued to our dramatic event. She straights up, smooths out her blouse, and grabs her coffee.

Turning smartly on her heels, she passes by me and whispers, "I'll call Corporate and fix your contest entry."

"Now ja-just wait a minute," screams Portia, but Eddie swipes his two waiting coffees from the counter and scurries out the door after Marilyn, grabbing my arm in the process.

"And that's a wrap everyone, goodnight!" He gives an exaggerated bow, nearly spilling coffee on both of us, then hauls me out the door with him.

"Quick, let's make a run for it before Portia really goes ballistic!" he says, flexing his wings for flight and half hovering in the air with me dangling by the arm.

I grab both coffees from him and keep my feet firmly planted on the ground. Marilyn is nowhere to be seen, but that's not surprising, she probably drove here and bolted to her car as well.

"Alright, but come down and walk with me, we can't both fly away."

Eddie chuckles and lands lightly beside me. He runs a hand through his air and looks down at me fondly.

"I can walk with you," he says lowly, but then keeps his distance with his eyes trained forward on the pavement. "So, um, is that true what you said to Portia, about you having two boyfriends?"

"Oh, um, yeah . . . it is."

"It's those two gorgeous roommates of yours, right?" He folds his wings in tightly to his body.

"Yeah, Chalice and Trent."

He looks down at me once more, just as we arrive at the entrance to our warehouse sized Candle Love.

"Well, I'm happy for you, Julie. You deserve it."

He places his hand on the small of my back just as we walk through the doors. It's a friendly gesture, just a gentle push as we both enter, and his hand is gone just as quickly as it appeared. But there's a warmth there I never noticed before and also a sadness.

A resignation.

I hope Eddie finds what he needs one day and that he's as happy as I am with Chalice and Trent. I really do.

CHAPTER TWENTY-THREE

My entire body hurts when it's finally time to leave work and go home. Rose and I had made premature plans to celebrate with dinner after completing the day, but somewhere around the mid-afternoon mark, we realized how tired and sore we were and promised we'd do it another day. Even Eddie was struggling and had at least five cups of coffee.

With Portia gone, we all had to take on extra work, but I'd be lying if I said it didn't feel, well, nicer without her being there. And while I don't like her at all, I do hope she's okay and that maybe she'll have time now to work on herself and being a little nicer to others.

I'm still perplexed about how it all went down. It all happened so fast and seemed like destiny or fate that Marilyn just so happened to be here when Portia said all those things. Maybe it was all a rebalancing act on the universe's part and Portia needed to learn a lesson. The universe just decided that today was the day and acted on it.

I'm glad I stood up to her, but she had insulted Chalice and Trent and I was not having that. Still, thinking about the whole interaction is making me squirm. I really hope I won't have to do something like that again. I'm not built for confrontations like that.

The old Julie would have given in and let Portia take the credit without saying a word, so I'm at least glad I told her how I felt, even if I didn't exactly call her out as an art thief in person.

The drive home from work is quick and easy with no traffic, a rarity for New California, but by the time I open the front door and stumble into the hallway, I'm ready to pass out. Luckily, Chalice happens to be walking by just as I come through the door and scoops my lazy butt up in his arms.

"Little Julie looks tired," he says softly, nuzzling my cheek and carrying me through the hallway toward the living room.

"It's been a long day," I mumble against his shoulder and snuggle into his chest. Usually, I don't like being carried around. Even as a child I didn't like it. Something about being able to do things on my own. But I'm tired and Chalice smells so good that I want to bury my face in his sweet amber chest.

When we get to the living room, Trent and Misty scurry off the couch to make room as Chalice carefully lays me down.

"How was work? I'm sure you all had a lot to do today," he asks.

"And did you talk to Portia?" asks Trent.

"Actual work was awful, there were . . . so many boxes. We're not even finished, it's going to take at least another day or two before we can open the temp location. And, well, the Portia thing worked itself out when she was openly insulting in front of our manager. She was fired, which is good, but that just made our jobs today that much harder."

"Well, she was caught stealing," says Trent with a flick of his tails.

"She was stealing candles?" asks Misty as she looks from me to her brother.

"No," I reply. "She put her name on something I sent into Candle Love Corporate. Not that the punishment for product theft would be any better, but at least she's gone now. She was always so hard to work with! But it almost doesn't make up for the fact that we have to pick up the slack for her now."

"What happened?" Chalice asks, and Trent leans over to hear my answer.

"I ran into her at that coffee place in the bookstore and she said some nasty things to me as well as mentioning the contest. Her biggest mistake was saying something like that in front of the entire cafe that Marilyn just so happens to be a frequent customer of. She heard everything and fired her on the spot."

"What did she say?" Misty asks, clearly involved in my drama now.

"She insulted Chalice and Trent," I say softly. "Said there's something wrong with them to want to be with me."

Misty's jaw drops open, Chalice tries to punch the wall, and Trent with his five tails waving aggressively has to hold him back.

"What do you want us to do about her," asks Trent, standing back once he's satisfied Chalice isn't going to put a hold through the wall.

"Nothing, she's irrelevant now and I doubt I'll see her around much anymore. I just want to move on and forget about her. Candle Love is much better off without her anyway."

"Are you sure?" Chalice catches my eye, and I nod.

"I'm sure."

"At least you're still employed," adds Misty in an effort to change the subject. "When Burger Bliss closed from the water main break, it was fixed quickly, but it wasn't like we could up and move to a temporary location."

"I suppose, but I'd rather have the days off." I laugh weakly and yawn. "I just need some dinner and time to rest, then I'll be as good as new. Hopefully. Maybe. We'll see."

"Well, I guess I'm glad everything worked out," says Chalice. "In the end, she got what she deserved, and you got credit for your art. It was fucked of her to pull something like that."

"I'm still perplexed as to why someone would do something like that in the first place, even if she did rationalize it in her mind," I let out a big yawn, "it still wasn't right."

"Agreed," says Trent as he wiggles back onto the couch and props my legs up in his lap.

Chalice sits on the arm rest behind my head and runs his fingers through my hair. With Trent slowly rubbing the soles of my feet and Chalice's careful strokes on my scalp, I can't help but let out a small moan of contentment.

Trent and Chalice exchange sly smile with each other, and I suddenly feel Trent's hands sliding from my heels to my calves and knees and an extra hand from Chalice as his fingers twirl around and tug slightly at my hair.

"Whoa, I can see when I'm not wanted," Misty announces suddenly and grabs her purse from the kitchen. "I've got plans tonight anyway."

"Where you off to, sister," mumbles Chalice, his focus clearly on his hands and my head.

I barely hear their exchange because I'm too busy imagining Chalice's hands in my hair as I kneel in front of him and take his giant cock in my mouth.

"Dinner with a friend, so don't wait up, though it's not like you would." She laughs and brings me back into the moment. "See you three tomorrow!"

I get a flash of her silver scales as she leaves the room and hear the door to the garage closing behind her. I feel a little bad from her quick departure; she is one of my roommates after all, just not one that I'm currently fucking.

But I hate that she may feel awkward. She's Chalice's twin sister after all, and I want to be respectful to his family.

"I hope we didn't go too far and weird her out," I say, tilting my head back and looking up at Chalice for confirmation. Trent gives my feet a squeeze as Chalice looks in the garage's direction.

"Doubtful," he responds. "She's into this kind of stuff, even if she doesn't really mention it. Um, multi-partner kind of stuff I mean, not brother-sister watching stuff."

"Fuck, Chalice, I don't think either of us were thinking that until you said it." Trent half laughs and half groans.

"Sorry, we're close, but not that close!" Chalice pouts, crossing his arms and looking down at me.

"Don't look at me, I'm with Trent on this one."

"You two," he kisses my forehead before getting up, "are ridiculous, but I love you both for it."

"Ridiculous and hungry, what do we have to eat around here?" I move my focus and attention to Trent at the other end of the couch.

"Nothing in the fridge!" calls Chalice from the kitchen.

I'm struck by my sudden inspiration.

"We could always do pizza? You know, to celebrate everything and all."

"That actually sounds pretty good." I shift around my weight so I can sit up on the couch.

"I'll take care of it," Trent says, sitting beside me and grabbing a blanket to drape around my shoulders. "Why don't you go take a nap while we wait for the delivery."

"I think I can manage that," I say softly, leaning into him and breathing in his scent. "Come get me when the pizza is here."

"Anything for you, Diamond," he whispers against my skin.

I sigh, tilting my head back and letting him trail a few kisses along my collarbone, but he respectfully holds back from more. My body shivers and aches from both wanting to submit to my urges and also rest from a hard day's work. In the end, though, my practicality wins out and I reluctantly pick myself up from the couch and go to my room.

There, I slip my CPAP mask over my face, curl up on my bed, and fall asleep fully clothed. I might be hot and bothered right now, but I'm no use to anyone if I'm half asleep the entire time!

I wake up to the smell of pizza wafting under my door and into my bedroom. It reminds me of my first night here and how nervous I was in my new home. But now, when I walk out my door and into the living room where I know the pizza will be, I won't be walking out to strangers. I'll be walking out to two guys that absolutely adore me.

They probably don't even realize how much they've helped me and how I know I simply can't imagine my life without them. I had expected big life changes out on my own, but I honestly didn't see this happening. Not that I'm complaining in the least, moving out turned out to be the best thing that's ever happened to me.

When Misty moves to her new place, we have to make this work because I don't want to complicate things. Chalice, Trent, and I have to stay to together. We just have to.

"Julie!" Chalice booms my name as soon as I enter the warm living room. As I suspected, pizza boxes have been piled on the coffee table and a stack of out of season paper plates, Lammas this time, have been placed nearby. It's just like my first night here, well, minus the porn. At least for now.

"I was just about to come get you," says Trent as he places a few slices of pizza onto a plate for me.

They've left me the middle of the couch and I have a difficult time controlling the rush of blood between my legs when I think about being sandwiched between them. But I somehow manage to take my seat by squeezing my legs together and concentrating. I detect the slightest flare to Trent's nostrils when I do, but Chalice seems focused on ensuring I have enough napkins.

"My stomach must have smelled it in my sleep and woke me up before you could." I laugh lightly and stretch. Two sets of eyes follow the slight rise of my shirt as it lifts from my waist as my arms go above my head.

"Should we watch a movie?" I suggest, even though that's the last thing on my mind right now. Sex and food being the top two and not necessarily in that order right now.

"Sounds good," says Chalice. "I, uh, took out the porn."

"Awww, really?" I laugh, nudging his ribs. "Now why would you do that?"

"I mean, I could put it back on if you want, but there's already a fantasy adventure movie loaded in the DVD player." His voice drips with light-hearted sarcasm but I can hear the tension lying beneath.

"I guess we could watch the porn later," I say dramatically, drawing out my words and giving him my best pouty face.

"Only if you eat something, Diamond," says Trent. "You'll need your energy if that's your plan for the evening."

I take a huge bite from a slice of pizza on my plate and look back at him with full cheeks. He's leaning back against the couch, both arms stretched out along the back. It makes his body impossibly long from his arms down to his feet. He's wearing a tight black shirt that is so worn I can see the definition of his tight ab muscles, and the jeans he's wearing leave little to the imagination. His five tails are pushed to his side with the tips twitching slowly in the air, and his black ears are turned and focused on only me. The bite of super sized pepperoni pizza nearly lodges in my throat when I swallow hard from just looking at him.

"Mmm hmm," I say through a mouthful of pizza.

I'm so smooth, I should write a book.

"I'm always down for porn," says Chalice. "If that's what the lady wants, of course."

I give him a playful nudge with my shoulder.

"I'll let you know if that's the case."

Chalice is dressed completely different than Trent with his loose t-shirt and beige shorts. His exposed skin glimmers softly in the dim light streaming from the kitchen and the dusting across his face glows against his hazel eyes. He really does earn the nickname of Golden God with his chiseled and muscular features.

"Fantasy adventure flick it is." Trent flicks a button on the remote and puts on some slow-moving fantasy movie. I assume the 'adventure' part comes somewhere near the end, but the movie looks like it was made fifty years ago, so their idea of 'actions and adventures' may be different from my modern day standards.

Still, it somewhat holds my attention as I finish three slices of pizza and two breadsticks. I probably could eat more, but I don't feel like stuffing myself silly. Besides, I could always sneak into the fridge later for a midnight snack of two.

Once we're mostly done eating, Chalice grabs the last breadstick and absentmindedly chomps it while leaning back against the couch with his arms behind his head. The breadstick dangles like a cigar from his mouth.

I'm taking the last bite of a pizza crust when Trent launches himself across my lap and snatches Chalice's breadstick with his mouth. His tails fly across my line of sight, but he keeps his weight mostly off my lap as he flips back over to his side of the couch, munching triumphantly on his prize.

"You want to play that game, huh?" Chalice rumbles, and I suddenly feel his hands wrapping around my waist and hoisting me on his lap, straddling his legs. His arms wrap around me securely as he holds me down.

His breath is heavy as he shifts under me, and I can feel his cock growing hard between us. I let out a little gasp when he shifts upward, pressing himself on me and groaning into my ears. Something happens in the movie before us, but I couldn't tell you what because my vision goes blurry with lust.

"Hey, I didn't steal your breadstick," I squeak breathlessly, caught up in the sensation and squeezing my eyes shut when one particularly rough thrust rubs me in just the right away. When I eventually open my eyes again, it's to Trent gazing at me from the other end of the couch and biting his lip. The breadstick forgotten and off to the side.

"Fuck, that's hot," he says with a scratchy voice. He slouches back and widens his legs before placing a hand on the growing bulge between them.

"That's because Julie is so fucking gorgeous." Chalice's fingers press into my hips. "She's the most beautiful creature in the world, and I never want to be without her."

"Ch-Chalice," my voice cracks as I push my back into his chest. His hips have stilled but he's still rock hard beneath me when he puts his arms around my shoulders and curls me around so I'm cuddled in his lap facing him. His face dips toward mine.

"I mean it," he says with his mouth hovering over my lips. "We belong with each other, I feel it in every cell of my body. We're together now, all three of us."

A hand slides between us and tilts my head backward so I'm looking at my other boyfriend upside down. Chalice has a wry smile as Trent leans in close and cups my face in his palms.

"Looks like you're stuck with us, Diamond," he breathes into my mouth before giving me a slow and torturous kiss.

When he pulls away, it feels too soon and I push my back against Chalice in protest.

"Let's go to my room." I can hear my own voice growing low and husky with the need of it all, and I wiggle myself up from Chalice so I can stand before the couch.

Trent leaps up next to me, trapping me in a hug that has the lower half of his body pressing greedily into mine. I reach around and give one of this tails a tug, and he purrs into my hair as his fingers clench into my skin.

"I'll follow you anywhere as long as you do that every day," he coos, his back arching with pleasure.

"Hmm, I wonder," murmurs Chalice, and I watch as he reaches over his with long arms and wraps his fingers around the base of Trent's tail, giving it a firm tug. Trent's eyes roll back in his head and his mouth drops open in a long moan.

Wow, I never thought a simple tail tug could be that steamy. I'm even more impressed that Chalice seems to be trying something new. That's going to take my wildest fantasies to a whole new level.

"Fuck." His tails thrash behind him. "Save it for the bedroom, you two."

I hear Chalice chuckle and rise from the couch, coming to stand behind us. I get that small and tiny feeling again, but know I'm in good hands with them.

"Come on then, you heard the lady," says Chalice. "Let's take this to her room."

CHAPTER TWENTY-FOUR

We've barely made it to the hallway before Chalice pins me against his chest and the wall. He begins to lay slobbering kisses up my collarbone to my ear lobes, which he teases with his tongue and causes my shoulder to hunch up from the ticklish feeling. Laughing, I grasp his forearms and try to push him away.

In response, he reaches up and grabs both of my wrists. Holding them together in one big hand, he pins them above my head and presses his forehead against mine.

"Are you okay with fucking both of us at once?" he asks.

While I appreciate him asking because consent is important, my willingness to respond positively is overwhelming and all I can manage is a simple, "Uh huh."

Sexy, Julie. Real sexy.

Chalice brings my hands down, spinning me around so that my back presses his chest now, and he's against the wall. Trent moves in next, closing the distance between our bodies until I'm sandwiched between them with my clasped hands pushing up against Trent's hardening bulge.

My hands ache to hold him and when Chalice frees them, I scramble quickly to push Trent's pants and briefs down to the floor. He springs loose against my palms and I finally get to wrap my hands around his throbbing member. I give him a few slow strokes, marveling at the velvety skin and length.

Trent hisses through clenched teeth.

"Careful, Julie, I want," he pauses and takes a deep breath, "to come in you and not on your hands in the hallway."

Chalice shakes in laughter from behind me.

"Don't worry, buddy," he says and grabs my hands again. "We're going to take care of her first."

Before I can say anything, he hoists me over his shoulder like I weigh nothing at all and carries me into my room. I giggle uncontrollably as he flips me down on my bed and crawls up beside me. Trent follows and slides up my other side. The bed frame creaks ominously under our combined weight, but I pay it no mind.

"Goddess, you're beautiful." Chalice sighs into my neck and trails a hand down my throat, between my breasts and to my belly. "And artistic, and creative, and kind enough to volunteer her Friday nights away. Fuck, Julie, how are you so perfect?"

"I don't think I am," I respond, my cheeks turning rosy from his praise. "No one is perfect."

"You're perfect for us," replies Trent as he nuzzles into the other side of my neck. "I knew it from the day we met."

"When you were naked out on the front lawn?" I gasp when Chalice's hand flutters back up and grabs one of my tits. He thumbs my nipple over my shirt and licks his lips.

"That's the day," replies Trent. His hand joins Chalice and grasps my other tit, massaging and kneading until I squirm beneath them. "I could tell there was something special about you."

I begin to feel Chalice inching across my bed, moving his big body further down until he's at my feet. He looks up and catches Trent's eye who gives a quick nod before repositioning himself.

Trent moves directly behind me so my head is resting on his lap, and his hands reach down to gently pull my shirt up and over my head. His shirt comes off afterward, and I stare dreamily up at his tatted chest.

"Help me with her bra, Trent." Chalice slips a finger between my breasts under the strap and waits for Trent to wiggle under my back to unhook the clasps. A second later, Chalice removes my bra by pulling his fingers up and tossing it to the floor.

"Fuck," Trent mutters from behind me, and I feel his body tensing, so I reach up and clasp the sides of his face in my hands.

"Deep breaths," I whisper, and he gives me a strained smile.

Chalice slips his shirt off next and hovers close above me, making me lose my grip on Trent. His golden toned skin is warm and silky when it rubs against my stomach as his lips seek one of my nipples and suckles greedily. He is not shy about the slobbering noises he makes and in my ecstasy, I glance up and see Trent biting his lip in concentration.

Chalice lifts his head up and looks at him. "You okay, buddy?"

"Ye-yeah," stutters Trent as he twists a fist into my hair. "I'll be fine."

Chalice chuckles, but instead of returning to my chest, he begins laying his slow, slobbering kisses down my stomach and over my belly button. Meanwhile, his hands make quick work of my pants and he pulls them, and my underwear, off. He kicks everything off the bed and spreads my legs before him.

"So perfect," he murmurs, entering me with two of his fingers and bending down to lick gently around them. I buck my hips into him as he stretches with his long strokes and soothes the slight burn with his dextral tongue.

Whimpering, I reach above my head and hold onto whatever I can get a hold of from Trent. My fingers find purchase in the flesh of his tatted forearms, and I grip him hard as pleasure builds within me.

"Shh, Diamond, we got you," murmurs Trent into my hair.

Chalice slightly lifts his head from between my legs and his breath is hot against my aching parts. I feel like a helpless puddle of mush beneath him.

"We're each going to take turns fucking this pretty pussy of yours," he says into me and my body shakes with anticipation. "And then we're all going to come together."

"Chalice," Trent says with a strained croak, "I don't know if I can . . ."

"You got this, I believe in you," he responds, gripping my thighs in his large hands. He pulls me from Trent's lap, and I slide along my bed until my legs drape over the sides. "Now, take off the rest of your clothes and join us."

Trent lets out a small whimper, and I twist my head at an awkward angle to see him wiggling out of his pants and down the bed so he's beside me again. Taking one of my hands in his, he grips his cock with the other and gives himself slow, measured strokes while gazing at the foot of the bed where Chalice already stands, naked and erect.

"Good boy," Chalice purrs before focusing his attention on me. "Let me know if anything is uncomfortable and I'll stop immediately, okay?"

I give him a firm nod and try to relax my muscles as much as possible. Chalice carefully wraps his hands around each of my ankles and spreads my legs apart, exposing myself fully to him. He sucks in a breath of air before lining up his massive, gold cock against me and slowly pushing inside. Inch by torturous inch, both Trent and I watch until he's flush against my body.

"Fuck, Diamond, you're deep enough to take all of him." Trent's eyes are wide, and his knuckles around his cock look white from his grip. "How do you feel with him inside you?"

"Full," I moan. "Goddess, I . . ."

I can't find the words and just moan some more instead. Trent gives a small laugh while Chalice begins to move his hips. Tilting his head back, he lets out a deep, long groan that has my toes curling and Trent squeezing my hand.

Past the point for more words, Chalice reaches down and presses a finger against my clit, rubbing in circles that time well with his thrusts. The bed creaks again under my back, but the sound is drowned out by my labored breaths as I climb higher and higher to a climax.

My tits bounce from the jostling position and when Trent reaches over to grab them and then quickly lower his head to take a nipple between his lips, I feel myself float away in an explosion of bliss. Muscles inside me clench around Chalice's cock and my hands fly out to grip Trent's hair, holding him against my chest as my body rocks with release.

When the sensation calms, I realize that Chalice has not and that his strokes have become quick and frenzied, only when he catches my eye does he bite his lip and slow down before extracting himself.

"I could spend eternity in your pussy," he gushes, flopping on the bed nearby and leaning in to kiss me deeply. "But, right now at least, I want to watch my best friend fuck you."

I feel Trent moving beside me until he's standing at the side of the bed. His breathing is labored, but his cock is still engorged and standing tall, just waiting for its turn.

"Get on your knees, Diamond," he commands and I scramble to make my body obey. Still coming down from my orgasmic high, I'm a little slow to reposition myself, but eventually make it so that I'm on all fours facing Chalice at the head of the bed.

Trent places his hands on my ass, rubbing my cheeks a few times before giving me a questioning, but light, slap. I purr in response and wiggle my hips.

"You can do it harder than that," I, somehow, manage to say.

He rewards my effort with a slap to my other cheek.

"We'll have to save this for next time, but it's good to know." His voice is strained, but his movements behind me seem smooth and polished.

"Are you ready for him?" Chalice asks softly. He kicks off the pillows from my bed and kneels in front of me.

I turn to look at Trent over my shoulder. We don't even have to say anything to each other because he just knows. I can feel his cock at my entrance, tentative and slow as he pushes inside me, and then followed by the tense full feeling when he rests inside me.

He doesn't start pumping right away and we stay joined together just like that as we both marvel at the connection between us. Chalice reaches around and threads his fingers through my hair, massaging my scalp and tugging gently as he stays quiet and respects the moment.

Suddenly, Trent's body tenses and I know he's close. His hips draw back and he thrusts forcefully back inside me, pumping himself in methodical rhythm. At the same time, Chalice rises on his knees for a better look and his cock rises to just the right level that I can take him in my mouth. He seems surprised at first, but recovers quickly and helps guide himself against my lips with his hands.

Hunching over my back now, Trent's hand shoots out and closes in on my clit, rubbing with quick movements in line with his cock pounding inside me. He then suddenly lets out a throaty growl and uses the hands on my hips to flip me to my back. His newly freed cock drips above me as I'm sprawled before him, and his face is mask of concentration.

The move throws off Chalice, who withdraws just in time from my mouth, but replaces his hands around himself, stroking his cock above my shoulder.

"Diamond." Trent groans, pushing himself slowly back inside me, his fingers pressing against my clit once more. "I can't hold . . ."

"Fuck." Chalice's hand quickens above me. "I'm going to come on your chest, if that's okay."

"Ye-yeah," I somehow manage to get out as another orgasm overtakes me like a burst of stars between my legs.

Words fail as all three of us release simultaneously. Chalice's hot stream coating my entire chest in pearly white just as Trent's speed quickens to a maddening pace. His tails fan out behind him like a starburst just before the final thrust that tightens every muscle in his body as he pours into me.

My own climax travels up my back and makes my spine arch upward toward the ceiling. I catch a quick glimpse of Chalice's head rolled back, eyes closed and mouth slack as the sensation pulses through him. The room's dim light hits the thin covering of scales and golden skin, making him truly earn the title of Golden God.

Waves of pleasure ripple through my body, continuing well after both my guys begin to collapse in exhaustion. Then, with one final thrust, Trent's body goes slack and he drops next to me, draping an arm comfortably around my midsection. Chalice shifts his weight so he's cuddled up against my other side and puts one arm around me, just above Trent's.

For a time, we lay there panting and spent as our bodies come down from their extraordinary high. It's a beautiful moment for about two and a half seconds, because there suddenly is another ominous creaking sound, followed by a rush of air as my bed frame collapses and the mattress falls flat on the floor of my room with all of us still on it.

We're silent for a stunned second, but then Chalice lets out a snort of laughter, which prompts Trent and me to join in with our own giggling. Then we're a naked, messy pile of laughter, tangled sheets and one very broken bed. Looks like I'm also joining the mattress on the ground club.

Trent takes his shirt and gently cleans me off while Chalice reaches over and grabs my CPAP mask, which he hands to me without a word.

After a little reshuffling of bodies, I slip the mask on and close my eyes. Chalice's golden body is protective and Trent's tails wrap themselves around me for extra warmth, and absolutely no one is bothered by the slight whooshing sound of my CPAP machine as we fall asleep wrapped in each others' arms.

TWO MONTHS LATER

"Julie!" Frankie's overly excited voice cries out as she charges me with a full-iced coffee in one of her hands. Most of the drink lands on my bare shoulders as she throws her arms around me and pull back to look at me with the love and affection of a best friend.

"Glad you could make it on such short notice," I respond.

"Of course, I'm always down for a pool party. Just as long as there's some eye candy around." She turns from me and surveys our packed backyard. "And I see there is."

We had a really good turnout for our backyard barbecue and pool party. Coworkers from Candle Love and Burger Bliss, plus some of Trent's friends, are mingling freely both in and out of the pool, playing games on the lawn or lounging in the hot tub.

There is even an embarrassing large poster board of the art I submitted for the Candle Love design contest. I didn't win or even place, but it's okay. The piece is still deeply meaningful to me and is destined for a place of honor in our home's barren hallway. I hope to create more artwork to accompany it in the future, with each piece celebrating the love Chalice, Trent, and I have for each other.

Even though the days have started to get cooler, it's New California and summer never really disappears around here. It's always prime weather for backyard fun with good friends, and we decided at the last minute to throw a backyard party to celebrate, well, everything.

"Only the best for my best friend." I laugh and grab a napkin from a nearby table to blot some of the coffee off my bikini. "Come with me and say hello to your new roommates!"

Frankie is set to move into our house in about a month and will take over Misty's mini-apartment above the garage. It all sort of worked out when Frankie's landlord, who was definitely over dealing with complaints from his other tenets about her midnight habits, handed over an eviction notice.

Am I a little nervous about it? Maybe. But Trent helped me to conduct a sound test of Misty's old room, and even if Frankie is struck by a lightening bolt of creativity at three in the morning, we shouldn't hear too much of it.

"Is that burgers I smell?" Frankie and I walk over to Chalice who is hard at work grilling burgers for a small collection of assembled friends.

That's kind of what you get when you work at a restaurant that makes burgers; everyone you know designates you as the burger chef no matter what.

His face lights up when he sees us approaching and, after setting his spatula down, he picks me up in a big bear hug and swings me around. After placing a sloppy kiss on the side of my cheek, he sets me down next to a pile of burger buns.

"My very own Burger Bliss," laughs Frankie.

"Don't get used to it," I respond, squirting a big dollop of mustard on one of the buns and moving out of the way for Chalice to place a steaming hot patty on top. I hand it to Frankie on a Beltane-themed paper plate. "He only cooks on special occasions."

"Such as my moving in?" gasps Frankie. She puts a hand to her chest and rustles her big wings. "What a kind creature to throw a whole party just for that. I'm truly touched. I might even have to get down and dirty after a few drinks in order to fully celebrate. Any of your friends up for a little friendly game of skinny dipping later tonight?"

Chalice startles when Frankie winks at him, but recovers quickly.

"Try Cyrus. He's the Demonnie with the blue horns, but I think he might still be dating Shawna. She's the human just getting out of the pool."

"I'll try 'em both," Frankie takes a big bite of her burger. "Thanks for the burger, Golden God!"

"You're, uh, welcome?" Chalice watches her go and turns to me. "This is going to be interesting."

I grab a plain burger for myself and take a bite before answering. "She's awesome, you'll love her."

"Maybe, but never in the same way I love you," he answers softly, pushing the burger away from my face and kissing me. It's slow and beautiful and sweet, all the perfect things you can get from a kiss between lovers.

"Never," I whisper back before he kisses my forehead and goes back to the grill.

Someone nearby jumps in the pool and two other creatures, a Demonnie and Fox Folk couple, team up and throw a Mousequeek in a red bikini in the water with them. Someone else turns the music way up when a group of Minotaur girls I don't know wander into the backyard.

Their loud voices over the thrashing of water and music pile onto my senses, and I feel a small bead of sweat crawl down my spine. But then there is a comforting hand on my back and the feeling of a black and white furry tail wrapping around my ankles.

"Wanna head inside, Diamond?" Trent asks, and I nod vigorously.

"I'll meet you there in a second, as soon as I'm finished out here," Chalice says, quickly throwing the last few veggie patties on the grill to cook. The two of them exchange a knowing look as Trent takes my hand.

He's been making himself busy crafting cocktails for our guests and smells like a mixture of citrus, berries, and vermouth. He could be a special edition candle.

Trent and I head inside, and it's blissfully cool and quiet. Staying clear of the kitchen and living room, we scurry down the hallway to my room and slip inside.

Before sitting on my bed, I have to move my CPAP mask out of the way. I've long since stopped hiding it and am glad I've become comfortable knowing it's nothing to be ashamed of. Even when I'm curled up with both Trent and Chalice all night long, I'm finally okay with it.

All three of us have taken to sleeping together in my room since my CPAP is set up here and it's not like we can break my bed any further, but have been considering modifying Trent's room to share since he has the biggest mattress.

"Julie," begins Trent, leaning over and pushing me down on the bed below him, "do you feel better now?"

"I do," I respond. "But I can think of a few things you could do to make me feel even better."

Trent chuckles and kisses my neck, his breath hot on my neck as his hips push into me. He's getting better at holding out, and it's been at least a few since I've made him come his pants.

"I love the way you feel under me," he murmurs into my skin. "And I love you."

"I love the way you feel on top of me," I whisper into his hair. "And I love you."

"Are you two getting started without me?" Chalice's deep voice rumbles from the doorway. I turn my hazy expression toward him as Trent continues on my neck, sucking the skin until I know he'll leave a mark that I'll have to cover up for work.

"Maybe," I coo at him.

He slams the door shut behind him and crosses the room in two strides before dropping to the bed with us and claiming my mouth his. Trent's hands circle around my waist, holding my body against his chest, and Chalice snuggles in close on my other side.

Frankie was right, this is a brand new life for me. Every now and then, I'll see or smell something that reminds me of my old life and the house I grew up in, but those memories quickly fade. I'm making new memories now, and I wouldn't have it any other way. These guys are my home now.

"Fuck, I kinda want to fuck you real bad right now," moans Trent from behind me. "Think they'll miss us outside if we stay in here for a little longer?"

"I think there's enough time to bury my cock in your tight pussy," Chalice breathes into my mouth, finishing his sentence with a gentle lip nibble.

"How does that sound, Diamond?" Trent's body grinds into my back. "Do you want that?"

"Uh huh," I respond.

Smooth Julie strikes again.

But I guess I'll get the hang of sexy talk one day.

There's definitely no rush.

THANK YOU!

Thanks for visiting Candle Love and have a great day! We hope you'll consider leaving an honest review on your preferred platform.

Interesting in a workplace romance involving everyone's favorite burger joint? Pick up BURGER BLISS, available now on Amazon!

Please give my Instagram a follow @Minty.Marie.Books

Or visit my website for links to all my works!

https://www.mintymariebooks.com

Thanks again, you're the best!

www.ingramcontent.com/pod-product-compliance
Lightning Source LLC
Chambersburg PA
CBHW021528250626
47154CB00006BA/2012